HER FORBIDDEN IRISH WARRIOR

MICHELLE WILLINGHAM

Recycling programs for this product may not exist in your area.

ISBN-13: 978-1-335-83190-3

Her Forbidden Irish Warrior

For questions and comments about the quality of this book, please contact us at CustomerService@Harlequin.com.

Harlequin Enterprises ULC
22 Adelaide St. West, 41st Floor
Toronto, Ontario M5H 4E3, Canada
www.Harlequin.com

HarperCollins Publishers
Macken House, 39/40 Mayor Street Upper,
Dublin 1, D01 C9W8, Ireland
www.HarperCollins.com

Printed in U.S.A.

1 2 3 4 5 6 7 8 9 10 HDC 28 27 26 25

The Legendary Warriors

History's most powerful heroes!

Robert of Penrith and his illegitimate half brother, Piers, were raised as differently as possible, but they've become reluctant allies since a deadly raid on their father's land left them exiled. Now, along with their friend Brian and the formidable MacEgan clan, they are determined to rise up, reclaim their birthright and become fierce warriors of legend that the world will remember forever!

But their journeys won't just be shaped by revenge and redemption. Because these warriors haven't considered the power of romance...

Meet the legendary warriors:

The Iron Warrior Returns
The Untamed Warrior's Bride
Her Warrior's Redemption
Her Forbidden Irish Warrior

Her Warrior's Redemption and *Her Forbidden Irish Warrior* are crossover stories, connecting The Legendary Warriors series with The MacEgan Brothers series!

All available now!

Author Note

I've been wanting to write another MacEgan book for a while now, and *Her Forbidden Irish Warrior* provided the perfect opportunity for a crossover between that series and The Legendary Warriors. If you've been wondering what actually happened when Mairead MacEgan was kidnapped, now you'll see who her true hero—or villain—actually was.

Balor Ó Phelan, nicknamed the Demon of Éireann, isn't a man known for heroism. But when Norman soldiers threaten a MacEgan princess, he won't hesitate to fight for her. Mairead is duty-bound to wed a nobleman, but she's deeply attracted to this fierce warrior who steals her away and makes her blood race.

If you missed previous books in The Legendary Warriors series, these include *The Iron Warrior Returns* (Robert and Morwenna), *The Untamed Warrior's Bride* (Piers and Gwendoline), and *Her Warrior's Redemption* (Brian and Velaria).

If you'd like me to email you when my new books come out, you may subscribe to my author newsletter at: michellewillingham.com/contact. I always love hearing from my readers.

RITA® Award finalist and Kindle bestselling author **Michelle Willingham** has written over forty historical romances, novellas and short stories. Currently, she lives in southeastern Virginia with her family and her beloved pets. When she's not writing, Michelle enjoys reading, baking and avoiding exercise at all costs. Visit her website at michellewillingham.com.

Books by Michelle Willingham

Harlequin Historical

The Taming of the Countess

The Legendary Warriors

The Iron Warrior Returns
The Untamed Warrior's Bride
Her Warrior's Redemption

Untamed Highlanders

The Highlander and the Governess
The Highlander and the Wallflower

Sons of Sigurd

Stolen by the Viking

Warriors of the Night

Forbidden Night with the Warrior
Forbidden Night with the Highlander
Forbidden Night with the Prince

Visit the Author Profile page
at Harlequin.com for more titles.

To Kendall—welcome to the family,
and I'm so glad you've found your happily-ever-after
with my son. Wishing you both many years of joy
and love together!

Prologue

Ireland, 1201

If Balor Ó Phelan didn't find his little brother by nightfall, Fergus was going to murder him.

The boy was barely seven years old—well past the age he should have been fostered with another family to strengthen alliance ties—and Kenneth had slipped outside the ringfort again. His brother loved exploring, and he was small enough to wander out unnoticed. Though Balor was only eleven, he blamed himself. He'd been distracted by chores, and he'd mistakenly believed their mother was watching the boy. But Orla hardly paid attention to anything anymore. She was lost in her own thoughts while her husband spoke with his council.

As the newest chieftain of the Ó Phelan tribe, Fergus was eager to prove himself strong and unyielding. Punishments were meted out swiftly, and Balor had borne the brunt of the man's temper more than once.

Truthfully, Fergus probably wouldn't care if he walked out and never returned. Balor wasn't the beloved son, like Kenneth was. He was the mistake—the reason why his mother cried at night and the reason why Fergus had despised him for every single one of Balor's years of existence.

For the chieftain wasn't the man who had sired him. Orla had been violated by a Norman soldier, and Balor was the result. Every time Fergus glanced at Balor's face, it brought back those terrible memories.

He would have welcomed the chance to be fostered elsewhere, but Fergus had never bothered to arrange it. Instead, it seemed that the chieftain preferred to keep him here, where Balor would face punishments for every minor infraction.

Although he understood the chieftain's hatred, there were days when Balor wished he'd been born to any family except theirs. He'd been the result of violence, not the cause. But no one could see beyond that except Kenneth. The boy didn't perceive a tainted bloodline—only an older brother he delighted in ordering around. But Balor didn't care—he'd gladly die to defend Kenneth.

Balor didn't truly know how his mother felt about him. There were times when Orla looked upon him with sadness, and other times when she looked away quickly, as though she couldn't bear to see his face.

But Orla didn't seem to have noticed that her younger son was missing.

And so Balor picked up a sack of grain, hiding his face as he joined a group of serfs walking outside the wooden gate. There wasn't much time before the sun set, but he knew a few places where Kenneth liked to hide in the forest. Balor studied the ground, searching for footsteps that were smaller than the others—anything to help him find his brother's path.

He needed to bring the boy home before Fergus discovered it and sounded an alert. If he could get his brother safely back inside the ringfort before nightfall, that was all that mattered. It was a vain hope to imagine that no one would notice the two of them were missing, but Balor clung to it.

He dropped the sack of grain into a wagon and followed the narrow path down the hillside. The grasses were dead, coated with frost. Balor clutched his threadbare cloak as a frigid wind tore through the thin fabric, a few snowflakes drifting in the air. The earth was hard beneath his feet, and worry knotted in his gut that Kenneth could freeze to death or be easy prey for the wolves. But Balor locked away the useless emotions, determined to find his brother first. He wouldn't stop walking until he brought Kenneth home, even if it grew dark.

When he reached the forest, he listened. That was the first lesson he'd learned when he'd eavesdropped among the hunters. *Stop moving, listen to the sounds of the forest, and be patient.*

But there was only silence. Which was probably a good thing.

Balor continued walking, his gaze searching for any movement, anything that could reveal his brother's presence. He continued through the forest for at least a mile, even knowing that it was too far for Kenneth to walk. His heart sank. Where was he? Had someone taken him?

The path ended at the top of Amadán, overlooking a narrow road that led towards Laochre Castle. From this distance, he could see the gleaming limestone walls that guarded the king's fortress. At the bottom of the hill, a group of riders passed by on horseback. Balor stopped for a moment and sat on the edge of the hill, shielding his eyes. The dying sunlight rimmed the horizon in a blaze of gold and red, but there was enough light that he recognized them—it was the MacEgans. Not the king, but it looked like one of the brothers and his wife. Behind them, two young girls rode side by side, and Balor couldn't stop himself from staring at them. They wore brightly colored clothing and were chattering to one another.

It wasn't the quiet wealth in their demeanour that caught his attention. No, it was the way their parents drew back their horses and smiled at the children. The MacEgan warrior reached down and ruffled the youngest girl's dark braid with affection, and she laughed at him.

The ache in his chest was a dull blade, reminding him that he wasn't like them. His father would never care for him in that way, and *that* was the envy that swallowed him whole.

The older girl spied him watching at the top of the hill and leaned in to tell the younger girl.

When she turned to look at him, Balor stood, realizing that he'd been wasting time when he should have been searching the forest. It didn't matter that they'd noticed him.

But the dark-haired girl smiled at him and lifted her hand in a wave.

It was the last thing he'd ever expected. For a moment, Balor gaped at her before his hand jerked up in an answering wave. By the blood of Danu, he felt like the greatest fool in all of Éireann. *Why* had he waved back at her? She was a nobleman's daughter. Their lives were so different from his, as distant as the sun from the earth.

They rode away, and it only heightened his embarrassment and loneliness. Most likely, he'd never see them again. If he had been the respected son of a nobleman, he might have been friends with the girls, for the MacEgans didn't live far away at all.

But he was the son of a Norman invader. Not the true-born son of a chieftain, the way Kenneth was. Balor knew his place.

He turned back to the forest to walk away, suppressing every emotion. It was better not to feel anything at all. Dead leaves crunched beneath his feet as he traveled back over the frosted ground. Now the snowflakes were beginning to fall in a regular pattern, and his worry increased. His brother couldn't survive a night outside in the snow.

Finally, he called out to his brother. 'Kenneth, where are you?'

He walked farther, hurrying through the woods as he raised his voice. 'Kenneth!'

Balor was starting to worry that his brother hadn't kept to the path. What if he wasn't here at all? He'd been so certain he could find the boy.

With every step, his dread increased. He called out, no longer caring if anyone else heard him. The last of the sunlight was dying, and he began to run back towards the Ó Phelan ringfort of Dunmalus. Panic turned his stomach rancid, and his blood chilled when he saw the flare of torches and a gathering of his father's men.

Balor cursed to himself, knowing what that meant. He slowed his pace near the edge of the forest, trying to decide whether to reveal himself.

Before he could take another step, he heard a sniffling sound through the trees. He tracked the sound to a sprawling oak tree with branches the size of his waist. When he glanced up, he saw his little brother hugging a large limb.

He didn't bother asking what Kenneth was doing in the tree—it was clear that he'd been climbing and wasn't strong enough to get down. Balor easily caught the lower branch and swung himself up, climbing towards the young boy.

Kenneth was openly crying, his arms shaking as he

clung to the branch. The moment he saw Balor, his sobbing grew louder.

'It's all right,' he told his brother. 'I'll help you down.'

'I'm scared,' Kenneth cried.

'I'm going to come to you. When I do, you'll let go of the branch and hold on to me,' he said. 'You'll be safe.'

'I wanted to be a bear,' Kenneth cried. 'Bears live in trees.'

Balor inched his way across the heavy limb. 'No, they don't. They live in caves.'

'I want to be a bear who l-lives in a tree,' his brother wailed.

'Well, you can't.' Balor reached out and took the boy around the waist, pulling Kenneth's arms off the branch and around his neck. 'Hold on as tight as you can. Don't let go.'

His brother squeezed him so fiercely, it was hard to breathe, but Balor moved towards the main trunk. It was difficult to move with his brother gripping him in front, but he eased his leg off the branch, holding on to a lower branch as he brought them both down.

His brother's tears dampened his throat, but he didn't mind much. 'I love you, Balor.'

'I love you, too,' he muttered, the ache inside deepening. No one else had ever said the words to him except Kenneth. And for that reason, he would do anything for the boy.

At last, his feet touched the ground, and Balor let go of the lowest branch. He could have set Kenneth down to walk, but he continued holding him. The scent of leaves and winter clung to his brother as Balor carried him back home.

But his footsteps turned heavy when the men saw him returning. Balor slowed down, not wanting to face what lay ahead. Instead, he tried to distance himself, wondering more about the dark-haired girl and her family. He thought of her smile and the unexpected wave.

When he reached the men, Fergus's expression held a quiet rage. 'So, you found him, did you?'

Balor lowered his brother to the ground, and the boy ran to his father. Fergus embraced Kenneth a moment before he said, 'Go to your mother, my son. She'll have food for you. You're hungry, aren't you?'

Kenneth's head bobbed in agreement.

'Go on, then,' Fergus urged. Balor started to follow, but the chieftain blocked his path. 'Not you. There won't be food for you.' The sneer on the man's face was as familiar as his fists.

Balor raised his chin and squared his shoulders, meeting Fergus's gaze. Despite his own raging hunger, it was a familiar punishment. He nodded obedience, and just as he turned away, pain exploded against his cheek as Fergus struck him.

'He's a child. Were you hoping he would die outside?'

'I was trying to find him—' he started to say.

'Liar.' Fergus landed another blow to his stomach, and Balor doubled over in pain. As the beating continued, a quiet rage began to bloom within him. He'd done nothing to deserve this life. Fergus might despise him, but one day, Balor vowed he would get his revenge. He would bide his time and grow up to become the man Fergus feared—a man of strength.

A man who would stop at nothing to gain vengeance against his enemy.

And a man who wouldn't stop until he ended Fergus's reign for good.

Chapter One

Nine years later

If there was one thing Mairead MacEgan enjoyed, it was helping her friends find love. Probably because her own life was nearly devoid of it, thanks to her overprotective father and uncles, who had driven away most of her potential suitors. But then again, most of the men only wanted to wed her because she was the daughter of a provincial Irish king—not because of who she was.

They didn't truly know her. No one did. They only knew the mask she wore, of the innocent maiden who smiled and lifted the spirits of others. The king's daughter who did as she was told.

Not the restless side of her that yearned for something more.

Someday, Mairead wanted to love a husband as deeply as her mother loved her father. Oh, she had been in love once—with a man her family didn't approve of. At the time, she'd believed it was the forever love she'd yearned for.

But it had only ended in grief and heartache.

She wanted someone who would know *her*, who would see who she truly was—not the woman they wanted her to be. Maybe one day she would find that kind of marriage and hold it within her heart.

For now, she intended to set aside her own wishes and help her cousin Velaria instead. Her cousin had only recently returned to Ireland from Constantinople—with one of the most handsome warriors Mairead had ever seen. And from the looks of it, Brian of Penrith was completely in love with Velaria, though her cousin seemed fearful of the idea of marriage.

So, of course, Mairead planned to intervene and bring them together.

She'd noticed the way Velaria stared at Brian with yearning, when her cousin thought no one else was looking. The way Mairead saw it, if she could nudge things along, both would be happier for it.

It was nearly Bealtaine, a celebration of May. The festival marked the beginning of summer, and Mairead loved watching the land transform into a vivid green. She and her mother had arranged for her older cousin, Alanna MacEgan, to tell fortunes while the young women made their May crowns out of branches and flowers.

'Where are you taking me?' Velaria asked.

'Alanna is waiting for us.' She kept her cousin's hand firmly in her grip, despite Velaria's groans.

Her cousin Alanna had always been an awkward maiden, painfully shy around men, and had never married. Instead, she used her talents in telling fortunes and making love charms for young women. Mairead wondered if she should ask Alanna to make one for Velaria. The thought intrigued her.

Still, the fortune telling and charms were simply for merriment. It was only a bit of fun to imagine which man would capture her heart or Velaria's.

And if that meant she had to pretend to be enthralled by Alanna's fortune telling and behave as if she were an empty-headed maiden, so be it. There was never any harm in bringing joy to others.

Although, from the young woman's swollen lips and the blush on Velaria's face, Mairead suspected Brian had already stolen a kiss. Her own cheeks warmed at the thought.

It had been a long time since she'd allowed anyone to kiss her.

The familiar hollow ache brushed her heart, but she forced it away. Diarmud was gone, and the loss of him had broken her innocent dreams, leaving a brittle shell in its place. There was no sense in dwelling on what would never be.

As they passed through the inner bailey, Mairead stole a glance at the men preparing for the competitions. Several were shirtless, wearing only trews while they strung their bows in preparation for archery.

Her mouth went dry at the sight of their carved muscles, and she swallowed hard. Although it was wicked, she sometimes missed being in a man's embrace, his body against her own—hard against soft. A tendril of loneliness wound its way around her heart as she passed by the warriors.

There had been a time when she had known what it meant to love someone. And that part of her wanted desperately to love again. She wanted so badly to forget Diarmud's death and move forward with her life. Maybe then, the empty grief would fade.

The only way it would happen was if she genuinely gave her suitors a chance, no matter how difficult it was. She *did* want to marry and bear children of her own one day. She simply had to blot out the past and force herself to greet a different future than the one she'd imagined.

Mairead led her cousin inside the Great Chamber where women were gathering around the hearth. Branches were strewn about several of the low tables, along with early spring flowers. Alanna was seated across from a young maiden, but she stood at the sight of them. After a nod to Mairead, she turned to their cousin. 'Velaria, it's so good to see you again.' She embraced her before turning back to Sinead with instructions on how to make a May crown. 'Take the blossoms you've chosen and weave them into a crown. If you rise at dawn, look through the center, and you may see the face of the man you will marry.'

If only it were that easy, Mairead thought. But she kept her thoughts to herself, hoping to simply enjoy the moment.

Sinead stammered her agreement and thanked her. Then Alanna turned back and asked, 'Which of you would like to go first?'

Though Mairead tried to encourage Velaria with a warm smile, her cousin deferred and said, 'Let Mairead go first.'

It didn't surprise her, but she humored Velaria and knelt down before the low table.

'As you wish.' Alanna set out several branches and named them as whitethorn, rowan, sycamore, elder, and hazel. To Mairead, she instructed, 'First, choose the wood for your May crown. Place your hands upon each one, and one will call to you.'

Mairead pretended to carefully consider each branch, but her thoughts wandered and the memory of Diarmud intruded before she forced it away and cleared her mind of everything. She took slow, deep breaths, trying to remember a time when she'd been free of heartbreak.

As a young girl, her life had been so simple and easy. She let her imagination drift back through the years, and the sudden image of another boy crept into her memory. It had been so many years ago, when she was hardly more than eight years old. She'd been out riding with Velaria that wintry day when her cousin had pointed out the boy sitting on the limestone ledge above them. He was thin, slightly older than herself, but it was the misery in his demeanour that had caught her attention. His shoulders were hunched over in defeat, and he looked as if he had no one left in the world.

Something within her had been drawn to him. Mairead didn't know why she'd lifted her hand in a wave that day, but it had seemed like something he needed. The boy had lifted his own hand back, then lowered it as if he were shy. He might be one of the Ó Phelans since they'd ridden so close to their lands.

But after that, she'd never seen him again, even though she'd gone out to the forest from time to time with her brother.

Mairead's hand stopped upon an elder branch as the memory faded. 'This one, I think.' The branch was a dull grey color, and it seemed to warm beneath her fingers.

Alanna paused and said, 'The elder will protect you from evil, yes. But you will need a strong guardian.'

Now, what did her cousin mean by that? She had no need of a guardian—she was surrounded by soldiers everywhere. Or possibly Alanna meant the man who would become her true love. 'My husband?' Mairead asked.

'You will meet him soon,' Alanna said. 'But not here. He is not one of us.'

It wasn't entirely surprising. But the words seemed to burn through her as she thought of the boy again. He was probably a serf, but something about him haunted her still.

She needed to turn her attention towards someone who would actually gain her father's approval. Perhaps one of the Normans from England. The idea of meeting a suitor with no connection to their people intrigued her. Her mother was Norman, and so were her Uncle Ademar and Aunt Katherine. Mairead wondered if she could travel back to England with her cousin Velaria and find someone there. Was that what Alanna had meant? The idea held merit.

Her cousin was asking her to choose flowers to weave in with the elder branch, and Mairead interrupted her. 'Where will I meet him?'

The woman fully ignored her and repeated, 'Choose.'

She sighed in frustration and selected dried heather, gorse, and yellow primroses. The bright colors made her smile as she arranged the May crown according to Alanna's instructions. 'And look through it at dawn?'

Alanna shook her head. 'You will wear your crown two days' hence, just after sunrise. And stay with Velaria.'

Two days from now? But that wasn't the tradition at all. Why would Alanna say such a thing? May crowns were for the ceremony, and it made little sense.

'But that's after Bealtaine,' Mairead argued. 'And it's not what you told Sinead.'

Alanna once again ignored her, refusing to provide further information. Then she nodded to Velaria. 'It's your turn now.'

With a sigh, Mairead took her branches and flowers, frowning as she took her place upon one of the stools. Her Aunt Katherine, Velaria's mother, joined them and was standing just beyond the circle of women. Worry lined Katherine's face, and Mairead watched mother and daughter closely. Her aunt's expression held sadness, whereas Velaria appeared weary.

Her cousin had been gone for years, believed to be dead. And now that she'd returned from captivity in Constantinople, Velaria wasn't the same young woman at all. There was a constant sadness that seemed to cloak her.

While Mairead wove the branches and flowers together, her own guilt magnified. She was starting to realize just how selfishly she'd behaved. She'd welcomed her cousin back with open arms, chattering on about Bealtaine and finding husbands. But the more she studied Velaria, the more she realized there was something in her that was broken. Mairead's heart ached, and she found herself wanting to mend it.

She'd been so centered upon her own dreams, she hadn't stopped to think of her cousin's suffering. Velaria was brave and bold and had travelled across the world to come home, whereas Mairead was sheltered and spoiled. As the king's only daughter, she'd never wanted for anything.

She knew nothing of the outside world. Nothing of pain or true suffering beyond heartbreak. And maybe it was time to crack open her shell and become stronger.

'You have journeyed far,' Alanna told Velaria, 'but your travels are not over.' The older woman released Velaria's hands, her face troubled.

Velaria ventured, 'Should I choose a wood?' She touched each of the different branches and finally selected a rowan branch.

The silence was uncomfortable, so Mairead tried to ease it. 'What about her husband?' she asked. 'Tell Velaria about how she will meet him.'

It was a desperate attempt to lighten the mood, and she hoped Alanna would tell Velaria about Brian. Instead, her expression turned grim as she studied Velaria. 'There is darkness around you. Darkness and death.' She shuddered at her own words, and her tone grew morose. 'You will not find the happiness you seek. Not until you face what you fear most and overcome it. You must take your sword into the darkness and accept what you are.'

Mairead winced, wishing she'd never brought Velaria to see Alanna. Today was meant to be fun, a way of lifting her cousin's spirits. And now, she'd made it so much worse.

Her aunt Katherine interrupted, 'I think that's enough. Velaria, choose some flowers and make your crown.' To Alanna, she warned, 'This is not the time or place to tell such a fortune.'

Mairead wholeheartedly agreed. There was something about the woman's predictions that unsettled her. But sometimes Alanna had a way of seeing things that weren't quite of this world.

She left Velaria and Katherine to speak alone while she tried to think of a way to mend the damage she'd wrought to her cousin's mood. Just as Velaria started to leave the Great Chamber, Mairead caught up to her and linked her arm with hers. 'It's going to be all right, Velaria.'

Her cousin tried to smile, but it wasn't real at all. Mairead guided her back outside. 'I know what will lift your spirits.' Right now, they both needed a distraction. And she knew exactly where to find it.

As they passed a servant, she handed her cousin a cup of mead and took one for herself. The fermented beverage would help both of them relax.

'Where are we going?' Velaria asked.

Mairead led her through the crowd. 'You'll see.'

It was now early evening, and all around them, men prepared to compete in the Bealtaine contests for the honour of being crowned the Horned One. Torch flames danced in the iron sconces set throughout the limestone walls.

Velaria took a sip from her cup and winced at the strong mead. But if the drink would dull the edges of her pain, Mairead intended to help her along. When they passed a servant with a pitcher, she refilled her cousin's cup and guided her up the stone stairs so they could observe the events below. What her cousin needed right now was to forget her troubles. She guided Velaria to sit on the stairs, and then she moved beside her.

Below them, the men had stripped to their waists, and in the firelight, their bodies gleamed. Each man would take turns lifting large stones, which made their muscles flex, revealing every carved line and sinew.

'Now, this is much better,' Mairead said. 'What a view.'

A startled laugh broke from her cousin's throat as Velaria finished her second cup of mead. Mairead studied the men and pointed towards one of them, nudging her cousin. The fighter had dark hair pulled back in a leather thong, and he glanced up at her, his gaze filled with wicked promise. She wasn't expecting it, and beneath her gown, her skin tightened. This man was nothing like the suitors she'd known before. There was nothing elegant or noble about him. He appeared wild, almost savage—and yet, somehow familiar.

She couldn't deny that a part of her was secretly fascinated by him.

But Velaria only remarked, 'Savaş is more handsome.'

'Who?' Mairead forced her attention away from the warrior and back to her cousin.

'Brian,' Velaria corrected. 'But I call him Savaş. It means war in the Byzantine language.' She gestured with her cup, and some of the mead spilled, revealing her cousin's slight inebriation.

Mairead wanted to feel affection again, to know that secret thrill of attraction. But the problem was, she couldn't seem to fall in love with the kind of man her father wanted her to wed. She found herself far more interested in someone who spoke the truth with brutal honesty or a man with a rebellious side. The fighter below offered a slight nod of his head as he turned back to the feats of strength.

'You should have seen him fight,' Velaria continued. 'No one ever defeated him.' From the wistful tone in her voice, Mairead suspected Velaria's feelings for Brian were stronger than she cared to admit.

'Not once?'

Velaria shook her head. 'If he'd been defeated, he would be dead. The same as me.'

Her matter-of-fact tone shocked Mairead as Velaria gestured with her cup and continued. 'We fought opponents in an arena to the death. Every three days, I never knew if I would survive by nightfall.'

Shame slid over Mairead in an invisible cloak of regret. Why had she ever been trying to cheer her cousin up with fortune telling or an evening staring at handsome men? Velaria was lucky to be alive.

Their lives were worlds apart right now, and it felt as if she no longer recognized her own cousin. She admired more than Velaria's lean strength and fighting skills—her cousin's courage was undeniable.

And maybe she was starting to wish that she could be more like her.

'I never knew,' Mairead whispered. 'I'm so sorry. Thank God you were rescued.'

She meant it in her heart. But from the way her cousin spoke about Brian, she could hear the yearning in her voice. Mairead suspected Velaria was in love with him, and she couldn't help but envy her cousin.

She finished her mead, while Velaria began looking for Brian in the crowd. Slowly, Mairead walked up the stone stairs to the parapet. Sometimes, when the wind blew hard enough, she could taste the salt from the nearby sea.

After she reached the top, she rested her hands upon the stone crenellation and stared into the distance. She saw the lights at Ennisleigh, the tiny island fortress across the inlet. Although she loved it here at Laochre, sometimes it felt as if her life was suffocating—like she needed to leave this place to find out just who she was.

In two days, she decided. Just as Alanna had predicted. She would bring her May crown to the hill of Amadán, look through it at dawn, and imagine the face of the man she would love.

Oh, she knew it was naught but a foolish superstition. But if she didn't leave the castle grounds soon, she might lose her wits. At the thought of leaving, a sudden sense of anticipation gathered within her, though she couldn't quite say why.

And she had the uneasy feeling that her life was about to change in ways she'd never imagined.

Two days later

Balor Ó Phelan had been trailing Lady Mairead and her cousin for the past hour as they walked towards the hill of Amadán.

He'd been among the fighters competing in the Bealtaine games when he'd seen Mairead MacEgan sitting on the stone stairs. She'd openly stared at him, and he'd stared back. Did she even remember him from all those years ago when she'd waved at him? Likely not.

But she'd grown into a stunningly beautiful young woman, innocent and bright-spirited. And so very far out of reach for a man like him.

Today her dark hair was bound back in a single braid,

and she wore a rose gown worthy of the king's daughter she was.

He didn't know how she and her cousin had managed to sneak out of the castle with the number of soldiers her father had on patrol. It must have been a secret way out, possibly a souterrain passage. Why in the name of Danu hadn't Lady Mairead brought an escort of guards? Was she truly that foolish to believe no one would harm her? Balor couldn't imagine that sort of naiveté.

The king's daughter walked alongside her cousin Velaria, both chattering as they climbed the hill of Amadán. Mairead carried a May wreath in one hand, and both women seemed entirely oblivious to the danger they were in.

They believe they don't need protection, he predicted. They were far too confident in their safety.

He both admired their spirit and knew it could be exploited by an enemy. They weren't safe at all, despite what they believed.

Balor tethered his horse within a nearby grove of trees and continued watching them from his position at the base of the hill. He waited for a time until the women reached the top of Amadán. Mairead turned towards the forest and raised the May crown over her face. Though he couldn't see her clearly, the sunlight silhouetted her dark hair like a goddess.

She'll never want someone like you, his brain warned. A tightness caught in his gut, but Balor shoved it down while he continued to watch and wait.

A sudden gleam of silver on the horizon made him pause. From a distance, it appeared to be chainmail armour. He moved his horse to the edge of the trees, resting his hand upon his bow.

A group of men—possibly a dozen—approached the hill from the coast. Norman scouts, he guessed, from their armour. Balor cursed beneath his breath, hoping the men would travel north without noticing the two lone women. He remained within the trees but selected an arrow from his quiver.

He already knew he couldn't fight all of them. Tension tightened inside him when six of the men started up the hillside. For a moment, he debated whether to interfere. The men hadn't threatened the women yet and, for all he knew, the Normans could be related to the MacEgans.

Even so, he didn't trust anyone. He held his position at the edge of the woods and nocked an arrow to his bow. If any man dared to hurt the women, Balor would put an arrow through his spine.

His blood raced as he watched, biding his time. From this distance, he couldn't hear what they were saying. But he could guess what they wanted from the women.

Moments later, two of the soldiers seized Mairead and began to take her away. Damn them for this. Fury blazed within Balor, and he dismounted, racing towards them. The horse would only draw attention, so he began climbing the opposite hillside.

Mairead's cousin stood alone, surrounded by four men. One wore armour trimmed in gold, probably one of the leaders.

For a moment, he was torn between protecting the king's daughter and protecting her cousin. A heaviness caught within him at the realization that one of them would die.

And for him, there was only one choice of who should live—Mairead.

She struggled against the men, while Balor took cover behind a large limestone boulder and readied his bow and arrows. When the men dragged her downhill, he took aim at one of them. But Mairead twisted against them, and he couldn't release the arrow without the risk of striking her.

At the top of the hill, Mairead's cousin had seized a sword and was fighting back against her attackers. Velaria struck down two of them swiftly, and from the way she moved, it was clear she knew how to defend herself.

In contrast, the king's daughter wasn't at all prepared to fight. Mairead stumbled upon her gown, and when they reached the bottom of the hill, the first soldier lifted her on his horse and swung up behind her.

Rage darkened Balor's mood. By the blood of Belenus, he would slaughter the man who dared to touch her. He hurried back to the trees, mounting his horse and preparing to follow. Cold fury brimmed within his veins as he imagined how slowly he would kill these men. They weren't going to take her—not as long as he could track them.

But after the rider passed the rest of the scouts, one of them shouted out a command in the Norman language to split up. Most of the group moved farther north on horseback, while her captors took Mairead towards the coast. The riders didn't remain on a straight path, weaving their way one direction, then another to cover their tracks.

Wait, he warned himself. If he broke through the trees too soon, it would attract the attention of the larger group. Stealth was his ally now. Balor leaned against his horse, urging it faster. He kept his attention on Mairead, trying to reach her swiftly.

There were only two soldiers, and he could easily take them down. He'd spent years training to fight, and he wouldn't stop until he got the king's daughter back.

Behind him, he heard the thundering sound of an approaching horse. Balor glanced back, and another rider began to close in on him from the south. A foul curse expelled from him as he fired an arrow towards the man.

But the rider lurched sideways at the last moment, and the shot missed. In the meantime, the other two men had reached the coast with Mairead as their prisoner. A small boat rested on the beach, and they were bringing Mairead towards it. If they reached the water, his chances of overtaking them were gone.

Just a little farther. Balor leaned in against his horse, needing to get there faster. But the moment he reached the strand, the other rider caught up to him. The man swung his sword, and Balor threw himself off the horse, rolling away before the blade could take off his head.

He jerked to his feet and unsheathed his own blade, furious because he was losing time while they were taking her away. The Norman soldier swung his weapon again, and Balor blocked the strike. He was at a disadvantage to the mounted rider, and he deliberately moved in front of the horse, trying to spook the animal.

Just as he'd hoped, the horse grew agitated, rearing up. The soldier fought to regain control, which gave Balor time enough to slash the man's thigh and bring him to the ground.

Damn the gods, he was running out of time.

Just as his enemy struggled to rise, Balor raced to the water's edge, past Mairead's fallen May crown on the sand. The men dragged her towards the small boat while she continued to struggle against them. One lifted the anchor and shoved the boat into the waves.

Balor took aim with his bow and shot the first man in the back, dropping him into the water. Mairead cried out in alarm, but the second man took his blade and brought it to her throat, making it impossible for Balor to shoot.

'If you release your arrow, she dies.' The Norman held her against him as the tide began pulling them farther away. Within seconds, the distance between them grew even more as the water pushed them back.

Balor didn't lower his weapon but waited for the right moment. All he needed was a clear shot, and the man was dead.

Mairead paled, her hands clenched in her skirts. Her gaze met his, and she blurted out, 'Please help me.'

The moment she spoke, her attacker struck Mairead across the face, bloodying her lip. She sank against him, and Balor released the arrow.

It grazed the soldier's cheek, leaving a line of blood as the man seized the oars, pulling hard against the water while Mairead lay slack against him.

And Balor didn't know if it was possible to swim fast enough to catch up to them.

It was the hardest thing Mairead had ever done, pretending to be unconscious and weak. Within her sleeve, she held a blade, waiting for the right opportunity to strike. Outside the boat, she heard more fighting before a man cursed and a splashing noise struck the water.

Then the boat rocked as another man climbed inside. Her heart pounded as she wondered if it was the Irishman. She prayed it was.

She'd already recognized him as the same fighter she'd watched on the night Alanna had told her fortune. But it also seemed as if she'd seen this man before, though she didn't know where. How had he known that she and Velaria had left Laochre? Had he been awake and followed them? She couldn't help but be grateful for it.

The waiting was agonizing, not knowing whether the

Irishman had come to rescue her. At last, she felt a hand reaching for her, and Mairead jerked at the unwanted touch, opening her eyes.

But the Irishman was gone, leaving her with two Norman captors. Dismay flooded through her when she realized she would have to break free of them and make her own escape. Her father and uncles had trained her to fight back, though she'd done a poor job of it earlier. But at least now she had a weapon they knew nothing about.

'You're a pretty one,' the bearded man said in the Norman tongue. 'I'll enjoy tasting you.'

She'd cut out his tongue if he dared try such a thing. They probably didn't realize she understood their language. And that might be an advantage. They might speak freely, thinking she wouldn't know their words.

'Stabfaidh mé thú,' she shot back in Irish, threatening to gut them.

The second man remained stone-faced. 'Hold her down.' She wanted to spit in his face, but she forced herself to keep her struggles to a minimum, just enough to make them believe they'd won.

Don't show your strength, she warned herself. *Wait for the right moment.*

She wished she weren't wearing a *léine* and overdress. Although the rose-colored silk was one of her favourites, it was better suited to her father's court than trying to run away. The skirts were far too long. Her mood darkened at the thought of what would happen to her now. Terror lanced what was left of her courage, even as she tried to remain cool and collected.

'We could give her to King John, after we've finished with her,' the first soldier said. He inched her gown higher, baring her legs. 'He'll enjoy this one in his bed when he arrives with his armies.'

Her blood chilled at the mention of the King of England. John had been named Lord of Ireland, but he'd mostly left them in peace. Why would he be returning now?

But all thoughts of the king fled when the first man tried to jerk her legs apart. Mairead struggled against him and let out a loud scream. While he was distracted, she gripped her blade behind her skirts, knowing she would have to wield it against these men.

Time seemed to go motionless, and her heart pounded. There was no choice except to fight back. She'd never wanted to kill a man, but if she didn't strike hard, he fully intended to violate her. And she refused to be his victim.

Her teeth were chattering with panic, and tears of rage slid down her cheeks. But before she could stab her attacker, the boat suddenly rocked violently. The man lost his balance and fell forward, just as the Irishman emerged from the sea, dripping wet.

He wasted no time in slicing his blade across her attacker's throat. The look in his dark blue eyes held intensity and a silent vow. He'd swum this far and would stop at nothing to defend her.

Something inside her warmed to the thought, and for a moment, she could only stare at him in shock. His features were handsome, but in a rough, unkempt way. His fierce jaw outlined a face that intrigued her. He wasn't like the polished noblemen her father had chosen as suitors in the past. Blue eyes of pure rebellion stared back at her and dark, wet hair hung against his nape.

Her thoughts scattered when the other Norman soldier withdrew his blade and slashed at the Irishman. Mairead backed away, still keeping the blade in her hand. The Norman struck out while the boat swayed dangerously. She questioned whether to let them fight—or should she intervene? Her question was answered when the Norman's blade sliced the Irishman's forearm.

'Is that all you can do?' he taunted the Norman soldier. He beckoned to his enemy, as if he relished the idea of a fight.

But the smug expression on the soldier's face made it seem as if he was only toying with his opponent. The Irishman slashed his own blade, and the Norman blocked the blow—just before he slid his own dagger between them.

In that vicious fragment of the fight, Mairead feared the worst. Her champion was going to lose, and after he did, this Norman would punish her. She couldn't let that happen. Her stomach roiled with terror and nausea, but she had to act now. Raw instinct and her father's training flooded through her as she stabbed her own blade into the side of the Norman's exposed neck. As her blade cut through flesh, she remembered her father's warning never to pierce it from the back, for fear of the knife striking against bone.

Blood spilled over her hands as she ended the man's life. The Irishman caught the Norman's body and tossed it overboard, the blade still in his neck.

'Good,' he murmured.

Her body shook with tremors, but Mairead dipped her bloody hands over the side of the boat, trying to wash them. Bile rose in her throat, but she choked it back.

Oh, God. She'd killed a man. Though she'd known that there might come a time when she would have no choice, it shook her to the core. Tears flooded her eyes, and she hardly knew what to do now.

Be strong, she warned herself. Now was not the time to fall apart.

She looked back at the Irishman, half expecting him to offer words of comfort or ask if she was all right. Instead, his gaze had turned thoughtful as if he was trying to make a decision.

'Thank you,' Mairead muttered, 'for trying to save me.' She dried her hands on her skirts and then asked, 'What is your name?'

'Balor Ó Phelan,' he answered.

The moment he revealed his identity, she struggled to veil her reaction.

She had heard a great deal about Balor Ó Phelan during the past few months—and none of it was good. She'd overheard stories about him, and some said he'd killed dozens of men.

'They call you the Demon of Éireann, don't they?' Mairead said softly. But for a demon, he was ruggedly handsome. Even now, his blue eyes held amusement, as if he knew a secret she didn't. Her gaze drifted over his broad shoulders and muscled forearms. She remembered seeing him without his armour, his abdomen ridged with strength.

And Heaven help her—demon or not—she liked what she saw.

Balor gave a single nod and took the boat oars as he positioned himself at the stern. 'They call me many things.'

'And are they true?' Among the tales she'd heard, the bards claimed that not only was he a killer, he was also reckless—a man who would stop at nothing to get what he wanted.

A slight smirk pulled at his mouth. 'Probably.' He began rowing, the oars cutting through the waves.

She didn't know what to say to that. Then she ventured, 'Today you behaved like a hero. I'm grateful for it.' She tried to smile, holding her knees as she regarded him.

'I'm not a hero, Lady Mairead.' He pulled the oars hard, and it was then that she noticed they were going in the opposite direction of Laochre towards the nearby settlement of the Ó Phelan tribe.

She didn't want to believe what she was seeing. 'But you saved me from the Normans. I thought—'

'You thought wrong. I'm taking you to Dunmalus.' His arms flexed against the power of the waves, drawing her eyes to his lean strength.

Then it dawned upon her what he was doing. 'Are you—you're not trying to take me as your hostage, are you?'

Balor's gaze drifted over her. 'That's exactly what I'm doing, my lady.'

Chapter Two

'Stop rowing, right now.'

Balor stared at the king's daughter, fully amused by Mairead's imperious command. Did she honestly believe he was going to let her go after all that had happened? He'd infiltrated the castle, rescued her from the Normans, and had successfully claimed her as his prisoner.

Fury blazed across her expression.

'Is there something you want, Lady?'

'Stop this.' She squared her shoulders and raised her chin. 'I refuse to become your captive. Put the oars down, and we'll start with you answering my questions.'

He found it somewhat entertaining that she honestly believed he was going to obey her. 'I don't answer to you, *my lady*.' He tilted his head slightly. 'But I might listen if you ask nicely.'

Her face blushed, even as her spine stiffened. 'Why are you kidnapping me?' she demanded. 'I thought you were here to rescue me.'

'The Normans took you first,' he pointed out. 'I was only finishing what they couldn't do.'

She gaped at him, her pale skin flushed with fury. 'My father will send an army after me. If you dare to bring me to your family's ringfort, they will tear it apart.'

Good. The idea of destroying Dunmalus was exactly what he wanted. Kidnapping the king's daughter would bring the wrath of the MacEgan tribe upon Fergus's head and undermine his authority. It would also allow his brother the chance to take command.

'It was the chief's idea to bring you to our ringfort,' he lied. 'My brother, Kenneth, wants to wed you.'

That part wasn't a lie. Kenneth had visited Laochre with Fergus on a number of occasions, and his brother had spoken of his fascination with Mairead. If Kenneth married the king's daughter, he would gain a MacEgan alliance. His brother was young and easily influenced. The match was a good one, for it would bind their lands together.

And if his brother agreed to this arrangement, he would become the new chieftain with a royal bride. Best of all, Fergus would either be banished or become a MacEgan prisoner.

The only problem was gaining Mairead's consent to the marriage. He'd expected her to be softhearted and fearful. It seemed she wasn't at all a gentle lady like others believed.

'Kidnapping me isn't going to get you very far,' she warned. 'I won't marry your brother. Or you,' she warned.

'Oh, believe me. I have no interest in marrying you.' He rested the oars across his knees and met her gaze. There was no denying her beauty. Mairead MacEgan's dark braid had come undone, with loose strands framing her face. There was a softness about her, and her green eyes and full lips demanded attention. But beneath her sweetness, he didn't miss the steel interior and confidence.

'We should talk about this before you make a terrible decision,' she said. Her voice turned gentle, and she said, 'You saved my life today. You saved me from being hurt by those men.' To his shock, she reached out and rested her palm upon his hand. The slight heat of her skin upon his was like nothing he'd ever felt before. No one touched him. They avoided him and cursed him.

It took everything in him not to jerk his hand back. She shouldn't lower herself to rest her hand upon his.

'What is it you want?' she asked quietly. 'There may be a way I could help you.'

His mind conjured up images of those lovely fingers moving from his hands to his chest. What would it be like if she explored his body with those soft hands? The very thought sent a flare of lust within him, and he gritted his teeth.

Quickly, he jerked his hand away. 'There's not. You're coming with me to Dunmalus.'

'Or you could bring me back to the island of Ennisleigh,' she suggested. 'It's not very far.' Her voice was alluring, and he knew exactly what she was doing.

'If you bring me home to my family, you will be rewarded,' she continued. 'My father, King Patrick, will gladly give you anything you desire for my safe return.'

Balor didn't believe that for a moment. He'd built a reputation as a cold-hearted warrior, and he wasn't about to play the hero.

Before he could pick up the oars, she took a breath. 'My father will be hosting another gathering before Lughnasa, with men from all over Ireland. Your brother could come then, and I would consider him among the other suitors.'

He doubted she would truly consider Kenneth for a husband. But then she added, 'If my father's soldiers attack Dunmalus, it will be war between our tribes. Innocent blood will be spilled, and that's not what either of us wants.'

'I've spilled my share of blood,' Balor admitted nonchalantly.

'Would you spill mine?' Her voice was barely a whisper. 'I am not a woman who will go meekly into marriage. I intend to marry a man I love, someone who loves me. And I will die before letting myself be forced into an unwanted union. Believe me when I say I will fight with everything in me.'

A darkness shadowed her words, making him fully realize the threat. If he took her to Dunmalus, Fergus might indeed try to take her prisoner. If she defied the chieftain, he wouldn't hesitate to punish her. And that was what made Balor reconsider his plans.

No matter that he wanted the MacEgans to attack Dunmalus and overthrow Fergus, Mairead was right. She would fight back, and he didn't want *her* to be harmed during this battle. If he brought her to Dunmalus, Fergus would only use her for his own gain.

He let out a foul curse. She was right—his plan wasn't a good one. If she had been weak or submissive, it might have worked. Instead, there was a warrior beneath that silken gown. Damn her for it.

Balor held her gaze for a long moment before he picked up the oars and changed their direction towards Ennisleigh. He pulled through the waves swiftly, wondering how she'd gained the upper hand. But it *would* be easier if she wed Kenneth willingly or if the king forced Fergus to step down.

And more importantly, she would owe him a favour.

'Before Lughnasa then,' he said quietly, 'I will bring my brother, Kenneth, to Laochre.'

Her lips curved in a soft smile that would bring most men to their knees. 'Then I will let him court me,' she agreed, 'and if he is a man of worth—if I believe I could love him—I will give him a chance.'

He rowed in silence until the island fortress grew visible. It was better if he didn't take her the entire distance. The MacEgans wouldn't believe for a moment that he'd rescued her. And Mairead might admit the truth to them—that he'd tried to kidnap her, just as the others had.

Balor slowed his pace and brought the boat slightly closer to the mainland. 'I'm leaving you here, and I'll swim to shore.'

She moved in closer and took his hands in hers. 'Thank you, Balor Ó Phelan. I am grateful for my life.' Her green eyes warmed, studying him closely. Then, she leaned in and brushed her mouth against his forehead in an unexpected kiss.

It was as light as a summer breeze upon his skin and just as brief. But Balor held her wrists captive, staring at her as the boat drifted. Though he knew this wasn't at all a good idea, he leaned in and stole a kiss of his own, taking her lips gently. Mairead froze in place while he explored that gorgeous mouth, softly claiming what she'd never intended to give.

And then, tentatively, she began to kiss him back. A groan caught in his throat, but he forced himself to gentle his grip on her wrists. She moved her palms up to his chest, as if she knew how forbidden this was.

He craved more of her, wanting to take her face between his hands. But when her arms went around his neck, he grew aware of how close they were to her father's fortress. This wasn't meant to be.

He took her arms away from him, stared hard into those innocent green eyes and said, 'Until I see you again, Lady.'

Then he dived off the boat and began swimming back to shore.

Late Summer

'Are you certain you want to do this?' her mother asked. 'There's no need to host an *aenach* to choose a husband so soon. Especially after…everything you endured. It could simply be a celebration.'

Though it had been nearly two moons since the Norman attack, Mairead had let her family believe she'd fought her way back to Ennisleigh alone. They had sent dozens of men after her, but by the time they caught up to her, she was already home.

No one knew about Balor's intervention, and something told her to keep that a secret. Her family wouldn't believe her if she'd told them the Demon of Éireann had rescued her. After she'd talked him out of kidnapping her, that is.

And yet… Balor had listened to her in the end and brought her back. Which meant maybe he was a man worthy of redemption. And now enough time had passed that she could invite his brother among all the other suitors and keep her promise.

'It will give me the chance to meet more suitors from all across Ireland.' Mairead kept her tone bright, even though it was a brave face to push aside her uneasiness.

'That's true,' her father agreed. 'And King John has also sent a few of his noblemen.' He exchanged a guarded look with Isabel, one that Mairead didn't quite understand. A few weeks ago, her father and his brothers had brought their forces north to greet King John. Although Patrick had claimed they had gone north to swear fealty, she suspected it was a show of force to answer for the Norman attack—and remind the king of their alliance and their strength in numbers.

It made her wonder if part of that alliance was meant to

be through her marriage. Was her father implying that she was expected to choose one of the king's men?

Even now she still didn't trust the Normans. Though she was trying to behave as if everything was normal, she still awakened at all hours of the night, remembering the moment she had ended the soldier's life. It haunted her, not because of what she'd had to do—but because of how easy it had been to kill him. In that moment, the choice had transformed her. And she didn't know how to go back to being the maiden she'd been.

Or even if she wanted to.

But she *did* want a husband and a family of her own, and this was probably the best way to get acquainted with possible matches. Perhaps the best way to remove the fear was to face it.

She smoothed her light blue silk gown and stood, pretending as if his words didn't bother her. 'I will consider the king's men, as well as the others.' Then she asked, 'Are all of the preparations ready for tonight?'

'Your mother has everything in hand.' Patrick sat back in a large wooden chair, his gaze suddenly turning thoughtful as Isabel came close and rested her hand on his shoulder. He softened and added, 'I have always hoped that we would live long enough to see you married.'

Her emotions tightened within her as she approached. 'Please don't talk like that, Father.'

'You were a gift to your mother and me,' he said softly. 'An unexpected one.' His tone turned to one of sadness.

'And a blessing,' Isabel agreed. 'The healer told me I would never bear another child. And then you came when I was past forty.' She shook her head in wonder. 'We never imagined such a miracle.'

Mairead came and drew a stool up beside them. To anyone else, Patrick and Isabel appeared old enough to be her grandparents. But she'd always adored them both. Seeing the way they loved one another was something she wanted for herself. She wanted a man to look at her the way her father looked at her mother.

And although Isabel claimed that Mairead's father had despised her when they'd first met, Mairead didn't believe that for a moment. 'I will meet the suitors, and if there is anyone I wish to wed, then we will set the betrothal,' she told them.

'After you choose a husband, I'm going to step down as king,' Patrick said. 'It's long past time Liam took my place.'

A sudden rise of fear caught her, but she pushed it back. She didn't really know why her father hadn't given up the throne years ago. Though most people said it was because Patrick was their most beloved king, she wondered whether her brother, Liam, would truly take the throne. Liam had been named *tánaiste*, the heir to the kingship. And yet, there was always a chance that the people could select someone else to reign over the lands. Provincial kings were chosen from among the people.

Mairead said nothing, not wanting to worry her father. 'Liam will make a good king,' she said, taking his hand. 'As for my marriage, I am grateful that you're allowing me the right to choose.'

'Within reason,' he said. 'I'll not let you wed a man who does not honour you.'

His words evoked the memory of the day she'd met Balor Ó Phelan. His kiss still haunted her, even now. It had been both gentle and tempting, coaxing her towards surrender.

It reminded her of Diarmud's kiss, and the grief rose up again before she pushed it back. *Don't think of him.* She'd paid the price once before, falling in love with a man her father didn't approve of.

Right now, she needed to push away all thoughts of Balor. He was exactly the sort of dishonourable man her father had warned her about. The Ó Phelan rogue had fully planned to kidnap her at first—but at least he *had* listened to her reasoning and had changed his mind. She had to admit to herself that it meant something.

The relations between the MacEgans and Ó Phelans were uncertain, at best. Years ago, Donal Ó Phelan had tried to seize the throne for himself. Was that the reason why Balor had meant to take her hostage? To challenge Liam and put their own tribesman on the throne?

Her blood chilled at the thought.

She had kept her word and had sent an invitation to Kenneth Ó Phelan. But why had Balor spoken on his brother's behalf instead of his own? He'd already said that he had no interest in marriage—not that she wanted someone like him. But something about Balor intrigued her…which probably meant that a part of her was wicked and rebellious, too. Her cheeks flushed at the thought.

'There is someone I've been wanting you to meet,' her father said. 'Lord Rogan Hammett, the Earl of Lowell, is one of the king's noblemen. He arrived earlier this afternoon, and I agreed to grant him an audience before the *aenach*.'

'Did you?' She wasn't at all certain about this—especially if the man was a Norman.

'Just meet him,' her father said. 'The choice is still yours.' He rose from the chair and offered his arm. 'Come, and I'll introduce you.'

Mairead took his arm, following him outside the solar, along with her mother. As they descended the stairs, she didn't miss the way her father slowed his steps, pausing to catch his breath. Sometimes it frightened her to think of his age. But she agreed that it was a good decision to let Liam take the throne at last.

When they reached the Great Chamber, her spirits lifted. She turned back to her mother and said, 'Mother, this is beautiful.'

Isabel had decorated the gathering space with fresh flowers, particularly those in Mairead's favourite color: yellow. Dried gorse, irises, and primroses adorned the tables and walls while new rushes lined the floors. A warm peat fire burned at the hearth, and several long trestle tables had been scoured. Throughout the room, light burned from sconces on the walls with fresh beeswax candles.

As they approached the dais, Mairead saw several men rising from their places. A sudden rush of nerves tightened in her veins at the thought of being the center of attention. She wished Velaria were still here. Right now, she wanted a trusted friend and confidante. But instead, her cousin had married Brian of Penrith in a quick wedding. Both were gone, and loneliness surrounded Mairead in a cloak of sadness.

Her father led her closer to a blond man dressed in a green silk tunic and trews. The nobleman was older, possibly near forty, and she suspected he might have been married before. He wore a heavy gold chain that crossed both shoulders, and his brown eyes warmed at the sight of her.

Her father introduced the man, speaking the Norman language. 'Mairead, this is Lord Rogan Hammett, the Earl of Lowell.'

Lord Lowell bowed and spoke in the Norman language. 'My lady Mairead, it is my pleasure to meet you at last.'

For a moment, she felt as if her mouth couldn't quite

form the right words to say. Only a few weeks ago, she would have been delighted to meet a handsome, wealthy suitor. But now she couldn't help but compare him with Balor. Lord Lowell's brown eyes seemed dull in comparison with Balor's piercing blue eyes. The earl didn't make her heart race, but she realized he was meant to be a safe, reliable choice of a husband. Likely one with strong connections to the English king—which made her wonder what they wanted from her.

Although she knew Lord Lowell and his men had nothing to do with the scouts who had attacked her a month ago—those soldiers had been part of King John's entourage before he'd traveled north—it was still difficult to trust any Normans. She managed to mumble a greeting, even as her father rested his hand against her spine. Probably to reassure her, but more likely to prevent her from bolting away.

Why was she so nervous all of a sudden? It frustrated her to feel so scattered. Mairead took a deep breath, then another, forcing her heartbeat to steady.

'I had heard tales of your beauty, and I am glad to see they were not exaggerated,' Lord Lowell continued. His compliment sounded genuine, and guilt weighed upon her, for she ought to give him a fair chance.

'I—thank you, my lord,' she managed to answer. Her father then brought her to meet the other men, but she could feel the earl's gaze upon her.

'Would you walk with me for a little while?' Lord Lowell asked, after she'd been introduced to the others. 'So we could get better acquainted?'

Mairead glanced at her father, and he inclined his head with permission. 'I suppose so.'

The earl offered his arm and led her from the Great Chamber to the large doors that led outside. 'It wasn't my intention to make you feel uncomfortable,' he apologized. 'I am sorry if I did.'

'All of this makes me uncomfortable,' she confessed. 'I was not truly thinking about what it would mean to have so many suitors here for my sake. It's overwhelming.'

They passed by her cousin Alanna, whose eyes had gone wide. A stricken look crossed her face as a basket slipped from her hands, spilling rushes and flowers everywhere. Mairead started to move towards her, but the woman bolted away.

At first, she worried about Alanna—but then, a sudden shock rippled through Mairead. Was this connected to the May crown she'd made several weeks ago? Was Lord Lowell the man she was meant to marry, and was that why Alanna had appeared so shaken?

'I am sorry,' Mairead murmured. 'We must have startled my cousin.'

The earl glanced in Alanna's direction for a moment before he turned back. 'You needn't be overwhelmed by so many suitors. I would hope that you would see it as an honour.' His mouth curved in a warm smile. 'A woman of your rank, a king's daughter, deserves nothing less than the right to choose her husband.'

Mairead didn't truly know what to say, so she said, 'Tell me about yourself and your homeland.'

Lord Lowell walked with her outside. 'I live in the northwest of England. It can be cold in the winter, but the hills are green, and the forests have trees so tall, you have to tilt your head back to see the tops.'

His voice was calm, and from his tone, Mairead could hear that he loved his homeland. She started to relax and ventured a smile. 'It sounds lovely.'

'It is.' They walked inside the inner bailey, and he added,

'My home is about the same size as Laochre, except the sea is farther away.'

It was a subtle way of speaking about his wealth. But she found herself feeling not quite so intimidated. And she supposed Lord Lowell could be a kind man if she gave him a chance.

Inwardly, she wondered what it would be like if the earl kissed her. Would it be gentle and inviting? Or only out of duty? She couldn't deny that Balor's kiss had awakened her, pushing away the months of grief. If he had continued kissing her, it might have become something more. A spark of heat had risen between them, kindling her blood hotter.

Immediately, she shut the thought down. She needed to stop thinking of Balor Ó Phelan when their lives were so different. Her father had given her this opportunity to get acquainted with a nobleman, someone who would offer a powerful alliance.

'I suppose you've heard that King John is here in the north of Ireland,' the earl was saying. It pulled her attention back to the present, and she wondered how much Lord Lowell knew about the attack.

'Yes,' she answered. 'My father and his brothers returned from the north, not long ago.'

'King John is asking all of the Irish kings to swear their fealty,' Lord Lowell continued. 'I suppose your father has already done so.'

'It's why he traveled there, I suppose,' Mairead hedged. But she wondered if King John intended to usurp the role of High King. Was that why he was here? To conquer and command Ireland? John had been named Lord of Ireland, but in years past, it hadn't seemed to matter since he spent most of his time in England.

Was that why her father wanted this alliance with the

earl? Had something happened with King John that Patrick felt they needed another means of protecting their family? She was starting to feel an invisible pressure, as if her freedom to choose was only an illusion.

The earl turned to face her. 'You speak my language very well, my lady. It's a welcome surprise.'

'My mother was Norman, and so was my aunt.' She ventured a smile, but then behind the earl, she caught a slight movement of someone crossing past her. Though she hadn't meant to glance at him, she immediately recognized Balor.

Despite her efforts not to react, her heartbeat quickened at the sight of him. He wore a grey threadbare cloak, and his dark hair was gathered back in a leather thong that emphasized his jawline. And when she saw his firm mouth, she couldn't stop the flush to her cheeks as she remembered the way her body had reacted to his kiss.

Balor Ó Phelan was entirely too handsome for his own good. And when his mouth curved in a wicked smile, she stiffened. He nodded in the direction of an older nobleman who stood beside a young man with reddish-brown hair—but Balor remained behind them at a distance. Mairead guessed the younger man was likely Balor's brother, Kenneth. From the look of it, Kenneth was slightly younger than herself.

'I'm boring you with conversation, aren't I?' Lord Lowell said. His eyes gleamed, and he glanced behind him at the young lad. 'I see that I will have to do more to gain your affections.' He lifted her hand to his lips, kissing it gently.

She was entirely too aware of Balor watching them, and embarrassment flushed her face. It was as if he knew how uncomfortable she felt, being the center of attention.

Mairead forced her attention back to Lord Lowell. 'No, you aren't boring me, my lord.' Her mind searched for an appropriate excuse. 'But I do have other suitors waiting to be introduced. Perhaps we could speak again later?'

'I hope so.' The earl bowed and stepped back.

No sooner had he left, than the older nobleman pushed his son towards her. He gave a slight bow and said, 'Lady Mairead, I am Fergus Ó Phelan, chieftain of our tribe. This is my son and heir, Kenneth.'

The young man gaped at her, his cheeks flushing. But he took a few awkward steps forward and bowed. 'It is an honour to meet you, Lady Mairead.'

She inclined her head politely. 'It is my honour as well.' When she glanced around, there was no sign of Balor. Though she didn't want to disclose that she'd met him previously, she asked, 'Am I wrong, or don't you have an older brother? Did he travel with you?'

Kenneth started to nod, just as Fergus cut him off. 'No. Kenneth is my only son.'

The chieftain's declaration startled her. Was the man not Balor's father? She hadn't considered that Kenneth was a half brother. Or had Fergus disowned his older son? Had Balor earned such a reputation that his own family would refuse to acknowledge him?

Their family troubles shouldn't bother her—especially since the bards had sung their tales of Balor as a fierce, bloodthirsty warrior. And yet...she didn't quite believe he deserved it. He'd saved her life, after all.

It was probably a good thing that no one here knew who he was, except the family who pretended he didn't exist.

With an apologetic smile, Fergus added, 'Kenneth is young, but he has spoken of nothing but meeting you. And I feel it would be a good match to join our lands together.'

Mairead kept her expression neutral. 'I will consider all of my suitors before making a decision.'

'Of course,' Fergus said. But she didn't miss the gleam of ambition in his eyes.

As she departed to return to the Great Chamber, she saw a shadowed figure in the threadbare cloak, just inside the doors. She turned, expecting to see Balor. But there was no one there.

There was no reason to be disappointed, Mairead told herself. She didn't truly need to see him again.

But it made her wonder why he had come. Unless...he had wanted to see her again. A flutter of nerves caught her stomach, just as she stomped it down with common sense.

No. She had extended the invitation to Kenneth, just as she'd promised. There was no logical reason for Balor to travel here, especially when his own family had denied knowing him.

So why *was* he here? He hadn't changed his mind about becoming one of her suitors, had he?

Her traitorous body grew restless at the thought, even though she knew better than to imagine he could ever be a match for her.

But one way or another, Mairead planned to find Balor and learn exactly why he had come and what he wanted from her.

After he'd slipped away from the keep, Balor watched over Mairead to ensure she was safe. He hadn't missed the way Lord Lowell had stared at her. Despite his age, the golden-haired Norman earl was exactly the sort of alliance she should have. He was powerful, wealthy, and an ally of King John's.

But something about the Norman earl made his fists tighten. Balor told himself it wasn't jealousy. No, he simply intended to protect Mairead from any man who tried to push against her boundaries. Or kiss her.

All right, so maybe it was a bit of jealousy. But although the earl might have kissed her hand, Balor took satisfaction in the knowledge that *he* had tasted those lips and felt the press of her body against his.

The memory curled within him like the wisp of a breeze—there for a moment, then gone.

He already knew he could never wed a woman like Mairead. A life of royalty was impossible to imagine, for his status was far beneath the dirt under her feet. Kenneth, too, had little chance of winning her hand in marriage.

Balor recognized Lord Lowell as a genuine threat. He was the sort of man who held the king's respect. The sort who might win her hand in marriage. Maybe even her heart.

Although he had retreated a slight distance, Lowell remained close by, watching over her.

It took an effort, but Balor forced himself to walk away from the woman he would never have. A sudden flicker of motion caught his attention, and Balor turned just in time to see a skinny young lad surrounded by other boys.

'You don't even know how to use a blade, Marcas,' one taunted. 'All you ever do is read.'

'I like reading.' The boy squared his shoulders and stared back.

'That's because you're too scared to fight,' another teased. 'You know you'll lose and start crying.'

The boy's posture tensed, and in that moment, it reminded Balor of his younger brother. It didn't matter that this wasn't his fight. Quietly, he took a few steps forward until he stood behind Marcas. The boy appeared unaware of his presence, and Balor unsheathed his blade, holding it firmly as he watched the other boys. The moment they saw him standing there, they stopped their teasing and appeared uncomfortable.

'Come on,' the first said. 'There's food near the kitchens. I'm hungry.'

The other two followed him, and the boy's shoulders slumped in relief. But the moment Marcas turned and saw Balor, he let out a yelp.

'I didn't see you there,' the boy apologized.

Balor shrugged. He was about to turn away when Marcas suddenly touched his arm. 'Wait. You were the reason they didn't try to fight me.'

'I was.' Balor sheathed his weapon and raised his hood, hoping that no one had witnessed the interaction. He'd followed Kenneth and Fergus here, but he didn't need them to be aware of his presence.

'I owe you a debt,' the boy said seriously. He straightened and asked, 'Are you here to court Lady Mairead?'

Balor didn't know quite how to answer that, so he said, 'I'm here to ensure that no one harms her.'

The boy stared at him as if making a decision. 'So, you don't want to marry her?'

He thought about lying and saying he didn't want to, but it seemed better to tell Marcas the truth. 'It doesn't matter what I might want. She wouldn't look twice at someone like me,' he answered.

'But if you *did* like her, would you—'

'I wouldn't waste her time.' He cut off the boy and continued, 'I'm not a wealthy nobleman like the others here.'

Marcas's brown furrowed. 'Then how can I repay my debt to you?'

'You owe me nothing.' He was about to walk away, but the boy stepped in and interrupted.

'Mairead's favourite color is yellow. And she likes walking barefoot by the sea at sunset when it's warm outside.'

Balor paused. 'How would you know this?'

The boy smiled. 'She's my aunt. I've known her all my life.' Then his gaze turned serious. 'Do you know how to use a blade? You look like you do.'

'I do. And so does your aunt.' He wasn't entirely certain what the boy wanted from him.

Marcas tilted his head to the side. 'If you teach me how to be a better fighter, I can take you to her when she's alone and introduce you.'

The boy's earnest desire to help was like a fist to his gut. Balor had never expected anything in return for the silent defence—but he couldn't deny that a moment alone with Mairead was indeed tempting—even if it was unlikely she'd ever want to see him again. But Marcas saw his hesitation and said, 'Or, if you don't think I'd be any good at fighting…'

'What about your father?' he ventured. 'Didn't he teach you to fight?'

Marcas nodded. 'He tried, but I wasn't any good. It would be better if you taught me in secret.'

'I'm a stranger to you,' Balor pointed out. 'How do you know I could even teach you? You've never seen me fight.' He shook his head, knowing that the MacEgans would never want a fighter like him near Marcas. 'It's better if you let your father show you how.'

'But if my father teaches me, then everyone watches,' Marcas said quietly. 'And they laugh at me. I embarrass him.'

The boy's pain echoed his own. Although Balor knew it was a terrible idea, he also couldn't deny that the boy could give him an advantage. He could ask Marcas to help Kenneth gain a private audience. 'How old are you?'

'I'll be ten soon.'

The yearning in the boy's voice pulled at him, and Balor let out a breath. 'Tomorrow at dawn. I'll be near the barbican gate. If you're not there…'

'I will be,' Marcas swore. With a mischievous look, he added, 'Follow me.'

'Now?'

The boy nodded. Balor kept his hood up to cover his face and followed the lad up a set of stone stairs towards the parapets. He walked past the guards, and the boy led him to one of the towers that overlooked the sea.

'Wait here,' Marcas said. 'I'm going to bring her to you.'

Before he could protest, the boy was gone. With a sigh, Balor leaned back against the stone wall. Despite the forbidden pull towards her, it wasn't wise to see Mairead again. Or else he might start thinking about the taste of her lips that first time. After she'd reached out to him, he'd been unable to resist stealing the kiss he'd wanted. Even now, it haunted him.

Outside, the moon was beginning to rise, casting rays of amber upon the dark seas. As Balor waited, he took a step forward and glanced down at the suitors gathering below. There were far more Normans than he'd imagined. Clearly, her father was looking for a match that would please King John and raise Mairead's rank even higher.

Or possibly they were here for another reason—to take command. Balor studied them, feeling a sudden uneasiness when he saw Fergus speaking to some of the Norman soldiers. Why would the chieftain do so? Fergus despised the Normans after what they'd done to Orla. Unless he hoped that somehow these men would help him gain an advantage with the MacEgans?

He didn't trust Fergus at all—and with good reason. The chieftain hated him for every breath he took and always had. The man had seemed to enjoy starving or punishing him.

Had it not been for Orla's intervention, Balor suspected he might not have survived at Dunmalus.

He'd understood exactly what it was to be a victim. And he couldn't help but see a glimpse of himself in the boy.

Balor hadn't known anything about fighting, except what it was like to be on the receiving end of the fists. He'd been just a little older than Marcas when Orla had sent him away to England, after a bad beating from Fergus.

At the time, he'd felt so abandoned and lost…but in her own way, his mother had saved him. He'd been allowed to dwell among a Norman lord's foster sons, and there, he'd learned how to fight, becoming more than the child he'd once been.

And whether or not they'd wanted him to return, he'd found the courage to travel back to Éireann, even knowing he didn't belong among the Ó Phelans. The years had forged his will into a weapon, one that would bring down Fergus Ó Phelan and put Kenneth in his place as chieftain.

Were it not for his brother, he'd have turned his back on all of them.

'Balor.' Mairead's voice was breathless as she stepped into the tower, escorted by Marcas. 'I thought I saw you earlier.' The softness of her smile only heightened his awareness of her beauty.

Don't, he warned himself. The last thing he needed was to let himself be allured by a woman he would never have.

The young boy released her hand and met his gaze

briefly, reminding Balor of the promise he'd made. Then Marcas disappeared, leaving them alone. So be it.

Lady Mairead took a step closer, and the scent of her skin flooded the air with a hint of rose. Balor wanted to bury his face in her hair before capturing that mouth again. Damn her for giving him a taste of forbidden fruit.

'You look…better than the last time I saw you,' he said roughly. The words weren't the compliment he'd meant to say, but whenever he was around her, he couldn't quite form the words he wanted to.

'So do you.' She didn't seem at all nervous, and there was a hint of amusement in her voice. 'I'm glad you decided not to cause a war between our families.'

'There's still time.'

At that, a slight smile tilted at her lips. 'Are you as bad as they say you are?'

The words felt like a challenge, and he rested one hand on the wall beside her. 'Far worse.' He needed her to remember that he wasn't one of her suitors. He wasn't here to win her affections or even her hand in marriage.

Her smile faded. 'Then why are you here?'

'Your nephew wants me to teach him how to use a blade. Marcas believed he owed me a debt and thought I wanted to see you alone.'

Her face had gone pale, but she lifted her chin. 'But you don't, do you?'

'I didn't at first.' He took advantage of his position and traced the line of her jaw with his thumb. When she exhaled, her eyes staring into his, he murmured, 'But maybe I've changed my mind.'

When she didn't speak, he continued moving his hand down her nape to her shoulder. 'Why did you kiss me that day, Mairead?'

Color flooded her face. 'It—it was nothing. I just wanted to thank you. I wouldn't be here today if you hadn't saved my life.'

'You did well enough with your blade.' He moved his hand back to her throat, and against his fingers, he felt her pulse beating wildly.

'Against one man,' she argued back.

He slid his hand against her braided hair while the other rested against the wall. If she wanted to pull away from him, it was easy enough. But she didn't move. And he was fascinated by the curve of that mouth, watching her lips part.

'I remember our kiss, *a mhuirnín.* Are you wanting me to kiss you again?' He cupped the back of her nape, leaning in close.

A cool blade slid beneath his chin. 'Leave me alone, Balor Ó Phelan. You only want to use me for your own gain.'

He smiled at that and pressed Mairead's blade away, not even caring that the edge sliced his fingers. 'I'm impressed.'

He expected her to shove him back, but instead, she moved to stand beside him, her shoulder brushing against his as she leaned against the wall. 'Why are you really here?'

'I told you. My brother, Kenneth, wants to wed you.'

She sheathed her knife. 'There are many men here who want to wed me.' She sent him a sidelong glance. 'Except you, I suppose.'

'Except me,' he repeated. 'I have no need to marry.' He also couldn't provide for a wife, even if he wanted one.

She paused a moment and said, 'I met your father and brother a little while ago. Fergus said that Kenneth was his only son. Why would he deny you?'

'Because it's true. I'm not his son.'

* * *

Mairead didn't understand what he meant by that. If Balor wasn't the chieftain's son, then…

'Who is your father?'

His demeanour tightened and he shrugged. 'A Norman who attacked my mother during a raid.'

Although his tone remained emotionless, she was starting to understand why he was so estranged from his family. 'I'm sorry. But that wasn't your fault.'

'Fergus blames me for it.' He turned to look at her. 'It's no surprise I'm not welcome among my tribe.'

'But you are close to your brother?' she ventured.

He inclined his head. 'Kenneth is a good lad and eager to please. He'll make a good chieftain one day.'

Even so, she already knew it was unlikely that she would marry someone like Kenneth. Not when her father had already arranged potential alliances with Norman noblemen, like Lord Lowell.

But she had no intention of revealing that. 'I will consider your brother, just as I will all the others,' she said. 'There will be a banquet tonight and dancing.' A mischievous thought caught her, and she asked, 'Will you be there?'

'I don't dance unless it's with a weapon.' His voice held a warning, but Mairead ignored it.

'You eat, don't you?' She took a step back and said, 'It's the least I can do for you after you saved my life.'

He didn't argue, and she moved towards the edge of the tower, staring out at the people below. She ought to rejoin her family inside—and yet, she wanted to spend more time here, with Balor. Part of her wished she hadn't drawn a blade on him—otherwise, he might have kissed her again. Her skin tightened at the thought.

A few moments later, he asked, 'After the attack…did your cousin live?'

She turned back and realized that he didn't know. 'Yes. My cousin has always been an exceptional fighter, thanks to her training.' Then she added, 'Velaria married Brian of Penrith, shortly afterward.'

He took a step closer and admitted, 'I'm glad she survived.'

She nodded and started to leave when he suddenly caught her hand in his. Before she could pull away, he pointed towards a group of soldiers. 'I know you are going to choose a suitor in the next few days. But before you do, consider how many Normans are here and why.'

'I know why they are here,' she answered. 'Many accompanied King John when he traveled north a few weeks ago.'

She kept her voice calm but couldn't suppress the chill that rose over her skin as she remembered the Normans who had attacked her and Velaria. One of the men had spoken about the king's arrival. And although those men had only been scouts, preparing the way for King John, she knew the monarch hadn't come to Ireland simply to visit.

Balor seemed to predict her next words when he continued, 'King John came to secure his power among the Irish kings. And a marriage between you and one of his noblemen would only strengthen it.'

'Maybe.' She didn't understand what he was implying. 'But if I choose a Norman husband, I'll return home with him to England.'

Balor's expression turned thoughtful. 'Your father is getting old. He won't be king for much longer.'

'And my brother, Liam, will take his place,' she finished. 'He was chosen as the *tánaiste*, and he's been ready to take the throne all his life. What of it?'

'Kings are chosen,' he said. 'Had you considered that some of your suitors might be here because they intend to depose both your father and brother?'

She shook her head. 'That's not possible. The MacEgan people would never choose a *Lochlannach* as king. They can elect anyone related to our family.'

'But what better way for a Norman to secure power than to wed the king's daughter? He would be family then, and able to take the throne.'

'They would never do such a thing,' she argued. 'I have plenty of family members who are Normans, including my mother. If there was anything to be concerned about, they would tell me. My father introduced me to a Norman earl today and—' Her words broke off as she suddenly wondered whether it had been her father's choice—or King John's command.

'How many Irishmen, besides my brother, are here?' Balor asked quietly. 'Among those who want to wed you.'

'There are several,' she started to say, but truthfully she didn't know. 'I still don't see why it matters whether they are Irish or Norman.'

His hand tightened on hers, making her aware that she hadn't pulled away the way she should have.

'Just ask yourself if they are here for you…or for your father's kingdom.' Then he released her hand and walked away.

Chapter Three

Balor was careful to remain in the shadows at Laochre Castle. He'd been here on several occasions, ever since he'd returned from England and mostly when he was trying to avoid his own tribe.

A few months ago, he'd competed among the others on the night of Bealtaine to become the Horned One, even though he'd known he wouldn't win the honour. It had simply been a moment to fight and pit himself against some of the strongest warriors in Éireann.

Fighting gave him a purpose, a way of releasing the years of resentment and hatred. It closed off his emotions in a way that drowned out any feelings of emptiness.

In the next few days, Mairead would choose a husband. It was the purpose of this *aenach*, and he'd wanted to bring Kenneth—even knowing that his brother was an unlikely match.

But worse was the thought of watching her pair off with another man. The dark sense of possession brewed within him, along with the desire to shred apart any man who dared to look at her.

Inside the Great Chamber, rows of trestle tables filled the room, loaded with platters of bread, fish, roasted meat of all kinds, and honey cakes. Fresh flowers were everywhere, and Norman soldiers gathered with the Irish for the feasting.

At first, Balor stayed near the back of the Great Chamber, far away from his brother or Fergus. The chieftain would want to be as close as possible to the MacEgans, and Balor didn't want to be anywhere near them.

He decided to join one of the tables filled with Norman soldiers. They paid him little heed, but one passed him a wooden goblet filled with ale. He drank and kept to himself, but two other Normans sat down beside him.

'Who do you think she'll choose?' the man asked.

Balor hadn't expected them to speak to him, but he shrugged and switched into their language. 'Probably the man King John chose for her. Whoever has the most wealth and power.'

His companion laughed. 'I suppose that's true enough.' He eyed Balor's clothing and added, 'You speak the Norman language well.'

'I was fostered in England,' he said, draining the cup. 'With Lord William Fleming de Beaumont.'

'Were you?' the soldier said. He exchanged a glance with the older Norman soldier. 'I am Gerald of Mowbray.'

'Balor Ó Phelan,' he answered. He noticed that the older Norman was staring at him now, his gaze piercing. 'Is something wrong?'

But Gerald shrugged. 'Not at all.'

'Did you know Lord Beaumont well?' the older man asked.

Balor shook his head. 'Only from a distance. My mother sent me to England, and I was fostered with a dozen others.'

The older one turned thoughtful and nodded. 'I did know the earl. He's a good man. I suppose you learned to fight among his men.'

He couldn't deny it. Beaumont's captain had forced all of them to train, night and day, until Balor was confident he could fight back against anyone. 'Well enough,' he answered.

Gerald motioned to the serving girl to bring them both more ale. 'And do you think you have a chance of winning the Lady Mairead's heart, Ó Phelan?' He nodded towards the king's daughter, who was sitting with her family upon the dais. Mairead wore a *léine* and overdress of deep green while a golden necklace set with green stones encircled her throat. Not emeralds, but he guessed they were polished marble stones from Connemara. Above her forehead, she wore her hair in a complex, braided coronet, letting the rest fall freely below her shoulders in soft waves.

'I've no chance at all.' Balor reached for the bread and tore off a large piece. He kept his expression and tone neutral, acting as if he had no interest in the king's daughter. Even if he was fully conscious of every move she made.

'Then why are you here?'

He shrugged. 'For the food?' Though it was an honest answer, the men around him began to laugh, and they raised their glass to him.

'I like you, Ó Phelan,' Gerald said, slapping him on the back.

It was strange to be welcomed among them, and a rise of uneasiness came over him. 'What of you?' he asked. 'Do any of you think you have a chance at winning the hand of an Irish noblewoman?'

Gerald shook his head. 'Not at all. We're here by the king's command. Well, *some* of us are.' He glanced at the older man. 'Others are here for their own purpose.'

Balor wanted to ask what he meant but held back. He would gain more information if he remained silent. With a light shrug, he lifted his glass and said, 'Then enjoy the food. *Sláinte.*'

While they ate, he started to count how many Normans were among them. Without armour, it was difficult to tell, but he listened to their conversations. It really did seem that the king was trying to infiltrate the MacEgan forces under the guise of sending men to court Mairead.

The feasting continued before several of the tables were cleared back to make space for dancing. Lady Mairead joined with several of her cousins, and Balor watched as she moved among her suitors. Her smile was genuine, and she moved like someone who had been surrounded by beauty all her life.

But then the men around him rose to their feet. 'Come on, Ó Phelan. You're coming with us,' Gerald said.

It would cause a greater problem if he protested, but soon enough, he realized they only meant to surround the dancers and watch. He tried to drift back behind them, but Gerald laughed and said, 'Oh, no. We'll see if another maiden chooses one of us. We have wagers on who's going to dance with you.'

'No one,' he started to say.

But their merriment had drawn attention, including the Ó Phelan chieftain's. Fergus stood from his seat at the table, his gaze furious. He strode towards Balor, murder in his eyes. 'You shouldn't be here. Get out.'

Balor ignored the chieftain, as if he hadn't spoken at all. Instead, he calmly took his place among the Norman soldiers at the edge of the dancing, his gaze fixed upon Mairead. Her expression paled when she saw him there.

Fergus apparently didn't care about causing a scene. But the moment the chieftain drew his *colc* sword to force him out, Balor reacted. He seized Gerald's goblet and dashed the contents into the chieftain's face. While the man was briefly blinded, he took a wooden stool and used it to knock the weapon out of Fergus's hand.

'You bastard,' the chieftain cried out, just as several MacEgan men surrounded him. 'You weren't invited here.'

'Don't you know better than to draw a blade in the presence of the king?' Balor countered.

As the men escorted Fergus out, two of them remained in front of him. One was a solidly built man, and Balor recognized Ewan MacEgan, the king's youngest brother.

'Is it true that you weren't invited?' The man's voice was quiet, but Balor didn't miss the underlying threat. When he glanced back at Mairead, he decided it wasn't worth it to answer the question. With a shrug, he stood and started to leave. He'd already eaten, anyhow.

'*I* invited him.' Mairead's voice rang out above the music, and the moment she spoke, all conversation died down.

Balor froze in place, feeling the eyes of everyone upon him. He hated being the center of attention, but he forced himself to face her. Her green eyes held worry, and she bit her lip as if she wished she hadn't spoken.

But it was the dark expression on the king's face that reminded him of his place. He gave a slight bow of deference and started to retreat.

A hand upon his shoulder warned that he was going nowhere. 'If my niece invited you, then you're not leaving,' Ewan MacEgan commanded.

He turned to face the man and waited. The Irishman stared at him while the Norman soldiers gathered around. All appeared quite interested in the conversation, and he didn't miss Gerald's smirk.

Although Balor itched to leave the Great Chamber, he

wasn't about to offend Mairead so publicly. Better to say nothing and blend in among the others.

The king watched him for a moment, as if casting a silent judgement. Then he signaled for music, and conversations eventually resumed.

Ewan switched into the Irish language. 'I'm wanting to know exactly why my niece would invite the Demon of Éireann to a feast in her honour. I suspect there's a story you're not telling us.'

Balor straightened and met the man eye to eye. It was clear that Mairead had not told her family of his role in her rescue, which didn't surprise him. He hadn't been a hero at all. He'd fully intended to kidnap her for his own purposes until she'd talked him out of it.

But an inner voice warned, *She didn't want them to know about you. She told them nothing.*

It was the reminder he needed, that he could never be a part of her life. She didn't want him the same way he desired her. He didn't belong in her world, and it was better if they knew nothing about him.

He straightened and answered, 'You're right. But that's her story to tell, not mine.'

Mairead tried to appear indifferent to Balor's presence, but she saw her uncle Ewan questioning him. She could also feel the tension from her parents, that she would dare to invite someone so unsuitable to wed. But that wasn't why Balor was here.

She told herself that, even as she excused herself from the dancing and made her way towards them. 'Uncle Ewan,' she greeted.

'Mairead.' His gaze softened upon her. 'I'll admit I'm

curious about why you invited this man here. Especially when his grandfather Donal tried to overthrow your father.'

She blinked a moment as the words fled, leaving her utterly unable to speak. Undoubtedly, her uncle was trying to make her question Balor's motives.

'Donal Ó Phelan is dead,' Balor answered. 'And his mistakes are not mine.' Without waiting for her to intervene, Balor took her hand in his and led her towards the dancing.

'I thought you didn't dance,' she protested.

'I don't. But that doesn't mean I don't know how.' He led her into the steps, his arm around her waist. 'I need to talk to you.'

She was fully aware of the heat of his hand against her waist as he moved her through the dance. 'What is it?'

He leaned in against her ear. 'I spoke to some of the Normans. Many of them are here at King John's command, not for your hand in marriage.'

The heat of his breath sent a ripple of sensation over her skin. 'Why? What do they want?'

He led her in a circle, and when she stared back at him, he answered, 'I think you already know the answer.'

A chill prickled over her at his words. She didn't want to believe that the men were here to claim her father's throne. But more and more, she was starting to believe that King John had chosen the earl to be her husband—and his soldiers were here to see it done. This *aenach* was an illusion, not a celebration. And she didn't know if she would have any choice in the matter of her marriage anymore. If she refused to wed a Norman, would her family be at risk?

'I don't want to believe it. But if they are a threat to us, what should I do?' His palm rested against her waist as they spun in a slow circle, and she grew fully aware of the heat of his touch.

His blue eyes were staring at her with undisguised longing. And his face was so close to hers, she wanted to reach up and touch the rough stubble on his cheeks. God help her, she wanted to feel his mouth against hers again, claiming a kiss she shouldn't want so badly. Her body grew restless, feeling those strong arms around her while he moved her amid the others, taking command.

Balor was dangerous, tempting her towards reckless decisions.

'Don't do anything yet,' he advised. 'Keep your ears open and tell your father what you hear.'

It was good advice, so she nodded. The dance ended, and he raised her palm to his lips, offering a faint smile.

Oh, he was far too handsome to leave her unaffected. Even after Balor returned among the others, her skin yearned for his hands upon her. She wanted him to kiss her again and sensed that it wouldn't be gentle at all.

Balor Ó Phelan was a temptation she didn't need right now. But when she glanced back to where he'd been standing, he was already gone.

Her brother, Liam, was standing beside their mother when she returned, along with her uncle Ewan. All were clearly awaiting an explanation from her. She was going to have to tell them the truth about the rescue, if for no other reason than to save Balor from their wrath.

When she started with a smile, Liam met her gaze and declared, 'Absolutely not.'

She feigned innocence while she considered what to say. 'What do you mean?'

He raised an eyebrow. 'I mean you'll not wed Balor Ó Phelan. I don't care what he's said to you or—'

'He rescued me from the Norman attack,' she interrupted.

All of them fell silent as they absorbed this new information. She was careful to keep her expression composed.

'Balor is the man who guarded me and brought me back to Ennisleigh,' she finished. 'I owe him my life. The least I can do is offer him food and dancing.'

Before she could walk away, her brother caught her hand and held it. Liam's stare turned discerning. 'Be careful, Mairead. I saw the way he was looking at you.'

'You're wrong. He's not here as a suitor, and I know I could never marry him.' Although they were the words everyone expected her to say—and she saw their visible relief—a pang of regret settled in her gut.

She had no illusions that any of her suitors were here for love. They wanted political alliances, and although most were kind, they cared nothing about her.

But Balor had been different from the moment she'd met him. He'd saved her during the attack, and he'd shown a bravery she hadn't seen in most men.

In their few stolen moments together, she'd sensed something happening between them. Balor had made her feel alive again, even if it was only raw attraction. After she'd lost Diarmud, she'd been living in a blurred world where life went on around her, and she'd had to pretend she had gotten over the loss of her first love. Even though she hadn't.

It wasn't wise to let her bruised heart fall for the wrong man again. Better to lose Balor now by pretending their stolen moments didn't matter. And she would deny the rise of interest she'd felt in his arms.

When Lord Lowell smiled at her and approached to offer a dance, Mairead told herself that she would give the earl a true chance at winning her heart. He had been kind enough—surely, she could learn to care for him.

If he was the match the king and her father had chosen—and if this marriage would please King John and protect her family—she saw no choice but to fulfil her duty.

Letting Balor go was the safe choice, the one that would protect him.

Even if it broke her heart.

It was dawn when Balor awaited Marcas at the barbican gate. He wasn't entirely certain whether the lad would arrive, but the only people walking around were the guards. If Marcas wanted privacy to practice, then he would have it.

Balor's sleep had been troubled last night. He'd dreamed of Mairead, of her being captured by more Normans while he was unable to save her. He'd awakened in a restless panic, his body sweaty and his heart pounding.

He reminded himself of all the reasons why it shouldn't matter. She would choose a husband, marry, and bear noble children like hundreds of women before her. Her life was her own.

But last night, he'd seen the troubled look on her face when she'd danced with the earl. It was the look of resignation, not hope. And he didn't know what that meant.

'Good morn to you,' a voice called out. He turned around and saw Marcas hurrying forward. The boy wore a tunic that was slightly too big for him with a colc sword at his waist. The weapon was short, but it still hung below his knees.

'Where did you get the weapon?' Balor asked.

'I borrowed it from my older brother,' Marcas said. 'He won't mind.'

'Does he know you borrowed it?' He kept his voice bland, wondering if the brother would come after him for it.

'He's visiting our cousins in the west. I'll return it before he returns at Lughnasa.' With a grimace, he added, 'If I don't, my sister Gabriella will tell him.'

'I want to see what you already know,' he said. 'Unsheathe your sword and show me what you've been taught.'

Marcas appeared uneasy, but he obeyed, holding it out. After a little while, his arm began to shake, revealing his physical weakness.

'Go on,' Balor said quietly. 'I need to see what you can do.'

The boy made a slashing motion, his feet unsteady as he jabbed at an unseen enemy. Without warning, Balor gave the boy's shoulder a light shove, and he went sprawling.

Marcas's face turned startled. 'Why did you do that?'

'You have no balance or support. It doesn't matter what kind of weapon your enemy wields if you can't stay balanced.' He reached out a hand and helped the boy up. 'Stand here with your feet apart like this.' He demonstrated a fighting stance.

Some of the guards nearby took interest and started watching. Balor took the boy's colc sword away and adjusted Marcas's posture. This time, when he gave the same slight shove, the boy held his balance better.

'Good,' he told the boy. 'During a fight, you have to be prepared to face a strike from anywhere. Keeping your balance is important.'

Marcas gave a nod, and Balor gave him the blade back. 'This time, hold the sword out and keep it steady.' He adjusted the boy's grip and moved it into a defensive stance.

'Now what should I do?' Marcas asked.

'Keep holding it until you can't hold it upright any longer.' The boy was lacking in physical strength, and he needed to develop his stamina.

'But what about during a fight?' His expression turned uncertain, even as he continued holding the sword.

'During a fight, you'll be holding out a sword for far longer than you'd imagine. And if you lower it, you die.'

The lad's eyes widened when Balor raised his tunic and revealed a silver scar across his chest and stomach. 'That happened when I wasn't fast enough.'

Soon, the boy's arm began shaking, and he struggled to keep the sword up. When he finally could hold it no longer, he lowered the weapon.

'Now switch hands,' Balor said.

'I can't use my left hand as well as my right.'

'Not many can,' he agreed. 'But it could save your life one day. And you'll also need strength to hold a shield.'

As he continued to work with the boy, he noticed a group of men hauling a stone chair towards the center of the inner bailey. A prickle of awareness caught him, and Marcas turned to look. 'That's for the morrow. When they choose my father to be the new King of Laochre.'

'King Patrick is stepping down?'

Marcas nodded, lowering his sword. 'The brehons will arrive today, and they will arrange for the choosing.' There was a solemnity to his voice. 'Papa spent last night at chapel, praying.'

'So, you'll become a nobleman, then,' Balor remarked.

'Me? No. That's— No, I can't.' Color flooded the boy's face. 'My father will be king, but that's all.'

It wasn't, and they both knew it. Once Liam MacEgan took the kingship, the boy's life would completely change.

Marcas sheathed his sword and turned back to him. 'Thank you for your help this morn. Will you show me more later?'

'If you like. But you should ask your father for help,' Balor said gently.

The boy shrugged. 'I haven't seen him since last night. He's too busy.' His gaze drifted over to the stone throne that would be used for the new king.

'Then ask him again when you see him next.'

In the distance, he saw his brother and Fergus walking together, and Balor decided to take his leave. 'Keep practicing on your own. You'll build strength but always remember your balance.' For a moment, Balor wondered what it would be like to have a son. The unexpected grip on his heart caught him unawares, but he forced it away, even as he watched the boy. The life ahead of him only had one path—as a mercenary to hire out his sword. He couldn't imagine having a wife and family…even if a part of him secretly wanted that.

The lad nodded. 'I will.' After a slight pause, Marcas added, 'You should compete for my aunt Mairead's hand in marriage. I think you would be a strong protector for her.' A cheeky grin lifted the boy's mouth. 'And then you could train me more often.'

Balor ruffled the boy's hair. 'Go on, then. Find your father.' Marcas walked back to the keep with his shoulders back while Kenneth and Fergus continued to approach.

Balor thought about returning to the Great Chamber but decided against it. The Ó Phelan chieftain wouldn't rest until he'd spoken his arguments, so he might as well be done with it. Fergus glared at him, while Kenneth appeared uneasy at his father's side.

'Why have you come to Laochre, Balor?' Fergus demanded. 'Are you trying to interfere with Kenneth's chances of marrying the king's daughter?'

'I was trying to help him,' he said, meeting his brother's gaze.

Kenneth had finally grown into his height, and his dark blond hair was neatly trimmed. He wore a silk tunic and was still thin for his age, despite his adolescent appetite.

'Lies. I know you're trying to insinuate yourself into Lady Mairead's favour,' Fergus said. 'But she will never wed a bastard, and you know it.'

'I do,' he agreed. 'Which, as I said, is why I was trying to convince her to consider Kenneth.' But Balor already suspected Mairead would never consider his younger brother as a husband. He'd seen it in her eyes—the look of sympathy.

He crossed his arms and regarded Fergus. 'And considering what happened last night, you should leave him be. My brother should speak to Lady Mairead alone.'

The chieftain grimaced. 'Kenneth knows nothing about how to speak to a lady of royal birth.'

'I'm still here,' his brother interjected. They both turned to look at him, and he straightened. 'Balor is right. I should be the one to talk to her and try to win her favour.'

'You should speak with Lady Mairead today before the new king is crowned,' Fergus insisted.

Balor gave a nod of agreement. 'I'll bid you luck,' he told his brother, even as he left them behind.

As he passed the stone chair in the inner bailey, he wondered whether Liam MacEgan would indeed take the throne this day.

But as Balor continued walking, an inner sense gave him pause. He grew alert to how many Norman soldiers were starting to gather. It didn't matter that this was a gathering for Mairead's sake. He couldn't shake the feeling that something was very wrong from the way they were speaking quietly amongst themselves.

And then, when Fergus went to speak with them, it seemed even more suspicious. Why would the chieftain do such a thing?

Balor walked up the stairs to the parapets, wanting to get a better look. When he reached the top near the tower, he glanced at the nearby island fortress of Ennisleigh. On the opposite side of the castle, he saw miles of green fields dotted with roundhouses.

He started to walk towards the tower, planning to survey the rest of his surroundings, when he heard voices coming from below. Lady Mairead was walking with the Earl of Lowell, and her smile was genuine.

She wore a blue overdress and *leine* trimmed with silver thread, and her dark hair was bound back in a barbette. He remained out of view, unable to stop himself from eavesdropping, even though he knew it was wrong.

She was far more fluent in the Norman language than he'd guessed, and Balor remained pressed against the interior of the tower while she spoke. 'I understand your family's lands are not far from my grandsire's lands where my mother grew up, Lord Lowell.'

'Indeed,' he agreed. 'I live half-a-day's ride north. You would be able to visit them often, if you wished.'

The conversation paused a moment, and Mairead fell silent. Balor waited for the earl to elaborate, but he, too, remained silent.

Ask her a question about herself, he wanted to tell the man. *What does she enjoy?*

But instead, the earl continued, 'The king believes our match would be a good one. It would bring together our family's lands.'

'It would be an alliance, yes, but Laochre belongs to my brother, not me,' Mairead corrected.

The earl cleared his throat. 'True.' After a slight pause, he added, 'Do you remember when your family rode to meet with King John, a few weeks ago?'

'Yes.' Her voice had gone cool, and Balor heard the slight trace of fear within it.

'Were you aware that—' another pause '—your cousin Velaria was sentenced to death by the king for killing one of his noblemen?'

God's bones. Balor's blood chilled at that, though Mairead had already said her cousin had lived and was now wedded to Brian of Penrith. He'd known that Velaria had killed the scouts, but he hadn't known there had been a nobleman among them. He leaned in closer, wondering what had happened after he'd left.

'We were attacked that day,' Mairead argued. 'Velaria was only defending herself. Both of us could have been killed.'

But the earl continued, as if she hadn't spoken. 'King John, in his mercy, agreed to spare her.'

'The king spared her because she married his bastard son, Brian,' Mairead argued.

'That wasn't the only reason,' the earl said. His voice grew pained as he continued, 'Afterwards, one of the conditions of saving your cousin's life was for your father to reaffirm his loyalty to the king...along with all his brothers.'

Balor didn't like the direction this conversation was turning. The earl knew entirely too much of the king's plans. And it only confirmed his earlier suspicions about King John wanting to secure another Irish-Norman alliance through Mairead's marriage.

'My father is a king in his own right,' Mairead said softly.

'A provincial one,' Lord Lowell corrected. 'He is not High King of Ireland.'

'My father has always maintained the peace between the MacEgans and the Normans,' Mairead continued. 'He married my mother to demonstrate his loyalty.'

The earl let out a heavy sigh. 'And the king wishes for you to do the same.'

'What do you mean by that?'

There was genuine fear in her voice, and that was enough to force Balor's hand. He wasn't about to stand aside and allow the Norman to threaten her.

'I mean that he wants a betrothal between us—'

'Lady Mairead.' Balor stepped out of the tower and kept a slight smile on his face. He flicked his gaze towards the earl but didn't speak to him at all.

'Balor.' Her voice held ice within it. 'What are you doing here?' It was clear that she wasn't at all pleased by his interruption. She appeared flustered and clenched her hands together.

'I was out walking along the parapets,' he said smoothly. 'And I thought it would be rude not to say hello.' He ventured a smile at her, one she didn't return.

'The lady was in the middle of a conversation.' The earl stiffened at the sight of him, and his expression grew wary.

'Oh, is that what that was?' He kept his tone innocent. 'It sounded like a threat. Like you were trying to force her into a marriage she doesn't want.'

Mairead's expression turned pained, and she shook her head slightly at him in a silent warning to leave her alone. But he wasn't about to listen.

'Come along, Lady Mairead,' Lord Lowell said. 'I will

escort you back to your father.' He held out his arm for her to take.

She lifted her chin, trying to veil the emotions on her face. But those green eyes held fear and uncertainty, as if she truly didn't want to walk with the earl. In the end, she let out a breath and took Lowell's arm, turning away.

Balor let them go, but in his mind, he had another plan. And apparently, a betrothal to disrupt.

Chapter Four

At nightfall, a loud knock sounded at the door of her bedchamber. Mairead let out a groan, for it had been a long day of endless conversations with men she barely knew. But her earlier conversation with the earl had bothered her deeply. If Lord Lowell had been chosen by King John as her husband, then it put her in a difficult position.

It felt as if invisible chains were locking her into a betrothal with a man she hardly knew. But what complicated matters more was that Lord Lowell had been kind. He'd done nothing to suggest that a marriage to him would be a hardship of any kind. She wasn't being fair to him.

But whenever she was near him, he didn't make her blood race. She didn't imagine his kiss or wonder what it would be like to feel his skin against hers. Not the way Balor did. Which was unwise since he'd already said he wasn't here seeking her hand in marriage.

The pounding at the door sounded again, and she went to answer it. But when she lifted the latch, she saw her nephew Marcas and Balor standing behind him.

'Have you seen my father, Aunt Mairead?' Marcas asked. His voice held genuine fear, and she didn't know why.

'No. I've been busy all day. Why do you ask?'

'The last time I saw him was yestereve,' Marcas said.

'My mother cannot find him, either. I hoped maybe…you knew where he was.'

She exchanged a look with Balor, and his expression was grim. Without another word, she understood the true problem. If her father stepped down as king and Liam wasn't there…

By the gods. She was starting to wonder if the Normans truly did pose a threat.

'We've been searching all day,' Marcas said.

'Have you told my father?' She tried to keep her voice steady, but the danger was very clear. 'The king must know if Liam is missing.'

'I was afraid to tell,' Marcas admitted.

'Go and speak with your grandfather now,' Balor advised, resting his hand on the boy's shoulder. 'It might mean nothing at all. He may have sent your father on a short journey.'

There was a hint of relief on Marcas's face, as if he hadn't considered that. 'All right.'

But Mairead doubted that her brother had gone anywhere. She nodded to her nephew in agreement, and Marcas hurried off.

As soon as he'd gone, she opened the door wider in a silent invitation for Balor to come in. His gaze fixed upon hers, and she suddenly flushed at the thought of him here, in her bedchamber. Her skin seemed to grow more sensitive, even as she tried to face him. 'They've taken Liam, haven't they? The Normans.'

Worry caught her at the thought of her brother being threatened. She drew her hands around her waist, ignoring the wish that Balor would hold her instead. The thought of being in his arms right now, of being able to rest her cheek against his chest while he guarded her, was a wistful imagining.

'I think so.' His tone was grim, and he added, 'The Normans may hope to crown the earl as the next king, with you as his bride.'

'They can't do that,' Mairead protested. 'It has to be a male from our bloodline.'

'Can you not become queen?'

She shook her head. 'It isn't our way.'

But she couldn't deny that Balor could be right. Maybe that was what this was—a form of vengeance. King John might be punishing her father for daring to give such a show of force when he'd traveled north with his brothers and their armies after her attack.

Although Patrick had claimed they had come to offer fealty, she suspected the truth. Her father had been angry about the Normans who had attacked her and Velaria. Arriving with hundreds of men was a silent message to King John that he did not fully control the kings of Ireland.

Which likely meant the monarch wanted to retaliate. Or perhaps he already had with Liam's disappearance.

Mairead sank down on a low stool, her stomach twisting. 'What should we do? Do I wed the earl, in return for Liam's life?'

'That's likely what they want you to do,' he said quietly, pulling up a stool beside her. 'But if you do wed a Norman, your family may lose control of the kingship anyway, and Laochre may fall under King John's reign.'

A coldness caught within her at the thought, followed by fury. All her life, she'd been soft and obedient, the daughter her father expected her to be. But Patrick had been a warrior, as had his brothers. They had fought for peace, and the last thing she wanted was to bow to a foreign king—especially if they had taken her brother.

She wanted to fight, just as her father and uncles had. And although she lacked physical strength, she had her wits. Mairead closed her eyes, trying to think of what to do.

'My family will not lose the kingship,' she said firmly. 'We need to gather men and find Liam.'

'I agree. Your father should ask his brothers to return here quickly, along with their men.'

He was right. If her father had time to gather his brothers together, they could defend Laochre from any threat.

'Until we find Liam, I'm not going to marry anyone.' She stood and regarded him. 'And you're going to help me leave Laochre.'

For if she was not here to wed any of the Normans, it weakened their ability to impose a marital alliance. They would have to take Laochre by force.

'No.' Balor stood to face her, refusing to play any part of this. 'I'm not helping you leave.' Although he'd previously wanted to disrupt her betrothal, it had been about dissuading her from marrying the wrong man or becoming a king's pawn—not running away with him.

'Why not?'

'I'm not about to abduct the daughter of a king, just so you can avoid marriage to a Norman,' he continued. Though he was well aware of his own hypocrisy, he knew better than to take her from Laochre with the number of guards and suitors watching over her. 'The MacEgans would murder me if I dared take you beyond those gates.'

'You already tried to abduct me at Bealtaine before,' she argued. 'Why would it be any different now?'

The gleam in her eyes made him uneasy. His previous

plan had been a reckless idea to remove Fergus as chieftain. She'd been right—it never would have worked. And now she wanted to become his hostage?

'You warned me, the last time I took you, that it could start a war. Why would we want your family to believe you're in danger?'

'But I would go with you willingly,' she argued. 'You'll escort me out of the castle and keep me safe. At least until my brother is found.'

'No.' He folded his arms across his chest and shook his head. 'If you defy your father and flee, everyone will think I've stolen you.'

'Or they might think I chose you as my husband.' Her voice held a note of teasing, but he didn't respond.

'Everyone would know that isn't true.'

His words were dull, emotionless. And yet, her expression shifted into one of sympathy. 'Why would you say that?'

'Because a king's daughter would never choose a bastard.' He knew the truth, even if she clung to her ill-placed belief in him.

Mairead studied him for a long moment. 'Are you afraid to travel with me?'

She took a step closer, her voice gentle, as if she were trying to tame a wild animal. Her dark hair rested over one shoulder, and he couldn't deny that she fascinated him. He'd tasted those lips once before—but it hadn't been nearly enough.

She drew so close, she was hardly more than a breath away. Her green eyes stared into his while she awaited his answer.

Balor slid his hand to her waist, wanting her to understand all the reasons why this was a bad idea. In the space between them, heat seemed to rise, and he was fully aware of the temptation to touch this woman and taste her lips once again. But he needed to push her away, back into the protection of her father and uncles.

Balor held his ground and stared back. 'Maybe I don't want to protect you. Maybe I'm the one you should be afraid of.'

'You wouldn't hurt me if I went with you,' Mairead said quietly. 'You're a man of honour.'

She was looking at him as if she truly believed that. As if she saw something in him of worth. And damn her, the words broke the restraints around him.

'That's the last thing I am, *a mhuirnín.* I have no honour at all.'

With that, Balor tangled his hands in her silken hair and claimed her mouth in the kiss he'd been craving since the first time she'd pressed her lips to his. He tasted the sweetness of her innocence, the softness of her mouth.

It was both an indulgence and a reminder to Mairead that he was not the man she wanted. He fully expected her to shove him away and demand that he leave her alone. Even as his tongue slid inside her mouth, he was waiting for her to strike him.

But instead, she wound her arms around his neck and kissed him back. *Damn her for it.*

Her kiss met his challenge and took apart his intentions.

He didn't know why she'd done such a thing, but he was starting to understand that Mairead was a woman of her own defiance. He'd issued a challenge, and she'd answered it back with one of her own.

When her tongue slid against his, desire roared through him. His shaft went rigid as her hips pressed close. Gods help him, this wasn't supposed to happen. She was supposed to be outraged, to draw her knife on him the way she had last time. Instead, she was pulling him closer.

God's blood, but he wanted her. Mindless need and longing tore at his control, and he pressed her against the wall, ignoring the voices of logic that reminded him that a king's daughter was far better than him.

But her response was more than he could bear. Her lips were soft, answering his fierce kiss with her own needs. He broke it off, keeping his hands upon the wall on either side of her.

Because if he succumbed to his own desire, he was going to peel back the layers and touch her bare skin.

Mairead's breathing was unsteady, but she stared at him unflinching. 'I'm going to talk to my father now and you're coming with me.' She seized his hand and pulled him towards the door.

But he remained in place. 'I'm not yours to command, *a mhuirnín.*'

She faltered at that. But there was no outrage in her expression. Instead, she changed her tactic and asked softly, 'Will you help me, Balor? Please?' She released his hand and waited.

The plea was quiet—and yet, it held the force of an invisible army, destroying his defences. She already knew he would never let her go alone.

It was a terrible idea to get involved with any of this. He didn't mind helping the MacEgans find Liam, but taking Mairead away from Laochre wasn't wise.

'There are dozens of others who would gladly help you,' he answered. 'Including my brother.'

'But you're the only one who doesn't want to marry me,' she said. 'It's safer with you.'

Her words struck a blow he hadn't anticipated, and he

felt compelled to respond. 'Why would you ever believe I'm safe?'

To underscore his words, he drew her close and grasped her hips. 'I may not be able to wed you…but it doesn't mean I don't crave your hands on me, Mairead.' He moved one hand up to her hair, threading it within the strands.

She appeared startled at his words and bit her lower lip as she considered it. 'Oh.'

Indeed. Mairead needed to fully understand exactly how bad this idea was.

'Will you at least escort me while I go and speak with my father?' She rested her hand on top of his and took it.

'For now,' he responded. Balor followed her into the hall but then placed her behind him for protection as they continued. If someone had taken her brother, then the culprit was likely still here.

He had no desire to be tangled up in any of this. Mairead was far safer remaining here, and he could never escort a king's daughter alone. Her father had over a hundred men, all better suited to protecting her. King Patrick's brothers and the MacEgan armies were enough to rival King John's.

But then Balor started to wonder if maybe that was why she wanted him to escort her. If she disappeared without choosing a suitor, Mairead was right—it disrupted any plans the Normans might have to claim the throne through her.

It was a quiet rebellion, one that would not implicate her father. He was starting to understand her reasoning—and it did make sense. But he still wasn't certain he would play any part in it.

'We'll go down this passageway and to the left,' she said. 'My family will likely be in the solar right now.'

She started to move ahead of him, but Balor kept her

guarded and opened the door for her. A serving maid had just delivered food and a flagon of wine before she retreated to stand against the wall, her head lowered in deference.

Inside the solar, Balor saw King Patrick, Queen Isabel, and a dark-haired woman he recognized as Liam's wife, Adriana. The woman's eyes were reddened from weeping, and Mairead rushed forward to embrace her.

'Marcas told us about Liam.' She drew back from Adriana and turned to her father. 'We need to delay choosing a new king until he's found.'

'I agree.' But King Patrick's voice was weary as he leaned back in his chair. The others stared at Balor in a silent reminder that he didn't belong. It was nothing new, and he strongly considered leaving, but Mairead's silent plea made him stay. Instead, he backed against the door and waited.

The king turned in his direction. 'Why is this man here, Mairead?'

She stood and walked to Balor's side. 'Because he has agreed to be my protector and escort.'

Agreed was a strong word. More like manipulated or coerced, Balor thought. But neither did he deny it. He couldn't argue that he wouldn't mind spending more time alone with Mairead—especially after she'd kissed him again. Yet, he hadn't made a decision on what to do.

'Your escort *where*?' Queen Isabel sent them both a pointed look.

Mairead folded her hands and regarded each of them. 'It's not safe for me here at Laochre anymore. I thought I could travel west to stay with one of my uncles until Liam is found and crowned king.' She squared her shoulders and added, 'Until then, I will delay choosing a suitor.'

Balor could see them considering her words. Her father

likely wanted to argue that Laochre Castle was the safest place for her...and yet, his own son had been taken.

He decided to stop being invisible and start asking questions. 'When did your husband go missing?' he asked Adriana.

The dark-haired woman glanced at the others. 'Last night. Liam went to pray at chapel, and he didn't come back to our chamber.' She stood and held her arms. 'When I awoke this morn, I was alone. I spent all day searching, and no one has seen him.'

King Patrick sobered. 'Why didn't you tell me this sooner, Adriana?'

Adriana's face turned crimson. 'We—we argued last night. I thought he wanted some time alone.'

The king turned to his wife and took her hand. 'I've already begun sending groups of men to search. We won't stop until he's found. I swear it.'

But Balor had his doubts. Someone must have seen the *tánaiste* being captured. Liam wasn't helpless or unable to fight. He had a reputation as a warrior, just like his father. Balor glanced over at the serving girl, who had not moved from her position by the wall. It made him wonder whether the other servants had seen anything.

'The men who took the *tánaiste* were likely already inside these walls,' Balor predicted. 'Possibly pretending to be suitors.'

'The Ó Phelans?' Patrick mused aloud.

Although the chieftain lacked the power to be any sort of threat, Balor agreed with the king. Fergus would indeed ally with the enemy if he thought it would bring him favour. 'Possibly. But the chieftain doesn't have enough men—and I don't know if he would take that risk because he wants

Kenneth to wed Lady Mairead.' After a pause, Balor added, 'I think it's more likely the Normans who were responsible.'

'I don't agree,' Patrick argued. 'They have no reason to attack us.'

When Mairead turned back to Balor, he could read the thoughts in her mind—why was her father defending them? He had his own suspicions but kept silent.

'I was already attacked by the Normans, only a few months ago,' she reminded her father.

'By a handful of men,' the king countered. 'And I have come to terms with King John about it.'

'What do you mean?' After a pause, she added, 'Did he threaten our family?'

Her father didn't answer, which only confirmed Balor's suspicions. The two kings had indeed made an agreement, and one that likely involved Mairead's marriage.

'Are you planning to give the English king control of Laochre through marriage to me?' she ventured.

Her mother took a breath and answered, 'King John wants only our loyalty and an alliance.'

'But an alliance of *his* choosing,' Mairead predicted. 'I presume it's with the Earl of Lowell?'

'The Earl of Lowell is a powerful man favoured by the king,' her father said quietly. 'He would indeed be a good match for you.'

Balor remained silent. He could see the trap closing around Mairead, and she saw it, too.

She took a step away. 'I don't even know the earl. And neither do you.' She clenched her hands together. 'What sort of bargain did you make with the king?'

When her father remained silent, she added, 'Or did you fail to keep an agreement with him? Is that why Liam went missing?'

Her father stood from his chair, his face furious. 'My alliance with King John has *nothing* to do with Liam's disappearance. John knows that if he threatens my family, it will be war between us.'

So there *was* an alliance.

Mairead paled at her father's words. 'If it wasn't the Normans, then who do you think was responsible?'

'There are others who no longer want a MacEgan king,' Patrick answered. 'They would be glad to take command of Laochre from us.' His expression fixed upon Balor, as if he still suspected Fergus might be among them.

'You've kept the peace for more than twenty years,' Balor said. 'There are many who support you.'

King Patrick seemed to consider it before he turned back to his daughter. 'Given what happened, I think it's best if I increase the guards who protect you, Mairead.'

'I don't think it's safe at Laochre,' she said. 'I will not be taken hostage like Liam—especially as a negotiating tool for another king.' She straightened and faced her father. 'I intend to leave, with Balor as my escort.'

Her father's gaze narrowed, his expression discerning. It was clear that the king hadn't missed Mairead's swollen lips or her flushed cheeks.

'Even if I agreed with your desire to go to my brothers,' Patrick said quietly, 'I would never send you to travel alone with one of your suitors. I am not a fool, Mairead.'

She cast an uncertain look at Balor in a silent plea for help. If he said nothing, then she would remain here with her family, which was likely the right decision. He shouldn't interfere with her father's desire to protect his daughter.

And yet—no woman had ever looked at him in that way before, as if she needed him. In Mairead's eyes, he saw her fear of becoming a prisoner in her father's castle and being locked away for her own safety. It would happen, too. He could see the determination on her father's face.

He shouldn't get involved. Not in this. The truth was, he didn't understand why she wanted someone like him. Most people, including his own family, believed there was nothing good in him. Nothing worth saving.

Except her.

Mairead treated him as if she saw beyond everyone else's opinions. And maybe that was worth his protection.

He chose his words carefully. 'I am not one of Lady Mairead's suitors.' He took a step forward and faced the king. 'Your daughter would be safe with me as her escort because I have no intention of marrying her.'

Queen Isabel blinked at his words in surprise and turned to her husband. But King Patrick was already shaking his head as he confronted his daughter. 'My brother Ewan could escort you, Mairead. Or any of my men. Why would I send you off with a stranger?'

'Balor isn't a stranger,' Mairead said. 'I told you before. He's the man who saved my life when I was first attacked by the Normans after Bealtaine. He brought me safely to Ennisleigh.'

The queen's expression softened at her daughter's words. But Balor wasn't entirely certain about the way Mairead was framing him as a hero. Not when they both knew his intentions hadn't been at all honourable that day.

Patrick studied him as if trying to take his measure. 'Are you saying you have no interest in my daughter?'

Far from it. But Balor crossed his arms and faced the king. 'She can do far better than a man like me, and we both know it.' Maybe he'd imagined it, but there seemed to be a faint gleam of approval in Patrick's eyes. Balor turned back to Mairead. 'Your father is right. You would be safer with a large escort to take you away from Laochre. But if you're trying to leave without anyone noticing, I am willing to guard you.'

The king didn't yield. 'What is your involvement with my daughter, Balor Ó Phelan?'

'She asked me to protect her from harm,' he answered as he stared back at the king. 'Which I have sworn to do.'

'And what do you want in return?' her father asked quietly. 'Silver?'

He hadn't considered that anyone would offer coins. And although he could use the money, it felt wrong. There was also something he wanted far more.

'If you're wanting to offer a reward for her safe travel, there is only one thing I want in return. I want Fergus removed from power.'

'That is out of my hands,' Patrick started to say. 'I cannot make you chieftain.'

'Not me. My half brother, Kenneth.' He regarded the king and queen. Isabel moved to her husband's side and rested her hand on Patrick's shoulder.

But the king only shook his head. 'I am sorry, but I won't interfere with the leadership of other clans. Unless the people want someone else, there is nothing I can do.'

To Mairead, Patrick added, 'We'll increase the guards around you. You won't be alone at any moment. I promise you'll be safe while we search for Liam.'

Mairead's face fell, and Balor could see the doubts written on her features. With a nod to the king and queen, he walked towards the door. 'Then I'll bid you good fortune in finding him.'

Mairead wasn't about to become a prisoner within her own home. Although her father was simply trying to keep her safe, she couldn't stand aside and let it happen. Balor walked alongside her towards her room, and she stopped him. 'I don't like this. None of it feels right. My brother was taken from his own home, and no one can find him?' She shook her head. 'It just seems wrong.'

Balor said nothing to her, but his hand paused on her spine. The warmth of his touch made her stop walking. But as they drew closer to her chamber, she slowed her steps. 'I feel like they will come for me next.'

'You defended yourself once before.'

But she'd had to kill a man. Mairead shivered and rubbed her arms at the memory. 'I know.' After a moment, she stared back at him. 'Do you think the men who took Liam were the same men who attacked me? The king's scouts?' She wondered if the two incidents were tied together.

'Probably not the same men,' he answered. 'Their reasons for attacking you and Velaria were quite different.'

The uneasiness deepened within her at the memory. 'I'm glad you were there that morning.'

His hand moved from her back to her waist, almost in the barest embrace. 'So am I.'

The timbre of his voice was an invisible caress, and Mairead tried not to succumb to the yearning that would only end in heartache.

She needed to step away, to remove his hand. And yet, she couldn't quite bring herself to do it.

'I still don't understand how Liam was taken,' she confessed. Her brother was much older than her, and in the same year she was born, he had married Adriana. In some ways, he'd been almost like another father, as well as a brother. As strong as he was, she couldn't imagine how anyone could have captured him. And he never would have left without telling anyone.

'Why would this happen?' she wondered aloud.

'It's about control and power, Mairead. That's all it ever was.'

She agreed with him. But to what end?

'Could we—walk outside for a little while?' she asked. 'I don't want to go back to my chamber just yet.'

Balor gave a nod, and they walked together in silence down the narrow stairs that led to the Great Chamber. Then he guided her through the doors and outside to the inner bailey. Night had descended over the castle, and the walls were illuminated every few paces by flaming torches set into iron sconces on the stone walls.

On the far side, Mairead saw a gathering of Norman soldiers talking in low voices. She exchanged a glance with Balor, who seemed to read her thoughts, and escorted her towards a staircase that led up to the parapets.

She was grateful for the dark cloak and hood that hid her features.

'Do you think they know anything about my brother?' she asked.

He took her hand in his. 'Let's find out what we can.'

They walked up the steps to the parapets, keeping their movements slow as they drew closer to the soldiers. Mairead brought him inside the first tower where he'd nearly stolen a kiss the last time. Balor pressed her back while he studied the soldiers. Then he guided her back out to the parapets, near the second tower. Just as they reached it, a smaller group of men broke away from the larger group.

They froze in place, not saying a word.

'We need to bring him to England,' one of the men was saying.

Were they talking about Liam? Mairead gripped Balor's hand in the darkness as she tried to listen to the men. His hand covered hers, his thumb rubbing her knuckle lightly. She tried not to think of how he was making her feel right now. Safe. Comforted. And she didn't know what to make of those feelings.

'I know,' the other Norman answered, 'but he won't go willingly. His home is here.'

'No, but he won't have a choice,' the first continued. 'You know our orders.'

A cold chill spiraled through her at their words. Who were they talking about? Was it King John's orders?

Their voices faded away as they continued walking. Balor led her inside the closest tower, and she leaned against the wall.

'What do you want to do?' he asked. 'Should I escort you back to your chamber?'

She thought about it, turning it over in her mind. 'The threat is already here, inside our walls.'

'It is, yes.' He paused, letting her make the decision.

She already knew her father would send men after her if she went too far. But her uncle Bevan's lands were not far away. They could spend the night there, and she could claim that she'd gone to visit her cousin Alanna. If she sent word to her father in the morning, he wouldn't be quite so angry.

'I want to leave,' she said at last. 'My uncle lives at Rionallís, and I know he and his men will protect us. It's a smaller castle, and Uncle Bevan knows every man.' She took a breath and added, 'I...would like you to escort me there tonight, if you're willing.'

Balor turned to face her. In his eyes, she saw a sudden flare of interest. But he ventured, 'Against your father's wishes?'

Her expression turned troubled. 'It might be against my

father's wishes, yes,' she admitted. 'But even if I told him what we just overheard, he probably wouldn't believe me.'

'And you're not afraid to travel alone with me?' he pressed again. 'Because I'm not a man you would ever marry?'

'N-no. You're not,' she blurted out. But the moment she said the words, she regretted it. 'It's not that I don't think you're handsome or the sort of man any woman would want—'

His expression turned wry. 'I know my place, Lady Mairead. And it's not at your side.' Balor lifted her hand to his mouth in a mocking kiss. And yet, the slightest touch of his lips made her skin burn with the desire for more.

She wanted to taste his wickedness, to cast aside all the reasons why it was wrong. Because a man like Balor Ó Phelan would know how to give a woman pleasure in the dark. Even being so near to him made her crave his touch.

'Will you come with me?' she whispered.

He hesitated for a moment, his blue eyes shadowed in the torchlight. She understood that she was using him, and it wasn't fair. But everyone else within these gates would tell her no.

'I will find a way to reward you,' she offered. 'I have jewels or gold, or—'

'I don't want your coins.' He lifted her hand to his face, and beneath her palm, she felt his bristled cheek. She saw a faint scar by his temple and stroked it with her thumb.

He closed his eyes, drinking in her touch. She wondered if anyone had ever touched him with affection, for he seemed hungry for it. Yet, when her fingers slid into his hair, Balor pulled back.

In a low voice, he said, 'I'll get a horse and wait by the stream outside the castle gates. If you're wanting to leave tonight—and if you can get out without anyone seeing you—aye, I'll escort you to your uncle's home. But you'll have to leave the castle grounds on your own.'

It was as if he wanted to be certain no one could accuse him of taking her. And maybe she owed that to him.

He released her hand and moved behind her as if he were a servant. Mairead glanced back at him, but his head remained low as she walked back inside the castle. The moment she reached the spiral stairs, he left her and returned outside.

Two guards stood at the far side of the hallway as she entered her bedchamber. Mairead lowered a heavy wooden bar to keep everyone out of her room, including her maid. Everyone would believe she had retired for the night.

But instead, she strode to the opposite side of her bedchamber and opened a wooden chest carved by her father's grandsire Kieran. She gathered a small bundle of clothing and all the weapons she could find. Then she changed out of her *léine* and donned a pair of trews and a man's tunic, along with her dark cloak.

Her father had built this castle decades ago, and she'd grown up at Laochre. As a child, she had learned all of the secret passageways built within the walls as a means of escape.

Mairead ran her fingers along the wall beside her bed until she found the loose stone and pulled it out. She opened the secret doorway and slipped into the darkness before closing it behind her, replacing the stone. Then she made her way through the narrow wall passage that continued downward. She walked through the darkness, keeping her hand on the wall for balance as she descended towards the souterrain passage that led outside the castle gates and into a wooded area.

The air was frigid at night underground, even though it was late summer. She clutched the edges of her cloak, even as she carried her bundle of clothing.

It was unbelievably dangerous to leave the castle grounds alone—especially now. But she walked silently to the stream within the forest and waited. When she heard a horse approaching, she froze and tried to hide herself.

'It's me,' a male voice said, and she breathed easier when she recognized Balor.

Mairead stepped out of the shadows and saw him leading a horse towards her. He was hooded, and he had a bow and a quiver of arrows over one shoulder.

He seemed on edge and kept glancing around them as if he expected to be attacked. Which, she supposed, was entirely possible—especially since she hadn't told her father of her plan.

Balor took her bundle of clothing and secured it to his saddle. Then he lifted her atop the animal and led the horse into the woods. He was careful to keep the horse at a walk, not wanting to draw any attention.

He followed the pathway of the stream, and moonlight filtered through the trees, casting a faint gleam upon the water. Sometimes he brought the horse within the stream, as if to hide their tracks. Even as the horse walked through the woods, the crunching of dry leaves and underbrush wasn't silent.

When they cleared the forest at last, he swung up behind her. His body pressed closely to hers, his arms around her. The feeling of his hard, muscled body made her breathless, and Mairead swallowed, forcing the unbidden yearnings away. Every part of him tensed as they left the forest, but she supposed that was to be expected. And then, he urged the horse faster.

Balor was an excellent rider, she realized. His body moved naturally with the horse, and he held her waist as they turned north. Thankfully, the moon was bright, reflecting on the surface of a small stream that cut through the land. After a few moments, Balor switched their path east before turning northward again. It was likely a means of deterring anyone from finding their path, and it eased her mind.

But as they rode, she grew more conscious of the powerful thighs on either side of her own. The scent of leather and pine emanated from him, and she leaned back, resting her head against him.

In his arms, she truly did feel protected. And she was starting to realize that being alone with this man wasn't wise at all, even if it was a short journey. Not because Balor had threatened her—but because she was fully conscious of his body. It kept evoking memories of his kiss, and something about this man tempted her into sin.

Her cheeks flamed and when the horse moved across a rough patch of ground, she lost her balance slightly and grabbed his knee. Balor caught her waist, keeping her pressed against him.

But it only made her aware that she wasn't the only one affected by this ride. His body was aroused, his length pressed against her spine. And between her legs, she grew sensitive and wet, imagining what it would be like to lie with a man like Balor. She bit her lip, pushing the thought away. They would arrive at her uncle's castle soon enough. She could already see it in the distance, shadowed by the moonlight.

And yet…he changed their direction again, moving towards a large roundtower and chapel that stood farther in the distance.

'What are you doing?' she asked. 'Rionallís is over there.'

But he ignored her and kept the horse on its path, his arm still tight upon her waist.

'Balor,' she insisted. 'We *have* to go to Rionallís. My uncle's men will guard us for the night.'

This time, he leaned in close to her ear. 'We're being followed.'

Chapter Five

Balor had kept their horse turned so he could see if anyone was tracking them. And just as he'd feared, he'd spied a small group of soldiers.

Mairead appeared taken aback by his prediction, as if she hadn't noticed anything. But he supposed he was more accustomed to sensing danger than she was.

'It's probably my father's men,' she said. 'He wanted me to stay.'

'Possibly,' he acceded. But he wasn't convinced. It could easily be the Normans they'd overheard earlier—especially if they had seen him taking one of the horses. 'We need to be certain who it is.'

She appeared uncomfortable and risked a glance behind her. 'I went through the hidden passageway from my room. No one saw me, I promise you.'

'They could have seen me,' he admitted. After a slight pause, he asked, 'If it *is* your father's men, do you want to go back with them?'

'No.' She turned away, resting against him as they continued riding. 'I don't.'

He kept her in his embrace as he rode towards the round-tower. Having her in his arms was a temptation he wanted to savour. Her head rested beneath his chin, and it was a sweet torment feeling her body pressed close against his.

'Will we go to Rionallís tonight?' she asked.

He didn't know. But he sensed the unrest in her tone. 'If it's safe, yes. But not until I know who followed us.'

'Why the roundtower?' she ventured.

'Because it's safe there. And I want to get a better look at the riders.' He glanced behind them, though it was still too dark to see beyond a patch of moonlight. If he helped her get inside, Mairead could pull up the ladder behind her, and no one could reach the entrance.

'They'll know we're there if they see our horse,' she warned.

He didn't share her concern. 'I'm not leaving the horse out in the open. I'm going to find out who it is while you stay here. Then after I return, we'll continue towards Rionallís.'

Mairead frowned. 'You're leaving me?'

'Not for long. I'll return soon,' he promised. His tone was grim, and when she turned to look at him, he traced his thumb down the edge of her jaw. 'If the Normans come for you, I won't let them take you without a fight.'

Liam had likely been taken as a way of manipulating King Patrick into obedience. Their political battle made no difference to him.

But Mairead was another matter. Aye, he knew she was far out of his reach. But he would slaughter any man who dared harm her—and that included the nobility.

His arms tightened around her as he increased the pace of the horse. A stone chapel stood beside the roundtower, and he led the horse towards it. It was a place to tether the animal until he could find out who was hunting them.

He helped Mairead down and took the reins of the horse

while she stared up at the tower. The entrance was higher than the height of a man.

'How will I get inside?' she asked.

'We should be able to find a ladder in the chapel. And then you'll pull it inside the tower until I return.'

Balor wasted no time in searching, and thankfully, there was a ladder nearby. He leaned it against the stone roundtower and held it steady, but before Mairead climbed up, she turned back to him.

'Be careful, Balor.' She rested her hands on his shoulders, and for a moment, he wondered if she meant to kiss him. If she belonged to him, he wouldn't hesitate to claim that kiss. But he already knew they were treading a dangerous line.

Instead, he tucked a fallen strand of hair behind her ear. 'I'll return soon. And don't lower the ladder for anyone but me.'

After she climbed up and pulled the ladder behind her, Mairead watched from the door as Balor retrieved their horse and began riding away. Was he being overly cautious? Or was the threat real?

She closed the door behind her, feeling the rise of fear and uncertainty. Inside, the stone walls were cool, and she shivered against the cool summer night air.

Mairead glanced at the stairs leading up to the top of the tower and the bells that hung there. She had visited her uncle at Rionallís countless times, but she'd never been inside the roundtower.

Exhaustion weighed upon her, but she couldn't imagine resting—not when Balor was gone. How long would it take him to return? And what would happen if he was followed here? She didn't know what to think. For now, she could do nothing except worry and wait.

Mairead gripped her cloak around her, already starting to question her decisions. It might not be the right choice to travel to Rionallís or disappear from her own home. Her father would be furious with her.

But she was tired of following orders blindly. She wanted to be in command of her own future, whatever that might look like.

She started to climb up the stairs to the top of the tower, following them up to the next wooden platform then diagonally in the opposite direction. After two flights of stairs, her legs began to burn with effort, but eventually, she reached the top of the tower by the bells.

From this height, she could see the dim light of torches in the distance. When she turned slightly, she saw a smaller group of riders with two torches. They were riding towards the tower, but then they turned and started in the direction of Rionallís. Perhaps they had followed Balor there.

Dread stretched out within her at the thought of him coming to harm. Fates help her, she kept imagining his hands upon her and the way he made her feel.

You're using him, her brain warned. She knew, full well, that a man like Balor was a forbidden temptation. Her family would be appalled that she was fascinated by a bastard warrior.

But his kiss had awakened her in ways she'd never experienced before. He had worshipped her mouth with his own, tasting her as if she were a cup of the sweetest wine. And the feeling of his body against hers had quickened her heartbeat, making her want to pull him closer. She'd gone breathless in his arms, and maybe it was because he was completely wrong for her in all the right ways.

Mairead climbed down each staircase. She needed to keep her distance from Balor Ó Phelan. He could escort her to her uncle's home, but after that, she had to let him go. It was the right thing to do.

But part of her wondered whether Alanna's prediction had come true about the May crown—that she had somehow met her future husband on the morning she'd looked through it. She *had* met Balor that day, after he'd saved her from the Norman scouts. And was it so wrong to let herself dream?

When she reached the bottom of the stairs, she sat upon the last tread and took a deep breath. It seemed she had a habit of choosing men she could never wed. First Diarmud, and now Balor.

The familiar tendrils of grief wrapped around her as she remembered him. Then she leaned against the cool stone wall and closed her eyes.

After what seemed like hours, she heard a voice call out, 'Mairead!'

She opened the door slightly and saw Balor standing outside the base of the roundtower. Relief poured through her at the sight of him. She struggled with the ladder but managed to lower it down. Within moments, he'd climbed up and pulled it back inside.

'Who was following us?' she asked.

He closed the door behind him. 'They were Normans, not Irish.' After a pause, he added, 'I think they might have been the men we overheard at Laochre. I led them towards Rionallís and waited for them to go inside the gates before I came back.'

'Do you think they were the ones who took my brother?'

'I don't know. But if they went searching for you, they won't find you,' he promised.

A sudden uneasiness flooded through her. There was no reason for a group of Normans to travel to Rionallís from Laochre in the middle of the night—not unless they were trying to capture her as a hostage. 'I don't like this.'

Balor sat beside her. 'I wish I could say they were your father's men, looking to bring you home again. But they weren't.'

'How did you even realize they were following us?' she asked. 'I never noticed anything.' It had been virtually silent, with only their mare walking through the forest. And yet, Balor had sensed an enemy was there.

'When we spoke to your father in the solar, the servant who delivered food to your father and mother was listening to everything your family said,' he told her. 'It's possible she was paid by the Normans to listen and send word.'

The thought of servants who might betray them was sobering. 'I'm starting to believe I should have stayed at Laochre,' she said quietly. 'My father was right. At least there, I would be surrounded by soldiers.' She met his gaze and added, 'I am sorry for asking this of you. It was wrong of me.'

'It's late,' he responded. 'We'll make a decision in the morning.'

Mairead leaned back against the wall, huddling within her cloak. But sleep wouldn't come, no matter how she tried. Her mind raced with fear and uncertainty. Although she knew she was safe for the night, it felt as if all their plans had been upended. The moment they left the roundtower in the morning, they would be found. She had no doubt of it.

But the idea of trying to sleep in this place was impossible. Balor seemed to sense her unrest when he reached for her hand in the darkness.

'Your hands are freezing.' He pulled her palms between his hands to warm them. 'Come here.'

Without asking, he pulled her onto his lap and drew his own cloak around her. Though she wanted to protest, his body heat and the extra layer of his cloak brought an immediate warmth that made her sigh with gratitude. She nestled in close and murmured, 'Thank you.'

And when she tucked her head beneath his chin and snuggled against him, his arms came around her in an embrace she wanted far more than she should.

After all the years of Fergus's abuse, Balor was truly in hell—all because of a beautiful woman.

Mairead was burrowed against him, and he could smell the faint floral aroma of her hair. He didn't really know what to do. This was, quite possibly, the worst torment he had ever endured—because with every moment, he craved her more. To have this woman in his arms, to hold her in a way that was utterly forbidden, was taking apart the only shred of honour he possessed.

He leaned back against the stone tower, keeping her in his arms while he stretched his legs out. After a few moments more, her breathing grew soft and even. She'd fallen asleep in his embrace. And it humbled him that she had given him that trust.

Mairead would be the death of him—of that, he had no doubt. And yet, there was a strength in her he admired, along with her endless belief that there was good in everyone. She even treated him as if there was something worth saving.

No one had ever really looked at him in that way. For a brief moment, he allowed himself to imagine what it would be like if someone like her cared for him. Or what it would be like if a woman nestled close to him like this, welcoming his embrace. She felt right in his arms, and he brushed a kiss against her hair.

The hollow ache of unbidden longing was like nothing he'd ever imagined. And maybe…a part of him wanted to be worthy of her.

He made a silent vow to himself to keep her safe, whatever the cost. If that meant laying down his life for hers, so be it. Mairead was lovely and good, worth fighting for.

And there was a battle coming—one for her father's throne.

Balor hadn't told her everything he'd learned tonight. After he'd left the horse near Rionallís, among the others in a stable, he'd waited and watched. The group of Norman soldiers had indeed been Gerald and Sir Edward. But they'd been led by the Earl of Lowell. A tightness caught his chest at the thought of the earl marrying her.

The Normans had gone straight to the gates of Rionallís, likely to search for her. He'd have done the same thing, if she'd been taken from him. Balor imagined the earl intended to bring her back to Laochre—but was Lowell also hoping to use her for his own advantage? It still seemed as if there *was* a betrothal that the two kings had arranged.

Balor was convinced that the English king had somehow ordered Liam MacEgan's disappearance. The *tánaiste* had been trained since birth to defend his father's lands. But if King John seized command of Laochre, he could then threaten the other territories controlled by the MacEgans.

Balor's mind was racing with all the possible outcomes as he tried to strategize what to do. But then Mairead turned in his arms and rested her hand upon his heart. That one motion stilled his thoughts.

A reckless part of him wanted to ignore what was right and just—and simply take the woman he wanted.

And with her cheek pressed against his chest, it made him wonder if she might be willing to go with him.

In the morning, Mairead stirred against him, and Balor realized that he had, in fact, fallen asleep. His shoulders and back were sore, but the warmth of her body had brought an unexpected comfort. When her eyes flickered open, she appeared surprised at where she was. He let his hands fall to his sides, letting her stay or go as she chose.

But she stayed. 'Good morn to you.'

'And to you.'

An awkwardness filled the space between them, and Mairead stood, stretching her arms. 'I'm starving.' Then a moment later, she winced, as if remembering what had happened the night before. 'What do you want to do?'

He reached inside a fold of his cloak and brought out bread and dried meat. 'Here. You can eat this while we make a decision.' Mairead was slender, and he didn't truly need to eat.

She tilted her head and asked, 'How did you know to bring food? We didn't take any supplies besides your horse.'

With a shrug, he said, 'Go ahead. It's yours.'

But she tore the small bit of bread in half and handed it to him. He didn't take it at first, but she opened his hand and pushed it into his palm. 'I am not eating unless you do, too.' With a slight smile, she added, 'You came prepared.'

He gave a nod. Though he didn't know why he told her, he added, 'I'm no stranger to hunger. I always carry food with me.'

At that, her smile faded. 'I am so sorry, Balor.'

He wished he'd never said it, for she would only pity

him now. Instead, he turned away, building back the invisible walls between them so he wouldn't appear weak in her eyes. He ate the bread and acted as if it meant nothing. 'You didn't know.'

Mairead ate a little of the bread and then ventured, 'Was it because your family suffered during the winter?'

He shook his head, not wanting to talk about it. But she stared at him for a long moment.

'Were you punished?'

Balor met her gaze. 'Why does it matter?'

She was trying to pry for more details, but he had no desire to talk about it. The last thing he wanted was for her to see him as vulnerable or helpless. His past didn't define him now. He'd become a fighter, a man who didn't care about anyone or anything. And he would gain vengeance against Fergus soon enough.

'I saw…the way your chieftain behaved towards you. And I know you want him removed from power.' After a slight pause, she said, 'I suppose he withheld food from you, when you were a boy?'

Clearly, she wasn't going to let it go. 'He saw no reason to waste food on someone like me.'

Her expression tightened. 'What a terrible person. Who would do that to a child?'

'Fergus never needed a reason. He's hated me from the moment I was born.' He paused a moment and said, 'But Kenneth often brought food to me in secret. And then I started keeping it with me, at all times.'

His brother had tried to look after him, though the food was never enough to satiate Balor's hunger. But once, Kenneth had admitted that their mother had given him the food and ordered him to give it in secret. Almost as if she cared.

Balor knew better than to truly believe it. His mother

rarely spoke to him or gave him any attention at all. He'd long ago stopped hoping for a trace of affection.

And he hated her inability to stand up to her husband. Whenever Fergus gave her orders, she'd obeyed—even if it meant turning a blind eye to his cruelty. Orla had defied her husband only once—when she'd sent Balor away to England for fostering.

On the day he'd left Éireann, he'd been eleven—almost twelve. Orla had given him into the care of a merchant, who had agreed to let him travel with him to England. She'd given the man coins, likely stolen from her husband. And she'd given Balor a silver ring, one he'd never seen her wear. She'd bade him give the ring to the Norman lord, in exchange for his fostering. It was hardly more than a twist of silver, but she'd promised him that once the earl saw the ring, he would agree to train him.

The last moment he'd seen his mother, just before he'd boarded the boat, she'd reached out to touch his cheek. 'Balor, I am sorry,' she whispered. 'I wish—' But she'd never finished the sentence. Instead, there had been a shadow of pain in her eyes before she'd given him an unexpected embrace and turned away. He couldn't remember the last time she'd hugged him.

Even so, he still blamed Orla for not defending him during his childhood. She could have stopped the abuse—but out of cowardice and fear, she'd chosen not to. A dark resentment remained buried within him for that.

Mairead tore off another piece of bread. 'I'm starting to understand why you want Fergus gone.' She held out the bread, and he ate from her fingertips, his lips grazing their edges.

Then she took a piece of the dried meat and tore it in

half, giving him the rest. Balor took it, but after he ate, she caught his hand and said, 'You didn't deserve to be treated so cruelly as a child, Balor.'

There was nothing to say, so he remained silent, only meeting her gaze as he held her hand in his.

'I hope you find your own happiness,' she continued. 'Truly, I do.' Then she released his hand.

Did she understand what she was doing to him? He wanted to capture that mouth, kissing her until he forgot all the reasons why he would never have someone like Mairead. But he held back, not wanting to frighten her.

'Should we go to Rionallís now?' she asked. 'Where is our horse?'

'I left it at your uncle's stable,' he answered. 'I didn't want to draw attention back to us by riding away.'

Her face fell before she said, 'I suppose it's not too far to walk.'

'We're not leaving yet. I want to get a better look from the top of the tower to make certain it's safe. We'll make that decision after we see our surroundings.'

She waited for him to lead the way up the stairs, but he gestured for her to go on. 'You first,' he said. 'That way, if you stumble, I'll catch you.'

She took a single step up and turned around to face him. It brought her face to his level, and he wondered if she understood the way she kindled the hunger for far more than a kiss. He held himself steady, meeting her gaze, even as every part of his body responded to her nearness.

'Be careful, *a mhuirnín*,' he warned.

But his words had nothing to do with the steep stairs and everything to do with the way her green eyes held a yearning that echoed his own.

* * *

They waited until nightfall to approach Rionallís on foot. Mairead was exhausted, but she agreed with Balor's belief that they shouldn't travel far during the day—at least, not yet.

Earlier that morn, after they'd climbed to the top of the roundtower, she'd seen the gleam of Norman armour in the distance, along with her father's men who wore dark leather. The soldiers had travelled to Rionallís while others searched along the coast and farther inland.

There was one moment when the soldiers had searched near the roundtower, and she'd held her breath in fear. But without a ladder, they could not investigate, and eventually, the men returned to Laochre.

After it was dark, Balor lowered the ladder and helped her climb down. They hurried together towards her uncle's castle, his hand upon her spine. She was grateful for his protection, even though she knew she shouldn't allow him to touch her.

It took nearly an hour as they made their way through the forest where they could stay hidden. Her stomach was roaring with hunger, but they'd already eaten everything Balor had brought. She imagined the food at Rionallís, and she continued walking alongside him towards the gates where torches in iron sconces flared in the darkness.

Two guards came forward, but this time, she stepped in front of Balor. 'I am here to see my uncle Bevan and my aunt Genevieve.'

'King Patrick's guards came to find you earlier, my lady,' one of the men said. She didn't miss the warning in his voice.

The tension tightened inside her, but she gave a nod. And

as the guards escorted them inside, thankfully, she didn't see any of her father's men or the Normans.

After they reached the stairs that led to the main keep, the guards returned to the gates. Mairead led Balor inside, and the interior of the Great Chamber was lit with torches and candles. When they walked towards another staircase, she heard the sound of harp music playing.

She risked a slight smile at Balor, whose expression remained emotionless as she led him up the stairs towards the solar. When she opened the door to the chamber, the harp music stopped as her aunt's fingers stilled.

'Mairead.' Her aunt Genevieve set aside the harp and caught her in an embrace. 'Your father's men have been searching everywhere for you. What happened?'

A slight relief flared through her at her aunt's worry. 'I chose to leave,' she answered. 'Liam was taken, and I think someone at Laochre was responsible. I do not feel safe there.'

'There is nowhere safer than your father's castle,' Genevieve argued. She kept her arm around Mairead, and the lines on her face appeared strained. Her snowy white hair was caught up in a jeweled barbette, and she wore a silvery grey overdress and *léine.* A moment later, the door opened, and Uncle Bevan came inside, followed by a servant.

Relief flooded over his face. 'Mairead, thank God you are all right. I'll send word to Patrick.'

'Wait a little while before you do.' She explained the reason why she wanted to remain in hiding, even as the doubts grew upon their faces.

'I am glad you came to us,' Genevieve said. She moved over to a small table and poured cups of mead for them. Then she gave quiet orders to the servant to bring food, and Mairead wanted to cry with relief at the thought of easing the hunger.

Then her aunt turned to Balor. 'And who is this?'

'My escort, Balor Ó Phelan,' Mairead answered.

'I've heard of you,' Bevan repeated. Her uncle's gaze darkened, and she could already read his thoughts—The Demon of Éireann. Although she'd heard the name before, now she was starting to wonder why he'd gained such a reputation. Balor did have a rebellious streak, but was there another reason or something he'd done? Or had it only been Fergus Ó Phelan spreading lies?

'I asked Balor to guard me on the journey from Laochre,' Mairead told them as she took a sip of mead. 'He followed my orders.' The last thing she wanted was any of them believing he was at fault for this journey.

'And what about your father's orders to stay at Laochre?' Bevan challenged. 'Some of his men came here earlier today to search for you.'

And others came last night, she thought. But she answered, 'I don't trust them. Liam was captured, and I believe they intended to take me as well. It's why we didn't come here sooner.' She stared back at her uncle. Then she asked, 'Has my brother been found yet?'

Her uncle sobered and turned to look at his wife. Genevieve sat down beside him and took his hand. 'No,' Bevan admitted. 'There's no trace of him anywhere. But we've been searching.'

The coldness inside her deepened. Liam was too strong to be overpowered without a trace—and the soldiers at Laochre would have seen an attack.

'They must have taken him by sea,' Mairead predicted. It was the only explanation that made any sense.

'But why?' her aunt questioned.

'Probably because King Patrick intended to pass the throne to him,' Balor said. 'And the Normans don't want that.' He revealed what they'd overheard the men saying about taking him to England.

Her uncle studied him for a long moment. 'And if Liam isn't there when Patrick steps down, he cannot be crowned.'

'Exactly.' Balor took a step closer to her, and Mairead moved to his side. 'There's something else I've been wondering. Why was the Earl of Lowell here last night?'

Mairead hadn't known that, and uneasiness filled her at the thought. If the earl had been searching for her… She didn't like to think of the reason. Especially if he was connected to her brother's disappearance. Why had Balor kept this from her?

'He travelled here to search for Mairead,' Bevan answered. 'To ensure her safety.'

'But no one knew I was gone last night,' she insisted. 'Not even my family.'

The door opened quietly, and she saw her cousin Alanna enter. The woman offered a slight smile of welcome as she joined her parents, Bevan and Genevieve.

Her aunt cast a sharp look at her husband, making Mairead wonder what was going on. 'When we spoke with Lord Lowell this morn, he was concerned that you had been taken against your will.'

'I wasn't,' she insisted. And she didn't want to marry a man who was intent on tracking her down like a wayward child. Lord Lowell was nearly as old as her brother, and she was starting to sense the age difference between them.

Alanna went to stand beside her parents, and she took her mother's hand in hers. 'I spoke with the earl earlier, and what my parents said is true. His intentions are honourable, Mairead.' Her cousin's tone was solemn, as if she believed there was no other choice.

But Mairead wasn't about to fall prey to Alanna's superstitions. Aye, she had woven a May crown, and true, her cousin had predicted she would wed an outsider. But that didn't mean it would happen. 'I will not be forced into an arranged marriage to please an English king.'

'Even if it saves the lives of your family?' a man's voice interrupted.

She turned and saw the earl standing at the doorway. It was clear that Lord Lowell had never left Rionallís. The earl's expression held worry and annoyance as he entered the solar and came forward to stand in front of her.

Mairead felt her skin prickle, and when she glanced over at her cousin, Alanna's expression held a glint of sadness. Oh, gods. Her cousin clearly believed this arrangement would happen.

'King John demanded a marriage alliance to ensure your father's loyalty,' the earl continued. 'My lands are near Thornwyck, and His Highness asked if I would consider the match.' A wry smile tilted at his mouth. 'It's no hardship to wed a beautiful woman, so I agreed.'

'I will not be a king's pawn,' she said softly. 'And I will not marry anyone until my brother is found.'

Balor moved closer, his hand resting on the blade at his waist as he regarded the earl. 'What do you know about all of this?' There was a trace of accusation in his tone.

'A small group of Normans left Laochre last night.' He met Balor's gaze with an open stare. 'Gerald of Mowbray and Sir Edward Baldwin. I think you know them.'

'We've met,' Balor answered.

'They saw you take the king's daughter,' Lowell continued. 'And I joined them in their quest to find you.'

'But it was my choice to leave,' Mairead corrected. 'I was not taken.'

The earl fell silent. 'Forgive me for the assumption, my lady.' But his expression held suspicion, as if he suspected her attraction towards Balor.

To break the tension, her aunt interrupted, 'You must be hungry.' It was an obvious means of turning the conversation. Genevieve gave the orders, and soon, servants returned with food and set it upon a low table.

'Please eat,' her aunt invited.

Mairead reached for a portion of hot stew with beef and vegetables, along with crusty bread and fresh blackberries, her favourite. She repressed a sigh and dipped into the stew with her bread. Balor sat across from her, but he was careful to take only small portions, as if leaving more for her.

The earl took nothing and moved back against the wall, not far away from her cousin Alanna.

'Have you eaten?' Mairead asked in their direction.

'We did earlier,' Alanna agreed. She risked a glance at the earl before she looked away.

It seemed as if her cousin knew something, but Mairead wasn't about to ask questions. The last thing she wanted was for Alanna to insist upon matchmaking.

She reached for another piece of bread and gave it to Balor. 'Here,' she murmured. 'There is plenty.' Earlier today, Balor had given up most of his own food for her. She wanted to ensure that he had enough now.

He accepted the food and ate, but Mairead suddenly grew aware of her aunt and uncle's attention upon her. After she finished her own meal, she stood and turned back to her uncle. 'I only intend to stay for a little while. I will return to Laochre after my brother is found and crowned king.'

Her uncle turned to Balor. 'Go back to Laochre and send word to King Patrick that his daughter is here at Rionallís.'

'Balor is not your servant,' Mairead corrected.

'Then what is he to you?' her uncle asked quietly. She didn't miss the disapproval on his face, but she also didn't know how to answer that. They were slowly becoming friends. And she couldn't deny her attraction to him. But it still felt as if she barely knew him.

Balor saved her from answering by saying, 'I am her protector.'

Lord Lowell took a step closer, as if to challenge Balor. The two men could not have been more different—one with wealth and power, the other with bravery and defiance. 'Lady Mairead has no need of your protection now,' the earl said quietly. When he turned to her, she saw the silent command that she should choose.

Although she didn't want to offend the earl, there was no question which man held her interest.

To avoid a conflict, Mairead straightened and said, 'I am grateful for every man who is willing to keep me safe. And now, if you will excuse me, I'd like to rest.'

'I will escort you to a chamber, Mairead,' her aunt offered.

'Sleep well, Lady Mairead,' the earl said quietly. 'And I promise you, we'll find your brother.'

His words were sincere, and she lowered her head in acknowledgement as she passed. But she couldn't deny her own confusion. Though she preferred Balor's company, Lord Lowell had done nothing wrong.

In fact, it sounded as if he intended to use his men to help her family, and for that she ought to be grateful. But when she turned back, her gaze fixed upon Balor instead. He stood at the doorway, and his eyes held hers with an intensity that stole her breath. It reminded her of the moment in the roundtower when he'd nearly kissed her again. Her face had been so close to his, it would have been effortless to lean in.

Her body couldn't help but respond to him, even though it was wrong. With reluctance, she turned away and went to follow her aunt.

Right now, the thought of a warm, soft bed was foremost in her mind. Balor followed behind them, ever vigilant even as he kept his distance. But he hadn't slept much, either—and he would not receive the same accommodations unless she intervened.

Mairead caught her Aunt Genevieve by the arm and murmured in her ear, 'Will you please make sure that Balor also has a place of his own to sleep? After all he did to bring me here safely, I would like him to be comfortable.'

Her aunt kept her voice low and whispered back, 'He means something to you. Doesn't he?'

Mairead gave a slight nod. 'I just…want to give something back. For tonight, at least.' Her cheeks burned, but she added, 'Do not worry. I know my duty.'

Her aunt's eyes softened. 'He could take Cavan's chamber for the night, since he no longer dwells with us.'

'Take us there,' she said. With a slight smile, Mairead added, 'He won't agree unless we bring him there first.'

Genevieve walked down to the end of the hall and opened the door. 'Here we are.' Then she leaned in and whispered to Mairead, 'Your chamber is next to his.' With a conspiratorial smile, she walked away and left them alone.

Which made her wonder if her aunt had guessed her wayward feelings.

Mairead ignored her burning cheeks and gestured for Balor to enter. 'You'll stay here tonight.'

His expression turned confused. 'I've no need of my own chamber. I can sleep on the floor with the rest of the guards.'

She ignored him and took him by the hand, bringing him inside. The brazier wasn't lit yet, and she turned to him. 'Will you light this, please?'

Before he could argue again, she closed the door. 'You helped me escape my father's castle and protected me last night. At least allow me to repay you with a bed of your own.'

He stared at her as if he couldn't imagine why she would offer this to him. But he said nothing and found flint and his dagger, lining up the tinder and peat, before striking a spark and coaxing a flame to light.

Once the brazier was lit, he turned back to her. 'Why are you doing this, Mairead?'

His demand made her question the decision. 'I…only wanted you to be comfortable while you are here.'

He kept his distance, his blue eyes piercing. 'Is that the truth? Or are you trying to imagine I'm like the earl or your other suitors?' He folded his arms across his chest. 'I don't need your pity, Mairead.'

But that wasn't it at all. Being here with this man evoked such long-forgotten feelings. He had defended her more than once, and she was starting to rely on him. Part of her didn't want him to leave—and she didn't understand what that meant.

'I don't pity you,' she said softly, taking a step towards him. 'It was never that.'

He stood his ground. 'I didn't come to Laochre to compete for your hand,' he said. 'I know you're going to marry a nobleman like Lowell, not someone like me. I know my place.'

'No, you don't.' Her own words surprised her, but they were true. 'A man who knows his place never would have come with me here. If anything, I think you don't know what you're capable of.' She moved in closer. 'Who you could become if you dared to reach for it.'

His face hardened, and he stood before her, framing her face with his hands. 'You're very fortunate, you know. That I haven't dared to reach for what I want.'

Her skin tightened, imagining what it would be to feel his hands upon her skin. 'And why haven't you?' The breathless tone in her own voice startled her.

'Because if I do, I won't let it go.'

Chapter Six

All her life, Alanna MacEgan had believed in fate. She'd learned, at a young age, that her instincts were strong. The people around her felt their emotions deeply, yearning for love or happiness.

And she truly did want to help them. As a girl, she'd believed in love charms and magic spells. As a grown woman, she believed in watching others—reading beyond their words and interpreting their actions.

Sometimes, a love charm gave a young woman courage to talk with a man she cared for. And sometimes when Alanna saw a dangerous infatuation, she could protect someone from a terrible fate by telling her that the match was not meant to be.

She'd always known Mairead needed a lover outside the MacEgan tribe. Her cousin was far too impulsive, despite her large heart.

But now, seeing the Earl of Lowell left behind in the solar, she felt unsettled. Her father had already left, knowing there was no harm in leaving the two of them alone. And although it was reckless on her own part, she felt the urge to nudge fate in the right direction.

'How are you, Lord Lowell?' she asked him quietly. 'Are you all right?'

The earl turned to look at her, and she noticed the weariness in his brown eyes. His blond hair was tousled as if he'd raked his hand through it in frustration.

'No,' he admitted. 'Not really.'

Alanna studied him closely, and she couldn't deny that she found him handsome. Not that it mattered. Men never noticed her. She had earned her reputation as a fortune teller, and everyone believed she was strange.

'Would you like some ale or mead?' she offered.

The earl's gaze lingered on the door as if he wanted nothing more than to push his way down the hall and follow Mairead. Though he didn't answer, Alanna poured ale and handed him a cup.

But she chose her words carefully as she spoke. 'You needn't worry. My cousin knows her duty, and she has always had a kind heart.'

'Is it kindness she feels towards her guard? Or something else?' he remarked. But she didn't miss the undertone of jealousy.

'It doesn't matter what she feels,' Alanna answered honestly. His feelings were easy to read, and so she reassured him, 'You are the suitor her father chose.'

He took a deep sip of ale and then asked, 'What is your name?'

'I am Alanna MacEgan,' she answered. 'You've already met my parents, Bevan and Genevieve.'

He walked over to the table and poured a cup of ale for her. She took it and sat in her chair, drinking to avoid saying something foolish.

'Do you and your husband live nearby?' he asked. 'Have you any children of your own?'

'I have neither,' she answered. Her heartbeat quickened with her own embarrassment. 'I live here with my family.'

At that, he turned to her. 'Did your father not arrange a marriage for you?' The expression on his face appeared confused, as if he could not understand why.

She wasn't about to confess that no man wanted to wed her. She'd shied away from men, most of her life, for they made fun of her.

'He tried,' was the only answer she could give. But she was fully aware that the earl was only a little older than herself. And although she knew he was meant for Mairead, there was a small part of her that wished she could have met someone like the earl, years ago when she was young and filled with hope.

Alanna leaned back in her chair. 'If you truly wish to win my cousin's heart, then help her find her brother.'

'We've been trying,' the earl answered. 'But aside from the group of Normans who left Laochre, we've found no trace of him.' He finished his ale, and she did the same as they sat in companionable silence.

And when she felt the eyes of the earl watching her, she couldn't help but dream of a very different future than the one Fate had chosen for her.

It was strange, lying in a bed. Balor had slept on the floor for most of his life. During his fostering, he'd slept on a pallet stuffed with fresh hay, and he hadn't minded so much. But here, the mattress sank slightly beneath his weight, and the coverlet had been warm. He hadn't been able to stop himself from thinking of Mairead, wondering what it would be like to share a bed with a woman. He could only imagine the softness of her skin, the heat of her body. And God help him, he couldn't stop the desire, the craving for her.

This had been a mistake. He never should have escorted her here. It had only awakened a different kind of yearning.

Her words had been a challenge to become more than what he was. Balor had never really considered it. All his life, he'd been tormented and abused because of the Norman who had fathered him. It had awakened a rage within him, a hatred of Fergus. It had been his sole purpose, his driving need for revenge.

But Mairead's quiet encouragement—*who you could become if you dared to reach for it*—made him suddenly question everything.

For a moment, he let his mind drift with daydreams. He'd lived in a castle before, during his fostering, so dwelling amid stone walls and guards was familiar. But when he was younger, he'd kept to himself, not wanting to be noticed. He hadn't wanted to befriend anyone. It was easier to remain alone and apart from the others.

But he'd still helped the younger boys with their training, guarding them from the older ones who had tried to intimidate them. It had been a way of remembering his own brother, Kenneth.

His thoughts drifted back to the present. What would it be like, having to defend an entire castle of people? An immense responsibility, no doubt. And yet, he thought of the young boy, Marcas. He could easily imagine defending the lad and others like him.

Fergus had used his position as chieftain to exert his own authority over others. He had gloried in the power, commanding his men. And yet, if they came under attack, Balor believed the chieftain would turn and run. Never would he pick up his sword.

Even if Kenneth tried to defend them, his younger brother lacked the strength and resilience to guard them.

Maybe that was why he'd come back to Dunmalus. A small part of him didn't want to abandon Kenneth, despite everything.

His brother needed help learning how to protect the Ó Phelans—he was too young and inexperienced to lead. If Fergus was gone and Kenneth became chieftain, perhaps it would be better to stay and guide him. It wasn't the life Balor had imagined for himself, but he would consider staying for a time if it meant securing Kenneth's future. He could become the sword wielded by his brother, protecting them from enemies.

The Demon of Éireann.

He'd earned that name. But despite the blood on his hands, he didn't care what everyone else believed of him. He'd had his reasons for killing so many fighters, leaving them to rot. And if no one but him knew the truth about what had happened that day, so be it. He refused to stand aside and let innocents be threatened. He didn't care if everyone believed he was a butcher.

All his life, Fergus had reminded Balor that *he* was to blame for his mother's misery. Orla had shrouded herself in grief, finding happiness in nothing. Certainly, she lived within her marriage as if she were a ghost. Her emotions towards her husband were empty, and the more she shied away from Fergus, the more the chieftain took out his rage on Balor.

Even though Kenneth had been kind, Balor couldn't get close to his brother without being severely punished.

And when your own family—the ones who were supposed to love you—treated you as if you were nothing but a burden, it was easy to believe.

Balor was torn between wanting to help his brother and knowing that no one wanted him at Dunmalus. Then, too, there was another problem if he stayed here. He might see Mairead again, married to a nobleman.

A tightness caught in his gut at the thought of another man kissing her. Touching her.

Lord Lowell was a far better choice of a husband for Mairead—Balor could offer her nothing. Not a home and not the life she deserved. And yet, jealousy slid through his veins. Last night he'd barely slept, fully aware that the earl was here, under the same roof. He knew, full well, what the earl wanted.

But Balor wasn't so certain about Mairead's desires. He couldn't understand why she had brought him here last night, demanding that he receive a chamber of his own. He wasn't used to anyone taking care of him.

He ran his hand over the coverlet and sheets, marveling at such a thing. Even something as simple as having privacy to sleep alone. The only time he'd ever had that was when he'd slept out of doors within a tent.

And this room had been warmed by the brazier. Balor stood from the bed, feeling the slight chill when he went to get dressed. He walked towards the window and opened the shutters, staring outside at the serfs who were unloading supplies from a wagon while soldiers trained in the inner bailey. Others brought trays of food from the kitchens, and his stomach rumbled at the thought.

Mairead deserved to live in a place like Rionallís, with a bed of her own and a warm room. In his mind, he imagined laying her down on a bed such as this, skin to skin.

In England, several of the maids had flirted with him. He'd been startled by their attentions at first, but they had quickly taught him how to please a woman. And although he'd enjoyed it, he'd never fully taken advantage of them, not wanting to sire any bastards of his own. It wasn't right or fair to the child.

But the thought of spending an entire night pleasuring Mairead brought an ache within him, a fierce craving to taste that sweet softness and drive her over the edge of fulfilment.

As if in answer to his daydream, a soft knock sounded at his door. Balor went to answer, not caring that he was only wearing trews. When he opened it, Mairead was standing before him in a dark green overdress and *léine* with her hair half up. She blinked a moment at his state of undress, and her face flushed. But she didn't turn away from him.

Her gaze was fixed upon his bare skin, and she let out a slow breath. 'Good morn to you.'

In answer, he opened the door wider, letting her come inside. She did, but instead of crossing the room, she remained next to him. 'I—I thought we could talk about what to do now.'

God, the scent of her skin reminded him of a field of fresh flowers. He wanted to bury his face in her hair, sliding his hands through that dark silk.

'What is it you want?' he asked.

'I don't know whether we should stay here or look for my brother.'

Balor rested his hand on the back of the door, shadowing her body. He was so close, he could easily steal a kiss if he wanted to.

And by the gods, he wanted to.

'What do you think we should do?' she said softly.

'That choice is yours.' He rested a second hand against the door so she was almost in his embrace.

Mairead tilted her head. 'Are you trying to make me feel uncomfortable, Balor?'

Uncomfortable, no. Pushing against the invisible boundaries? Yes.

'Is that what you feel?'

'I don't know what I feel.' Her gaze drifted downward, and she studied his bare chest a moment before she laid her hand upon his heart. 'Only what I want.'

The moment her soft fingers touched him, he went hard. He craved her beyond all reason, especially because she had sought him out. *She* had touched him first, and a wicked side of him wanted to seize everything, even as his brain warned him to grasp the last shred of honour he possessed. Which was almost nothing at the moment.

He reminded himself that she hadn't come here for seduction.

'What is it you want, Mairead?' The words came out rough, revealing the frustration curled within him. He certainly knew what *he* wanted.

Her, naked on his bed, laid out for him to savour with his hands. And his mouth.

She threaded her hand into his hair and pulled his face down. 'The freedom to choose.'

Balor didn't ask permission but crushed his mouth to hers, taking what she'd dared to offer. Her arms went around his neck, and he pressed her back against the door, resting his knee between her legs. She kissed him back, opening to him, and touching his tongue with her own.

He was desperate to have her in whatever way she offered. He explored her, teasing her lips and letting instinct guide him. Already, his pulse was pounding, the need aching beyond anything he'd ever imagined. He wanted this woman with every breath he took.

'Does your family know you're here in my chamber?' he murmured against her lips.

'No.' Her voice was a breathy whisper. 'My uncle would murder me if he did.'

A soft laugh escaped him. 'So, you didn't just come here to talk about what you want to do next?' He was starting to wonder if Mairead had a sensual side of her own. Or whether he'd simply been acting like a bastard, exploiting her innocence.

Her cheeks flushed, but she didn't rise to his bait. A blend of emotions passed over her face—fear, uncertainty, and her own yearning. She kept her hands on his chest, as if to feel his heartbeat. But she moved her fingers across his muscles, sliding them over the silver scar across the ridges of his abdomen in the barest caress that took him apart.

'Tell me what you want, Mairead,' he urged.

'You're talking too much,' she said and pulled his mouth back to hers. His thoughts scattered, and he fully agreed with her. To bring her closer, he lifted her to straddle his thigh, despite her twisted skirts.

Now that he had better access to that sweet mouth, he plundered it, even knowing that the kisses were stolen. 'I enjoyed the bed last night,' he said against her lips. 'But I wanted you in it with me.' He shifted his weight, and a startled cry broke from her as his thigh pressed against her intimately. Instantly, he stopped. 'What is it?'

She shook her head, her eyes pleading with him. And then he realized that…the movement of his thigh between her legs had caught her unawares, awakening her own needs. He caught her hips, watching as she closed her eyes and a gasp caught in her throat.

'Do that again,' she whispered as she clung to him.

Slowly, Balor rocked his thigh against the center of her womanhood. Her fingers dug into his shoulders, and she trembled against him, as she leaned her head back. 'Balor, I—'

Her words broke off, and one of her legs grazed his own erection as she arched. He was going to lose control if he continued pleasuring her, and he didn't care. Despite his own raging need, his desire to arouse her was stronger. He moved his hands to her waist, gentling his kiss as he moved his thigh in a slow, shifting rhythm.

He reasoned with himself that he could claim her like this, and no harm was done. She was still a virgin, still untouched.

But she was biting her lip, her breathing unsteady as he moved. What he was doing was good, but it wasn't enough. Slowly, he moved one hand higher, resting it just beneath her breast as he shifted his thigh.

And when she moved his hand to cover her breast, cupping the generous curve of her, his body turned to rigid stone. He was thankful the door was bolted, so no one could come in and interrupt this. He traced her breast, finding the cockled nipple, and gently began circling it with his thumb.

Another moan broke from her, and she was gripping his hair now, nearly undone by what was happening. She had never looked at him like this before, and he was determined to drive her into the sweet darkness of oblivion.

It didn't matter that his own body was grazing the edge of honour. He intended to explore her body, learning everything he could. He loosened the laces of her bodice, adjusting her clothing until his hand covered her bare breast.

There was an immediate change in her demeanour, and she kissed him again, her tongue tangled with his as he stroked her nipple, wishing he could expose her flesh and see that beautiful breast.

'If I could, I would have you naked right now,' he said.

'I would lay you down on that bed and spend hours with my mouth on your skin.'

He moved his hand to her other breast and found it as erect as the first. He teased it mercilessly, watching her as she continued to move against his leg. 'Would you like that, Mairead?'

She gave a slight cry as he circled her nipple with his thumb. And then, without warning, she pressed herself hard against him, rocking and moaning as she trembled. She gripped his neck, and he pressed his mouth to her throat, watching as she came apart with her pleasure, a cry breaking forth from her throat.

More than anything in the world, he wanted to be inside her at this moment, feeling her body surrounding his as she shuddered. He pressed her back, and she seemed to sense what he wanted, wrapping her legs around his waist.

'Don't stop,' she pleaded, her breathing unsteady.

Balor groaned, driving himself against her, through the folds of her gown, while he held her against the wall. Instinct guided him, and she kissed him hard as he gripped her hips. Despite the barrier of their clothing, she arched, shattering a second time as he ground himself against her. He could barely breathe, the raw needs coursing through him until abruptly, he found release and saw stars.

It felt as if he'd just touched a piece of heaven, and nothing could have prepared him for this. Slowly, Balor lowered her down. Mairead's cheeks were flushed, her eyes glazed with the aftermath of her own release. She looked stricken, as if she couldn't believe what had just happened between them.

He let her go, not knowing what to say or do. Maybe it was best to say nothing at all. He stepped away, reaching for his fallen tunic on the floor.

But when he turned to face her, she had already fled, closing the door behind her.

Mairead remained inside her bedchamber, questioning what to do now. Her face was still flushed, her body satiated in a way she'd never felt before. Her heart had never pounded this way, not even with Diarmud.

She sat down, her breasts aching, while she longed for more. Although she never should have gone to Balor's room, it had been an impulse. She had truly meant only to talk to him. But the moment he had come near, he'd tempted her.

The sight of his body had stolen her breath. Every ridged muscle, the sun-warmed skin, had awakened her own desires. She wished she could have kissed a path over his muscled chest with her mouth, learning the edges and planes of his warrior's body. The silver scar across his abdomen revealed his fighting past, and she'd traced it with her fingertips, needing to touch him.

A shadow of loss crossed over her mood. She had loved Diarmud, only a few months ago. At least, she'd believed it was love. Now, she wasn't so certain. It felt more like a maiden's infatuation instead.

No one knew Diarmud had been her first lover. She'd told no one at all.

But she was starting to realize it had been a mistake. Her feelings towards him were nothing compared with the fiery storm of breathless need Balor had conjured. Or was it simply lust?

Diarmud had treated her as if she were something precious, and it had warmed her heart when his face had lit up to see her.

Foolishly, she had believed they would marry, even knowing that her father would never accept a soldier as her husband. And yet, she'd allowed herself to daydream of a simpler life.

Diarmud had promised that he would become worthy of her, that he would fight in battle to defend the MacEgans' honour.

Never in her life had she imagined that they would bring back his broken body.

Diarmud had been so determined to prove his worth to her family—and now he was dead. Guilt suffocated her with memories of her own past mistakes. It was *her* fault that he'd died.

Perhaps she should simply accept whatever marital alliance her father wanted. She didn't deserve love or passion.

And although Balor had given her a taste of that forbidden passion, he and Diarmud were completely different. There was a ruthless air to Balor, a silent confidence in his fighting skills. And when he'd turned that intensity towards her… Her heart thundered at the memory.

Yet, he'd never once spoken of a future for them. Her heart faltered, for he'd said he wasn't interested in marrying her.

Was that the truth? If so, then why had he touched her so intimately? Was it desire or was he only using her?

Mairead lowered her head and exhaled, afraid of being spurned. Maybe this wasn't real, and she only wanted it to be.

But did it make her wicked for desiring him, hoping to soothe the loneliness that haunted her?

A knock sounded, and her aunt Genevieve came inside. Her wrinkled face held a warm smile. 'I thought we would see you below stairs to break your fast, Mairead.'

She *was* hungry, but she didn't quite feel ready to face

her family. Or especially Balor, after what had just happened between them. 'I'll come down in a little while.'

Her aunt paused a moment and then ventured, 'Are you well, Mairead? You appear troubled.'

She was. And restless. And afraid she was about to make another mistake with her life, giving her heart to someone who didn't want it.

'I don't know what to do,' she admitted. 'I don't know whether to stay here or return to Laochre.' It was a feeble excuse, and she knew it.

Genevieve drew closer. 'Either is fine, my dear.'

But she shook her head in disbelief. 'I don't really feel safe at home.' She glanced at her aunt. 'And I don't know what to do now.'

'It seems to me that there are two men who want to keep you safe.' Genevieve's voice softened as she sat down on the bed beside her. 'I know Lord Lowell's family. He's one of the most powerful men in England and would be glad to watch over you.'

'I know. Everyone wants me to wed him.' Mairead gripped her hands together, trying to keep her voice calm. 'But I just…don't think I can.'

Especially after she'd just experienced an awakening at Balor's hands. Her brain warned her not to place the desires of her body over the rational decision of whom she should marry.

Her aunt reached out to take her hand. 'Has the earl given you a reason not to consider him?'

Mairead didn't know how to answer that and could only cast her gaze at the floor. No, there was no reason she shouldn't wed a man like the earl…except that she wanted Balor instead.

'Or is there someone else?' Genevieve asked softly, with a knowing gaze.

She lifted her eyes to her aunt's, letting her expression speak for itself. The older woman's face grew solemn. 'Mairead, be careful. I felt as you did once.'

'But you married the man you loved,' she pointed out. Was it so wrong to want a husband who loved her?

'And Bevan nearly died trying to defend me from the monster I was betrothed to.' Her tone was solemn, and she reached out to take her hand. 'Believe me, I *do* understand what you're feeling. But I'm not certain you would…have the life you want with Balor Ó Phelan.' When her cheeks reddened, her aunt squeezed her palm. 'I see the way you look at him.'

Mairead turned away, not denying it. But she spoke the words her aunt wanted to hear. 'It doesn't matter what I think. My family would never accept him. And I suppose they fear we would have nowhere to live.'

'Your father would give you a place,' Genevieve corrected. 'But what does Balor want? Does he hope to lead the Ó Phelan clan?'

He wanted his younger brother to become chieftain—she knew that. But never once had Balor spoken of his own future. It made her wonder what his plans were. And whether he even wanted her to be part of them.

'I don't know,' she admitted. 'Is he below stairs with the others?'

Her aunt shook her head. 'He is with his brother, who arrived a little while ago. I suspect Balor will return home with him soon.'

Why had Kenneth Ó Phelan traveled here? A sudden uneasiness caught Mairead as she wondered whether the young man had come to find her or Balor. 'Did his father travel with him?' She hoped not. She had witnessed for herself the hatred that Fergus bore for Balor. The last thing she wanted was for another fight to break out between them.

'No, he is alone,' Genevieve answered.

Thank goodness for that. But it still made her question why Kenneth was here.

'I will join you for the morning meal,' she told her aunt. It was the best way to get the answers she needed.

The older woman led the way, and when they arrived in the Great Chamber, Lord Lowell rose at the sight of her. 'Good morn to you, Lady Mairead.' There was relief in his expression, as if he'd half expected her to flee last night.

There was no sign of Balor anywhere, which bothered her. As she walked closer to the dais, she asked her aunt in a low voice, 'Will you invite Balor and his younger brother to join us?'

'I will. But you should sit beside the earl,' her aunt countered in a whisper, 'and have a conversation with him. Then make your own decision about whether to consider him as a potential husband.'

Mairead gritted her teeth. 'Fine.'

She would do what was necessary if it meant Balor would gain her family's hospitality. But she feared her impulsive visit to Balor's chamber might result in his sudden departure. And she didn't want that at all.

She raised her chin and climbed the steps of the dais to where the earl waited. Lord Lowell offered her the chair beside him, and her cousin Alanna sat on the opposite side.

'I hope you are well.' The earl offered a warm smile.

'And you.' She returned it and greeted her cousin. 'Hello, Alanna.'

Her cousin answered the greeting but there was a speculative look in her eyes. Mairead prayed Alanna wouldn't speak of betrothals or love charms, and thankfully, her cousin made only ordinary conversation.

The earl offered Mairead pottage, bread, cheese, and summer berries. She took some of each, but even as she spoke to him with politeness, her attention was shifting, searching for Balor. *Please let him not be gone.*

'Do you have children from your first marriage, Lord Lowell?' Alanna was asking.

At that, the earl brightened. 'I have three sons, yes. The oldest, Peter, is fifteen. Samuel is twelve, and my youngest is Mark.'

Mairead was startled to realize that the earl had no need of heirs. It meant that he didn't truly have to marry anyone.

Then the earl added, 'King Patrick offered to allow my sons to train at Laochre. It would be a good opportunity for them.'

She didn't quite know what to say but managed, 'They would all be welcome, of course.'

'And what of me?' the earl asked quietly. 'Would I be welcome?'

'I—I suppose so.' She distracted herself with food, feeling like a terrible person. Her aunt was right—Lord Lowell did seem like a good man. Just as Diarmud had been kind. The only problem was that her heart was falling for Balor.

She couldn't think of what to say and so ate in silence. The earl grew solemn, and for a long while, he didn't speak, either.

Thankfully, Alanna intervened. 'My lord, I would enjoy hearing about your home.' The earl turned to speak with her, and it was then that Mairead spied Balor standing on the opposite side of the Great Chamber. Her cousin's conversation was a good distraction, and Mairead murmured an excuse as she left the table. Slowly, she crossed through the rows of tables until she reached the opposite wall.

Balor's gaze was fierce and filled with heat as he regarded her. It evoked all the memories of what they'd done only a little while ago, and her face flushed.

He leaned in and murmured, 'Your father has just arrived at Rionallís.'

She held back a curse. Of course he had come. She had no doubt that her uncle Bevan had sent word immediately. And undoubtedly, Patrick would blame Balor for her disappearance, no matter that it had been her own idea to leave Laochre.

Despite her desire to keep him here, she understood that it would only incite her father's anger.

'You have to leave,' she urged. 'It's not safe for you here anymore.'

'I can take care of myself.' He continued holding her hand and asked, 'What do you want to do now?'

She squeezed his palm. 'I don't have a choice. My father won't allow me to stay here.' Mairead closed her eyes and took a breath. 'His men will force me to go back home.'

But her mind sharpened at another idea. If she played the role expected of her, if she pretended to be frightened, her father might believe it.

'I think you should go back to Dunmalus with your brother.' She let out a heavy sigh. 'If I beg my father's forgiveness—and if you're already gone—he won't harm you.'

'Is that what you want? For me to leave?'

She shook her head. 'I don't, no. But—'

'Good.' Without another word, he took her hand in his and led her towards the entrance to the Great Chamber.

What was he doing? This wasn't part of her plan. 'Wait, Balor. I can't just leave with you. Not with everyone watching.'

'Do you want to find your brother or not?'

She stared at him, not understanding. 'What do you mean?'

He kept her in the shadows as he led her outside. 'I mean that I think Kenneth knows something that will help us find Liam. Come with me.'

Chapter Seven

Balor gave her his cloak, and she raised it over her head, keeping her face and hair hidden as he led her outside. His brother remained near the inner bailey wall, and as soon as Kenneth caught sight of them, he walked forward.

'In here,' Balor warned, bringing them inside one of the towers. He didn't want King Patrick to catch a glimpse of his daughter just yet.

Kenneth appeared uneasy about Mairead's presence, but he mumbled a greeting to her.

Mairead answered it and then asked the young man, 'What do you know about Liam?'

He exchanged a glance with Balor and then said, 'I think my father knows what happened to your brother. Fergus didn't take him—there's no sign of Liam at Dunmalus—but I overheard him arguing with our mother. He…' Kenneth broke off, as if he couldn't find the right words.

'It's all right,' Mairead reassured him. 'You won't be punished for your father's misdeeds, I promise you.'

The young man's shoulders slumped. 'My father paid someone a great deal of silver. After my mother learned of it, she confronted Fergus to find out why.' He looked out at the soldiers in the inner bailey and admitted, 'He said something about gaining the throne at Laochre.'

'He paid someone to take Liam into captivity, didn't he?'

His brother shrugged. 'I think so, but I don't know where. Or who has him now.'

Balor didn't press his brother further. Fergus had made it no secret that he'd envied the MacEgans. His own father had tried—and failed—to take the throne. As a child, Fergus had been fostered with the MacEgans as a hostage to keep his father from attempting a second coup.

It stood to reason that the chieftain would want Liam to be an Ó Phelan prisoner, to offer leverage against their own claim to the throne.

'We need to question Fergus,' Balor said. 'Find out who took the *tánaiste* and where. King Patrick should know of this.'

'No,' Kenneth protested. 'The king would kill my father immediately. I'm begging you…as my brother, don't tell Patrick.'

Fury stretched the limits of his patience, for Balor didn't care what happened to Fergus. He *wanted* to bring about the man's downfall. But he also cared about his brother.

But Mairead spoke softly, 'Thank you for telling us this, Kenneth.'

The young man regarded her for a moment. 'I would… want someone to help me find Balor, if he were missing. I don't know if anything I've said will make a difference. I think my mother knows more.'

She released Balor's hand and took a step closer to Kenneth. 'I am grateful to you, and I pray that we will find Liam soon.'

Balor reached out and embraced his brother. 'Go now, before anyone sees you.'

Kenneth's gaze lingered upon Mairead's, but there was

a sad resignation, as if he realized he had no chance of winning her heart.

Balor understood that feeling well.

The stolen moment between them had caught him unawares. He'd known that Mairead hadn't come to his bedchamber for that reason—and yet, he'd fallen under the spell of desire, needing to touch her.

For that fleeting moment, this woman had belonged to him. And he'd savoured every touch, especially the way she had responded to him.

He couldn't deny how badly he wanted her. A good man would stand aside and let her have the life she deserved by wedding a man like the earl. Or a wealthy nobleman.

But the problem was he'd never been a good man. He was starting to question whether letting her go was the right decision.

Honour would give him nothing but loneliness and jealousy.

His fingers brushed against hers, and she took his hand, holding it while they watched to ensure that his brother made it safely outside the gates.

'Do you think the chieftain hid my brother somewhere near Dunmalus?' Mairead ventured.

He turned back to her. 'I don't know. But my mother might know more about what Fergus did. I'll go and talk to her.' He could return to Dunmalus and talk to Orla while Mairead remained here with her family.

'I want to come with you.'

He tightened his hand upon hers. Aye, he wanted that, too. But it wasn't wise—especially now that her father was here.

'You wanted to be safe,' he reminded her. 'Travelling with me is dangerous, and you know it.'

Before he could stop her, Mairead slid her arms around his waist. 'Don't you think I see the prison they are making for me? I see the earl, the man they chose as my husband. My father and uncle are here, along with the others. If I stay, I worry they will force me to wed Lord Lowell immediately. And that's not something I want.'

'Then tell them no.' He rested his hands at her waist, unable to push her away. 'They cannot force you to make a vow.'

'I don't want to stay behind.' She rested her forehead against his. 'Don't leave me, Balor. Take me with you.'

He didn't want to be caught in the middle. Especially since it would enrage her family and they might learn nothing at all about her brother. Bringing her with him meant defying orders.

But he also knew he couldn't stand aside and walk away from her. Not if she needed him.

He cupped her face, stroking his thumb down the edge of her jaw to her throat.

Maybe it was time to truly become the villain everyone believed he was.

Mairead could feel Balor's gaze upon her back as she walked towards her father and uncle, leaving him in the shadows. She'd considered her choices, and it would buy them more time if Patrick believed she was being obedient.

She kept her steps slow and even, as if she had come outside to greet him. After a slight pause at the door, she waited for the king to acknowledge her.

King Patrick was dismounting from his horse while his brother Bevan stood nearby. Her father's gaze tightened at the sight of her. Mairead lifted her chin and offered a slight smile, despite the exhaustion of the past two days weighing upon her.

Patrick came closer and crushed her into an embrace. 'Mairead, why did you leave Laochre?'

'Because I overheard Normans plotting against my brother. I believed they would come for me next, so I came here instead.'

Her father blanched at that, but she continued on. 'Did you not teach me to be aware of those around me? To be ready to defend myself at all times?' She shook her head. 'I was unprepared the last time I was taken. I wasn't about to let it happen again.'

Patrick exchanged a glance with his brother, and she could see the strain on his face. 'You shouldn't have left without several men to protect you.'

'It would have drawn too much attention,' she argued. 'Instead, I commanded Balor Ó Phelan to bring me to Rionallís.'

He appeared uncertain about her words, but her uncle Bevan confirmed it. 'She did have an escort when she arrived.'

'And where is Ó Phelan now?'

'I sent him back to Dunmalus with his brother,' Mairead lied. She walked alongside them back to the keep, behaving as if she hadn't openly defied her father. To redirect the conversation, she asked, 'Have you found Liam yet?'

'Not yet. Our men are still searching. And stop trying to pretend as though I'm not fully aware of what you're doing, Mairead.'

'And what is it you think I'm doing?'

'Avoiding your betrothal.' His gaze sharpened.

'You offered me the right to choose my betrothal,' she said quietly. 'Has that changed?'

When her father didn't answer, uneasiness curled within her stomach. This was the reason she'd feared. But before he could speak, she blurted out, 'Why? Are you afraid I won't choose the right man?' she ventured. 'Like Diarmud.'

Patrick appeared pained at her words. Probably because there was some truth to it.

Her father let out a sigh. 'I know you were fond of him,' he said at last. 'But he was a soldier, Mairead. You are my daughter. He could offer you nothing at all, except his heart.'

'I loved him. I had planned to marry him in secret.' The words blurted out from her lips before she could stop them. It had been true, once, even if that love hadn't lasted. She still remembered the rush of giddy emotion when she'd seen Diarmud smile at her. He had been so kind, treating her as if she meant everything to him. At the time, she'd been delighted with their forbidden union.

But he'd never made her blood race the way Balor had.

Balor had changed her, in ways he'd never guessed. Before he'd come to the *aenach*, she'd been resigned to marrying a man she didn't love and pretending to want an ambitious marriage to a man who would expect her to rule at his side.

And now she couldn't bear the thought of it.

Her future felt so uncertain right now. Worse was the fear that Balor didn't truly want her for anything more than stolen passion. He'd yielded to her plea of letting her travel with him to Dunmalus, but he'd made no secret of his reluctance.

She risked a glance back at the shadows, even as her father was saying something she wasn't paying attention to. Despite their differences in status, Balor had fought at her side and defended her.

And yet, there was a difference between them. Not because of their social standing, but because Balor had made it clear that he didn't want a life at her side. And it hurt to know it. He'd always been careful not to make any promises.

She turned back to her father, who was waiting for an answer to a question she hadn't heard. 'I am not ready to wed anyone, Father,' she admitted. 'I've hardly slept in the past two days, and my brother is still missing.' She shook her head. 'I need time.'

Her father escorted her back within the castle keep. 'I promise you'll be safe at Laochre. Gather your belongings, and we'll go back.'

Mairead could feel the invisible net, snaring her back to her family home. She gave him a slight nod to pacify him. Then she excused herself and walked away.

Her thoughts were tangled up, for she had no intention of returning home. Instead, she intended to be defiant with Balor and risk losing her heart a second time.

It wasn't hard to see that Mairead had been coerced into obedience by her father. And so, Balor had made plans of his own.

He'd spent part of last night exploring Rionallís, for he'd anticipated having to make his own escape. Not for one moment did he believe he was safe here, and he'd wanted to know the best way to quietly leave. Now that Mairead's father was here, his time had run out.

And so, he'd waited for her inside her chamber.

The moment Mairead entered the room, he lowered the bar across the door and stood in front of it.

'Balor!' she gasped and stepped back. 'You frightened me.'

He pointed towards her bed where he had set aside serf's clothing for her. 'I brought you these to wear.'

She blinked a moment and stared at him. 'Why?'

'Because if we're going to find your brother, you need to blend in with the others.'

Her expression turned thoughtful, but she laid the clothing back on the bed. 'You should turn around.'

He started to move, but then her green eyes locked with his as she began to loosen the laces of her gown. His throat went dry, even as honour demanded that he turn away from her.

'I should, shouldn't I?' The words revealed a trace of rebellion.

Mairead answered his defiance as she slowly raised the overdress and *leíne* over her head, wearing only her shift.

He couldn't tear his gaze away as she reached for the trews and pulled them on beneath her shift. Then she turned her back on him and lifted the shift away, giving him a slight glimpse of bare skin and the curve of one breast.

God above. The sight of her was a temptation that silenced his honour while she dressed in the tunic and cloak. It took everything in him not to reach for her and press her down to the bed, feeling that softness beneath him. She awakened a hunger in him, a craving that would never be satisfied.

Mairead hid her gown within a trunk on the other side of the room and turned back to him. She braided her hair and stuffed it down the back of the tunic.

'Should we leave?' she asked coolly.

He managed a nod. 'Lift your hood first. I'll go down the stairs, and you'll wait before following. Find a group of men to trail behind, if you can.'

He lifted the wooden bar across the door and left. He

didn't see any guards, which meant they hadn't seen him enter Mairead's chamber earlier.

When he reached the bottom of the spiral stairs, he heard her footsteps behind him. He kept his pace even, as if nothing was wrong.

But just as he reached the door leading outside the castle keep, a hand seized his arm. 'And just where are you going, Ó Phelan?'

He turned and saw Bevan MacEgan. The older man's gaze was shrewd, as if he fully expected Balor's defiance.

Behind him, the footsteps stopped, and he prayed Mairead would remain out of view. 'I'm going home to Dunmalus,' he answered honestly. 'Unless you'd prefer that I stay?'

The Irishman's expression held a warning. 'Leave my niece alone.'

He pulled his arm free and faced the man. 'I've done nothing except obey her orders.'

Bevan ignored the response. 'She needs to remain safe with her family. Stay out of this.'

Something about the man's warning felt like a challenge. Balor simply smiled and walked past the man through the doors. He didn't turn back, not wanting to reveal Mairead's disguise. He walked towards the inner wall, fully aware of the soldiers trailing behind him, likely from MacEgan's orders. Balor knew if he drew the men away from Mairead, it would be easier for her to leave.

And then what? his mind prompted. It wasn't as if she could stay with him after they found her brother. He was her protector; that was all. After that, he had to return her to her family, where she could wed a nobleman.

But a rebellious side of him wanted to keep her. He

wanted to shatter Mairead's carefully constructed world of royalty and steal the woman he wasn't meant to have.

He didn't know what sort of madness this was, to even consider it. But he'd never really been a man of honour—he'd been a man bent on learning to fight. And learning to survive. He'd been told by Fergus, time and again, that he was worthless. Even now, the MacEgans wanted him to stay away from her. And yet…

Mairead had asked to come with him. Not the earl. Not another nobleman.

Him. The Demon of Éireann.

Maybe it was time to stop believing what others said about him—and time to seize what he truly wanted. And if being wicked gave him Mairead MacEgan, so be it.

Balor walked forward, keeping his hand on his sword hilt as he silently passed the guards and continued to the stables to retrieve the horse he'd taken from Laochre.

After he mounted the horse, he rode outside the gates alone. It wouldn't be long before someone discovered Mairead's disappearance, so he searched for a sign of her. She was no longer with the serfs she'd followed, and he studied the forest nearby.

He kept his horse in a walk, still searching. Then, at last, he saw her emerge at the edge of the woods. After ensuring that no one was watching, Balor dismounted and helped her on the horse before swinging up behind her. Within moments, he urged the horse into a hard run, moving swiftly towards the coast.

'Your father will have me whipped for this if we're caught,' he murmured in her ear.

'Then let's not get caught.' She leaned back against him, and her words made him tighten his grip around her as they rode hard towards Dunmalus.

He was careful to hide their tracks as best he could, riding through forests and streams. But during the journey, all he could think of was that he'd given her the choice to return to her safe world—and she'd chosen him instead.

No one had ever chosen him. Ever.

She didn't know, couldn't understand, what that meant. This was no longer about finding her brother or learning the truth about King John's plans amid the Irish nobility. She had trusted him with her life, and he no longer cared about what was right or honourable. If Mairead wanted him, then he would keep her until the last breath was ripped from his body. No one would take her from him.

The sun was high in the sky by the time they neared Dunmalus. Balor slowed their pace slightly, unwilling to risk Mairead's safety. He had no interest in speaking with his father, but his mother might have the answers they sought.

There was one place where the Ó Phelans might have hidden Liam, if he *was* their prisoner—and it was not at the fortress.

They continued riding past Dunmalus before he turned the horse towards the coast. 'Where are we going?' Mairead asked. 'I thought—'

'We're travelling to the place where the chieftain keeps his prisoners,' he finished. 'The mound of hostages.'

He continued past the fortress, keeping the hill of Amadán behind them, until they reached a smaller hillside. The earthen interior had been hollowed out with an iron gate.

But the moment Balor saw it, his hopes faded. 'There are no guards.' Fergus would never keep a high-ranking prisoner such as the *tánaiste* unguarded.

'We should look inside anyway,' Mairead said.

Her suggestion held merit, for it was still possible that

they might find evidence that her brother had been there at one time.

He obeyed her wish, and they dismounted and approached. Mairead walked downhill towards the entrance of the mound. Balor shadowed her, and as they drew close, his heart sank.

There was indeed a prisoner inside. And it was his mother.

Balor wrenched the iron gate open, and Mairead saw that the woman's hands and feet were tied together. Sympathy rose within her, and she reached for the blade at her waist, intending to cut the woman's bonds.

'Why did they do this to you?' Balor demanded.

The woman glanced up, her face paling at the sight of her son. 'You shouldn't be here. Fergus will kill you.'

'That's not what I asked.' His voice remained tight with fury. And when Mairead took a closer look, she noticed that the woman had Balor's same blue eyes. It had to be his mother. But for whatever reason, there was anger between them.

'Are you hurt?' she asked.

The woman's gaze turned tired. 'No. Only hungry and thirsty.'

Mairead used her blade to cut the woman's ropes while Balor pulled out food and drink to offer her. He gave her a flask of mead, which she accepted gratefully, along with the bread. Afterwards, Balor repeated his earlier question. 'What happened, Orla?'

She leaned back against the earthen wall. 'The Normans came to Dunmalus.'

Mairead's gut tightened, and she feared that they had taken her brother to England. It wouldn't be hard to sail away from these shores.

'Why? What did they want?' Balor asked.

Her face paled, and she drew her knees up. For a long moment, it appeared as if she was trying to gather courage. Mairead moved beside her and took her hand. 'Don't be afraid. No harm will come to you.'

'I've always been afraid,' Orla said quietly. 'And I despise myself for it. None of this would have happened if I hadn't been so afraid.' Her gaze passed over to Balor, and it held only regret.

Balor sheathed his knife and came to sit with her. 'Did Fergus pay the Normans to take Liam?'

She held her silence, as if trying to find the right words. Then she shook her head. 'These men weren't the same Normans who took Liam.' She swallowed hard. 'They… were sent by your real father, Balor. To find you.'

His posture went rigid, his jaw tightening. In the shadows of the mound of hostages, Mairead sensed his fury. 'I don't need to be found by the man who hurt you.'

Tears rolled down Orla's face. 'You don't understand. I—'

'I don't *want* to understand,' he shot back. 'I have no father. I never did.'

'You do,' she whispered. 'And your father didn't—he didn't violate me. I loved him.' Tears rolled down her face, and she admitted, 'Everything I did was to protect you.'

'You did nothing.' His words were cool, emotionless. 'Except look the other way when Fergus raised his fists to me.'

Orla flinched, as if the words sliced her to the bone. 'I was afraid Fergus would suspect the truth if I tried to defend you.'

An uneasiness crept within Mairead. 'Does he know about…your lover now? Is that why he imprisoned you?'

Orla bowed her head. 'When the Normans came, he… learned some of it. Not all.' She rubbed her raw wrists and then swiped at her tears. 'I am sorry for being a coward, Balor. You're right. I should have stood up to him sooner.'

His mother took a deep breath. 'I couldn't…let Fergus see what you meant to me. I had to keep you at a distance to protect you. But I have always loved you, Balor. I swear it.'

Balor stood and retreated to the entrance. It was clear to Mairead that he didn't believe her. His face might as well have been made of stone as the afternoon sunlight silhouetted him against the shadows. 'I don't care.'

Although his words were cold, Mairead could see the unrest beneath his eyes. Despite his callous words, she suspected they were far from the truth. These words held years of hurt, years of abandonment. And he had every reason to be angry with Orla.

He folded his arms across his chest. 'The only thing I care about is finding Liam MacEgan. Tell me where the Normans took him. The ones Fergus paid.'

Orla rested her head against her knees, as if she realized her son was lost to her. Words meant nothing and could not undo the years of neglect. An ache caught within Mairead's heart, and her own eyes burned with tears.

'At a ruined fortress near Banslieve,' Orla said at last. 'Fergus paid another group of Norman soldiers to take Liam there a few days ago.'

Mairead's heart pounded, for she had been to Banslieve before. It wasn't far from her uncle Connor's lands, but it was at least a full day's journey by sea.

'Fergus wants to claim my father's throne,' Mairead predicted. 'And if my brother is far away…' Her words drifted off.

'Then Liam can do nothing to stop Fergus,' Orla finished. She cast another look at Balor, but her son's gaze remained hardened.

Though she knew there was nothing that would console him, Mairead went to his side and took his hand in hers. She couldn't blame him for the tension in his body, the barely concealed fury.

But for the first time, she'd caught a glimpse of his ruthless nature. The sort of man who could cut an enemy down without remorse. And she didn't know how she felt about it.

'Thank you for telling us,' she told his mother.

But Orla didn't speak another word. Silent tears slid down her cheeks, and she clasped her hands together, not moving.

Then Balor turned his back on her and left.

They barely managed to get a boat into the sea before MacEgan soldiers emerged in the distance, approaching Dunmalus on horseback.

Balor kept the sail down, rowing out into the open water with Mairead, who crouched low in the boat. Better if they believed he was a fisherman out alone. They couldn't see who he was from this distance. As he cut through the waves, he emptied his mind of his mother's revelation. He didn't want to know about the Norman who had sired and abandoned him.

His muscles strained as he rowed, keeping his gaze fixed upon the shore. The MacEgans had surrounded Dunmalus. He wished Fergus had been there, but he was glad Kenneth was not.

'Are you all right, Balor?' Mairead asked. She was watching him from her hiding place, and the tone of her voice held wariness.

'I'm fine.'

He told himself it wasn't a lie. It didn't matter what words his mother had spun. Her actions mattered more. All his life, he had hungered for someone to care about him. But Orla had hardly ever looked at him. She certainly gave Kenneth the affection and love he'd craved.

How could she imagine that he could ever forget that? Or forgive her for the years of Fergus's abuse? The loneliness was the worst, even beyond the hunger or the thirst.

He rowed hard in the water, needing the physical exertion to calm his anger. Though he resented his mother for her cowardice, he couldn't allow himself to believe that she truly felt affection towards him. She had made her choice, years ago. And although he should pity her for facing the consequences of Fergus's wrath—or feel guilt for leaving her behind—he felt nothing, save resentment.

After an hour of rowing, he finally raised the sail. The wind immediately helped them gain speed, and he used an oar as a rudder, steering them west.

'You can sit up now,' he told Mairead. 'They can't see us.' The sun was rapidly descending, and soon it would be nightfall.

When she lowered the hood, her dark hair whipped around her face. He watched as Mairead braided it swiftly, tucking it back within her clothing. Then she rested her hands upon his, and he stopped rowing.

'Is something wrong?' He couldn't understand why she'd reached out to him.

To his shock, she moved in close and embraced him hard. Balor tucked her head beneath his chin, holding her close. The embrace reached beneath the shell of his anger, softening it. She didn't speak, didn't offer any explanation.

'You didn't deserve what your family did to you.' Mairead rested her cheek against his, and her actions were an unexpected comfort he'd never imagined. He held her in his arms, breathing in the scent of her hair. The quiet embrace slipped past his own defences, pressing against the heart he shielded from everyone else.

It only strengthened his resolve not to let her go.

Balor stroked her hair back and brushed his mouth across the top of her head, fighting back against the ache in his chest. 'It doesn't matter anymore.' The past couldn't be changed. 'But I won't allow Fergus to threaten your brother's throne.'

She pulled away, and in the fading sunlight, her face was bright and lovely. She glanced back at the mainland, her expression pensive and hopeful. And he was an utter bastard for taking her away from her family and home, even if she'd asked him to.

'I pray that we find Liam,' she murmured, keeping her eyes fixed on the horizon. 'Do you think he's alive?'

'I hope he is.' He didn't say that it was more likely her brother was hurt or even dead. Better if she didn't imagine the thousand things that could go wrong if they tried to rescue him.

But he didn't care.

Whenever Mairead looked upon him, she didn't seem to see what everyone else saw. She treated him as if she saw the man he wanted to be—instead of the man he was. With every moment he spent at her side, the more he wanted her to have faith in him. He wanted to give her the joy of seeing her brother alive again. And maybe it would close up the invisible wounds that his own family had sliced, leaving him with only pieces of himself.

This journey with her might be his only chance to spend time alone with Mairead. But the moment they reached

Banslieve, they would have to find allies. Possibly her uncle.

'Even if we find Liam, we can't save your brother alone,' he reminded her. 'We're outnumbered.'

She gave a nod. 'We are. But it couldn't have been a large force who took him—otherwise, my father's soldiers would have seen them.' She paused and added, 'We don't have to fight them—we would only need to help my brother escape. If we go together, I could be a distraction while you free him.'

Balor already knew there was little hope of a rescue—not with only two of them. They could track down her brother, but even if they found him, it was unlikely he could free Liam without being caught.

He didn't know if the MacEgans had seen their escape by water, but if they had, Balor was starting to wonder if he *should* give them a chance to catch up. If his mother was right about Liam's location, they would need those forces to free the *tánaiste.* By hunting Mairead, they could lead the king's men to save his son. It was worth considering.

'I'm not putting your life in danger,' he told Mairead. 'But we will try to find Liam.'

'How long will we sail?'

'It depends. If the wind holds, we should arrive within another day.' But it could take longer since they needed horses and more supplies to travel inland.

'Thank you,' she said, reaching out to touch his hand. He stopped rowing a moment and squeezed it in return. Her green eyes warmed. 'I owe you a debt for this.'

Balor gave a shrug, as if he didn't have every intention of keeping her. He wasn't helping her out of a selfless desire to help the *tánaiste.* It was purely for his own gain.

And from the way Mairead was looking at him now,

so full of hope and gratitude, he couldn't bring himself to say anything at all.

After Balor released her hand, Mairead leaned her face into the wind and smiled. 'Is this what it feels like to be free?'

No. It felt like wanting something he was never supposed to have. But instead, he gave another nod and focused on rowing.

For a time, she said nothing, simply staring at the horizon. A shadow seemed to cross her face when he kept them clear of Ennisleigh and continued rowing west. It hadn't escaped his notice that the last time they had been in a boat together, he'd intended to kidnap her then, too.

'Balor, could I ask you a question?' she asked softly. He turned to look at her, and sadness seemed to slide across her face. 'Why did your mother marry Fergus if she loved someone else?'

He hadn't wanted to think of it. For so long, he'd believed the story she'd told—that a soldier had attacked her. All her life, Orla had been withdrawn from everyone. He'd assumed it was because of the attack, not because she'd lost someone—his father.

He'd suspected that she hadn't loved Fergus, that she'd married him out of desperation instead of desire. 'I suppose she thought she didn't have a choice. Especially if she was pregnant with me.'

'Did Fergus know about her pregnancy when he married her?'

'Maybe. She didn't marry him right away, and she let him believe she'd been attacked.' He stared out at the sea, silencing the rise of his own questions. 'But he knew I wasn't his son.'

And Fergus had blamed him for Orla's anguish.

It didn't matter if Orla had loved a Norman, years ago. She'd made her choices and so had his real father. Balor didn't want anything to do with the man who had abandoned both of them.

'She should have left Fergus years ago,' he finished. Although part of him understood that she'd also been left behind, it angered him that Orla had never stood up to her husband. At least, not until the day when Fergus had lost his temper, blaming Balor for something he hadn't done.

His mistake had been trying to defend himself and fight back. Fergus had struck him, and without thinking, Balor had pushed the chieftain away. After that, he had little memory of what had happened, aside from the vicious beating and losing consciousness. His mother had somehow stopped Fergus—and after that, she'd sent Balor away to England.

Before that night, she'd always shied away from conflict, trying to talk Fergus out of it. But words had never been enough.

Mairead drew her knees up, studying him. 'I can understand why you wanted my father to depose him as chieftain and put your brother in his place.'

'Anyone is better than Fergus.'

She gavc a single nod. 'After we find my brother and bring him home, I will find a way to help you.' He gave no response, for he didn't know if that was even possible. But then she tilted her head and regarded him. 'Why don't you want to become the chieftain yourself?'

He hardly knew how to answer that. He'd never even considered it in all these years. After he'd left home, he'd never imagined wanting to come back to Dunmalus. It had never been a true home to him.

He'd grown up in the shadows, feeling like no one cared

about him. As a child among the Ó Phelans, he'd been told for years that he was unworthy because of his birthright. He couldn't simply ignore the years of believing he was less than the others and suddenly decide he wanted to be a leader. They would never accept him. And perhaps that was the easiest answer to give.

'Because the people would never want a man like me.'

Chapter Eight

Sometime during the night, Mairead became dimly aware that Balor had brought them closer inland. They had slept within the boat with his cloak covering them against the chill. The heat of his body had warmed hers as they remained anchored off the coast. The sea had been calm, lazily drifting against the vessel.

She'd slept hard, comforted by his presence beside her. Balor had slept just as deeply, his arms and legs tangled around her. And she'd found that she didn't mind it at all.

She didn't know what to think of this man. He was troubled, born into a family who didn't want him. And yet, he'd survived. He'd used their neglect to drive him towards becoming a different man, someone strong and confident.

Unlike her suitors, he had not been born into a life of wealth or status. He'd clawed his way from nothing into a man who had become a strong warrior. She couldn't help but admire that.

But even more, with every moment at his side, her attraction grew stronger. Being so close to Balor had only made it worse. Right now, Mairead was fully aware of his body and the position of his hand so close to her breast. Against her spine, she could feel the hard shaft that made her grow soft and weak with wanting him. Was it so wrong to desire a man's touch?

Mairead slowed her breathing, wondering if she dared confess her longing. She pushed her backside against him and didn't miss the tension in his body when she felt the rigid evidence of his need. He didn't speak a word, behaving as if he were still asleep. But his hand was perilously close to her breast. She shifted slightly until his fingers were upon the curve.

'Are you wanting something, *a mhuirnín*?' he whispered against her ear.

Yes. But she was afraid of what he might think of her if she was honest. He was so wrong for her…and yet, her body wasn't listening to her mind. She craved a moment for herself, despite all the reasons it was wrong.

Silently, she took Balor's hand and brought it beneath her tunic, loosening it until his hand cupped her bare breast. His thumb brushed against the erect nipple, and she bit her lip, the sensations of desire aching with every stroke.

'Is this what you want?' He rolled the nipple between his fingers, gripping her waist so she could feel every last inch of him against her backside.

It was, but she didn't dare say it. There was a part of her that yearned to be touched, to feel like a woman instead of a king's daughter. She knew this wasn't fair to use him. But he also didn't seem to mind.

She rolled over to face him, though she couldn't see his face in the darkness. He continued exploring her breast, and the echoing ache between her legs made her skin grow hotter.

'What do *you* want, Balor?' she whispered, resting her hands upon his thundering heartbeat.

'More than you can give,' was his answer.

She didn't know what to say to him. Her future felt as if it was out of her hands, no matter that she was trying to grasp control of her own life. But she had this stolen moment with him. His hand stilled upon her breast, though he didn't move it away. 'I know that I don't deserve anything.' He cupped her face with his other hand. 'I'm the villain, remember? I haven't earned the right to be with someone like you.'

The darkness in his tone was a warning. But she didn't care. Sometimes darkness was soothing, a quiet night that haunted her dreams with yearning.

'We have time right now,' she whispered. 'Let it be enough.'

Balor's mouth claimed hers, even as he tempted her with his teasing fingers, her nipple rising against him. When his tongue slid against her own, she opened to him, no longer caring that she was giving in to temptation.

'But you came with me when I asked you to,' she murmured against his mouth. 'You've fought for me these past few weeks. And I've never really known why.'

He rested his forehead against hers. 'Maybe because you seem to think there's a part of me worth saving.'

A piece of her heart broke off at his words, and she kissed him this time, moving her hands over his face and down to his shoulders.

'You *are* a man of honour,' she said, her hands moving against his skin. 'No matter what they say.'

'I don't feel honourable at all right now.' The edge of his voice held a hint of frustration as his palm slid against her spine.

'I don't want you to be.'

At her words, his mouth claimed hers again with a fierce need, heating her skin until she was wet and aching.

'I want to touch you,' he murmured against her mouth. 'Everywhere.'

She loosened the ties of the trews she wore and reached for his. Her hands were shaking, but she forced herself to admit the truth. 'So do I.'

'Your family would slit my throat if they knew what I was thinking right now,' he said roughly. He reached back for the anchor and pulled it up, letting the tide pull them back out to sea.

The sky was still dark and clouded, but the faint crease of dawn had begun illuminating the edges of the horizon. Their time together was slipping away, and she drew him back down to her. 'I think you are the only man who has ever treated me like a woman instead of a pawn. You've kept me safe, even when it brought you into danger.'

He pressed her back against the boat, his hard body poised over hers. 'You are no man's pawn. Not even mine.'

'It's hard to breathe when you touch me,' she whispered. 'And yet, I can't catch my breath with the fear that you won't.'

A hint of a smile caught his mouth. 'Then let me discover exactly how to make you forget how to breathe, *a mhuirnín.*'

Balor had never imagined that this woman would desire someone like him. And her soft acquiescence was an offering that humbled him.

He would never dream of claiming her virginity—that was a husband's right. But he fully intended to claim the right of a lover, tasting her skin and giving her pleasure.

She'd mistakenly believed he was an honourable man. Right now, honour was the furthest thing from his mind.

He helped her loosen the tunic, sliding it over her head until she was naked from the waist up. Gods above, but she was exquisite. In the faint dawn, shadows guarded the soft pink of her nipples. The generous curve of her breasts made his shaft rigid at the thought of touching her.

He kissed Mairead again, palming her breast and using his thumb to arouse her nipples. She was breathing heavier, arching against his touch.

And it was only natural when he trailed a path from her throat to one breast, covering the erect nipple with his tongue and mouth. She gasped, her fingers digging into his hair while he explored her. Oh, she most definitely liked that. He could feel her body trembling, and he drifted his mouth to the other breast, continuing to stroke the sweetness of the first.

He was so focused upon her, on tasting that soft skin and watching her unravel, that he didn't notice until her bare palm closed around his erection.

He nearly shouted at the pleasure, and she squeezed him gently. 'Does that…hurt you?'

'No. But I'm not finished with you yet.' He moved her hand away and slid her trews away, baring her womanhood. He caressed her stomach, inching a path lower, until she guided his hand between her legs.

She was slick and ready for him, something he hadn't expected so soon. The moment he touched the hooded flesh above her entrance, she moaned.

She was so unbelievably sensitive. As he circled her, using her own wetness to smooth the touch, she grew more agitated. He paused, wondering if he should stop.

'Balor,' she pleaded. Her fingers were digging into his shoulder, but when he pressed a little too hard, she winced.

'Show me,' he demanded. He idly wondered if she had ever touched herself before.

But she brought his head back to her breast and demanded, 'Kiss me here.' Then she guided his finger inside her while she circled the flesh with his thumb.

He obeyed, and the change upon her was instantaneous. She shuddered as he moved his finger in and out, and he added a second finger, stroking her from within.

'Gods above,' she breathed. But she was moving against his rhythm, moaning as he suckled her nipple.

Mairead reached for him again, and this time, his trews loosened until his erection rested against her hip. 'Don't stop,' she pleaded.

But he still wouldn't dare take her offering. Instead, he continued his siege upon her womanhood, watching as she raised her knees, her body straining.

If he didn't gather the threads of his self-control, he wouldn't be able to stop. And so he withdrew his hand. His own breathing was unsteady, but he had an instinct of his own.

Without asking permission, he lifted her hips and tasted her intimately.

Mairead shattered at the first brush of his tongue upon her swollen flesh. She arched deeply, crying out as he licked and suckled her. 'Balor, you— Oh, gods.'

This was heaven, he decided. She was utterly at his mercy, and he held the power to drive her over the edge until she found her fulfilment. Her hands dug into his hair, and he tasted her again as she came apart, her body trembling.

She was so responsive, he gloried in the way she gave herself to him. And although his own body was raging for more, he held himself back. This moment was for her.

Even if it was all they'd ever have.

Whatever Mairead had thought of Balor before, she'd been wrong. This man was nothing at all like she'd expected. He had no reason to travel with her across Éireann to find her brother. It wasn't his responsibility. But he'd somehow become her protector, and it warmed her.

Balor had hidden the boat amid the rocks past the shoreline before they began travelling on foot.

Although she knew her father would never allow her to wed someone like Balor, she was starting to question everything about her own future. Her heart flinched at the thought of being with anyone else. Especially now.

The memory of his hands on her body, his mouth on her skin, made her flush. But she refused to feel embarrassed or guilty over what they had done. She had wanted him to touch her, and it had been as wonderful as she'd imagined it would be.

She was distracting herself with finding her brother, but the true dilemma was Balor. He'd said nothing about this morn or the way he had pleasured her. She couldn't discern his emotions, and he seemed almost like a stone wall, utterly unreadable.

Dozens of questions roiled in her mind about what to do now. Should she tell him that her feelings had shifted beyond attraction and desire? Would he ever consider staying with her? Or would he refuse, claiming that she had to marry a nobleman?

As they walked inland, he barely spoke to her. His silence bothered her even more. Did he feel anything for her in return, or had it only been a stolen moment of pleasure? What if he wanted her body but nothing else? It frightened her to wonder whether it had been a terrible mistake to lower her defences.

But she wasn't brave enough to ask. Better to keep the vulnerable thoughts to herself than face the risk of rejection.

She gripped her arms, trudging doggedly across the

fields while he never stopped searching for enemies. His hand rested upon his sword, and she grew aware that he was always alert. He truly was one of the strongest fighters she'd ever met.

She needed to know if her feelings were one-sided. But the thought of baring her emotions was too much.

Instead, she matched her pace with his, letting her fingers brush against his left hand. Without hesitation, he took her hand in his. She silently exhaled with relief.

And when he lifted her palm to kiss it, his gaze still fixed on the horizon, she had her answer. A smile slid over her face, a smile of relief that she wasn't so alone. His blue eyes turned to glance at her, and though he didn't smile, she saw the answering hunger in them.

It was enough.

They walked for hours, stopping only for a short midday meal, before they continued inland. Her feet were aching, but Mairead made no complaint.

In the distance, she could see the ruined fortress as the sun descended lower in the sky. Was it possible that her brother could still be there? She hoped he was still alive and unhurt. But her greatest fear, one that turned her heart into ice, was the fear that Liam was already dead. It had been days with no sign of him.

She kept her hood up to hide her face as they walked closer. She'd braided her hair back, and at her side, she wore a blade. Nerves rippled within her, but Balor pressed his hand to the small of her back, and she relaxed slightly. He wasn't going to allow anyone to harm her. They would find out what they could and make a decision afterwards.

'Do you want to get horses from the village?' she asked him, nodding at the roundhouses in the distance.

'We haven't the silver for that. And besides, it would draw too much attention to us.' He nodded towards a small village nearby. 'We'll ask them questions about whether they have seen any Normans in the area.'

'And what will we tell them?' she asked.

'That you are my wife, and we are travelling to meet your kinsmen at Banslieve. We'll ask for a place to stay while I go and scout out the fortress.'

'Don't ask me to stay behind in the village,' she insisted. 'Let me come with you to find Liam.'

But he shook his head. 'One of us should stay behind in case the other is captured. If I don't return, go north for another half day and you'll reach Connor MacEgan's ringfort.'

It sounded as if he believed she would have to go to her uncle for help. 'Do you think the Normans are still a threat? Or possibly the king's men?'

Balor gave a nod. 'I don't want to risk both of us being captured.' Then he lowered his voice and added, 'And we were followed by your father's men. Be assured of it.'

Mairead took his hand in hers, feeling as if their time together was slipping away. But worse was the thought of losing him. Past and present seemed to merge together, and she prayed that Balor would be safe from fighting. 'Promise me you'll be careful.'

Balor stopped walking briefly and stroked the side of her face without saying anything. His eyes burned into hers before he led her towards the village.

They were greeted by two boys who eyed them and then ran off, calling out to their parents. Mairead lowered her hood, feeling self-conscious for wearing trews and a tunic.

An older man came forward from one of the roundhouses. He was broad-chested, and his brown hair held streaks of grey. Possibly the chieftain, she guessed.

Balor looked uncomfortable, but before he could speak, Mairead greeted them. 'Good eventide to you. My husband and I are travelling north and wondered if we could share your fire and take shelter for the night?'

The man glanced at each of them, and Mairead added, 'We won't stay longer than that. We are travelling north to my family with the Ó Duinne tribe.'

Before the man could refuse, a plump woman pushed her way forward, a broad smile on her face. 'Of course. You're both very welcome.' She patted the man on his shoulder and said, 'My husband, Seamus, isn't so very friendly to strangers. But we have a place where you can stay. Our son is away, and you can sleep in his home tonight.'

'But—' the man started to protest.

The woman sent him a pointed look and, without waiting for an answer, she led Mairead and Balor towards the roundhouse on the far end of the ringfort. The dwelling was made of stone with a thatched roof and a low door. She opened it, and despite the darkness, it was warm and dry.

'Here, now. Will this suit you?' The woman stepped back and gestured for them to go inside.

'It's perfect. And it's very kind of you to let us stay,' Mairead said. She kept her words polite, though she wondered why they had offered such a place to strangers.

The woman smiled broadly. 'Will you be needing any food or drink?'

'We have our own,' Balor answered. Then he added, 'But you have our thanks.'

'Of course, of course,' the plump woman said, as they followed her back outside. 'My name is Edena, and my husband, Seamus, is chieftain of our small clan. We're cousins to the Ó Duinne family, so you're like kin to us.'

Seamus didn't look as if he agreed with his wife, but he didn't argue.

'The stream is just past those woods if you need water. And we've hot stones in the fire over there.' Edena pointed towards one of the hearths. 'You may want to bring some inside. It can get cold at night.'

Mairead repeated her thanks, and then they went back into the roundhouse. After she'd gone, she said, 'I feel rather like I've been tossed around like a storm cloud. But she was friendly, I suppose.'

'She recognized you,' Balor said. 'She knows your father is the king, and she will send word to Patrick.'

Of course. Her heart sank at the thought. 'How long do you think we have until they arrive?'

'A day. Possibly less.'

He rested his hand against one of the wooden beams and regarded her. His gaze was intense, flooding her with memories of his touch. She was suddenly aware that their time together would draw to a close. More than anything, she wanted it to last as long as possible.

'I don't want this time with you to end,' she said. 'Even if it's wrong for me to feel that way.'

He palmed her spine, and she closed her eyes. His touch was searing, making her resolve crumble. She knew it was such a terrible idea, but she couldn't stop herself from resting her hands on his chest.

'Is that what you think?' He took a step closer, and the heat of his body seemed to warm her. 'That what we have together is wrong?'

She didn't. Not at all. But she also knew that she was putting him in an impossible situation, the same as Diarmud. And selfishly, she wanted him anyway.

'I don't want you to face any consequences for my decision,' Mairead answered softly. 'Especially punishment because I forced you to come with me.'

'You didn't force me to do anything, *a mhuirnín.*'

Balor moved his hand to her face, caressing the line of her jaw. Then he reached back to unbind her braid. Gently, he loosened the strands until waves of dark silk surrounded her shoulders, falling down her back. He sank his fingers into her hair, savouring this moment with gratitude that she was here with him this night.

He traced her hair and the outline of her face with his hands before he rested them on her shoulders. Mairead kindled a hunger in him that he could never satiate. She was the feast he wanted to devour...but he was willing to take any crumbs she would offer.

'No matter what happens in the next few days, I need you to stay alive,' Mairead whispered. 'I couldn't bear it if anything happened to you.'

In the faint light, she began unfastening her garments until she wore only a shift. 'And I want to share this night with you. No matter what lies ahead.'

He was well aware that it could be their last night together. And although he had already trespassed beyond the boundaries that belonged to a husband, he no longer cared. He craved Mairead MacEgan more than life itself.

He kissed her roughly, pressing her back against the wattle and daub wall. 'And what is it you're wanting from me, *a mhuirnín*?'

She answered his kiss, threading her tongue with his. Then she took his hands and guided them to her breasts. 'I want everything I'm not supposed to have. And more.'

He cupped her generous curves, brushing his thumbs over the erect nipples as his mouth devoured her. Instinct claimed him, and he lowered her shift to her waist, baring her skin. His body was rigid with need, but he was determined not to waste this gift of her innocence. And that meant exploring her, learning more about what she liked or didn't like.

Balor traced her bare skin, noting the way it pebbled with the chilly night air. Her breathing grew unsteady, and he found himself wanting to explore that silken skin with his mouth once again.

And he told her so.

'I want to kiss you everywhere.' He bent to slide his mouth over the column of her throat, noting the way her hands gripped his nape. He inhaled sharply when she pressed too close to him. His body responded with a ferocity that was nearly visceral.

'Are you all right?' she asked.

He gripped her waist and nodded. 'Just on edge.'

She rested her forehead against his. 'You were the man I wanted to choose for my betrothal. Not Lord Lowell. Not anyone else. Only you.'

The words washed over him like a benediction. 'And I would have fought to claim you as my bride.' He lifted her up and brought her down to the pallet of furs, gently laying her beneath him. The fallen *léine* hung at her waist, exposing her breasts and the swell of her hips.

She reached out to stroke his bristled face. 'If we cannot stay together, then will you give me a memory to keep for the rest of my life?'

His heartbeat thundered even more. And when she lifted her *léine* away, the sight of her naked body silenced every word he wanted to speak.

* * *

It was everything she could do not to tremble. This was the greatest risk Mairead had ever taken, for she was so afraid that Balor would turn her away, despite how badly she wanted him. His gaze was piercing as he studied her. Her heart was pounding so hard, she wondered if she dared reach for the man she craved so desperately.

She wanted him to know how much she cared, how much she needed him.

And so she was reaching for the last weapon she had. The only question was whether he would fight for a life together.

Slowly, he sat up and rested his hands on her bare hips. 'I know I should tell you to cover yourself. Your body belongs to your future husband, not me.'

A flush came over her, and she wondered if he was truly going to turn her away.

'But right now, *a mhuirnín*, the sight of you destroys my honour.' He cupped her breasts, gently caressing her until warmth bloomed between her legs. 'I haven't forgotten what it was to watch you come apart. And now I want to be inside you when that happens again.'

The wetness between her legs surged at his words, for she hadn't forgotten, either. His talented tongue had stroked her over the edge when they were on the boat. She bit her lip, trying to calm her racing heart at the memory.

Mairead began to pull at the laces of his tunic, lifting it away until she revealed the hardened muscles beneath. She touched his warm skin, sliding her hands over his shoulders. His strength fascinated her, and she lowered her mouth to his shoulder before her hands drifted over the scar on his chest, down to the ridges of his stomach.

She was about to explore his body with her own mouth,

but then he kissed her throat, his warm breath causing gooseflesh to rise over her skin.

'I've never taken a woman before,' Balor murmured. 'But I swear I'm going to spend every moment of this night learning what pleases you.'

His words only deepened her blush, and Mairead drew her arms around his neck.

It startled her to learn that he was a virgin, especially after the way he'd touched her before. If she were still innocent, she would be terrified of these feelings coursing within her. She would be so afraid of what was to come—when instead, she was eager.

A flush of guilt passed over her, for Balor didn't know she wasn't a virgin. He was afraid of ruining her—but that wasn't possible, for she was already ruined.

She had given herself to Diarmud, only a year ago. They had fumbled in the darkness, and she hadn't minded the awkwardness of their lovemaking, fully believing that they would be married after he proved himself to her father. Diarmud had promised to love her forever and make her his bride.

The loss of him had been more than the loss of her innocence. It was the loss of the man she'd loved and the future she'd dreamed of. Maybe it had been her fault for daring to seize what she wanted instead of remaining obedient.

Now, in Balor's arms, she wanted to reclaim that missing part of herself. She wanted to experience hope and dreams of a different kind of future. It was a risk, yes.

But she believed it was worth it. *He* was worth it.

Balor seemed to know exactly what she craved, and the thought of joining with him sent a rush of desire racing through her veins.

She didn't care if it was wrong. She was tired of obeying the rules, tired of being the woman everyone else told her to be. For one night, she wanted to be disobedient and reach for what *she* wanted.

And what she wanted was Balor.

'Lie down,' he ordered.

She knew he wanted to be in command while he touched her. But she intended to be his equal in every way—and that meant pleasuring him as well.

'Not until you've removed your clothes,' she countered.

Balor moved his hands to the ties of his trews and swiftly removed them. The sight of his body and hardened muscles made her breathless at the thought of what would happen between them. Between her legs, she grew wet with anticipation, her body trembling with need.

Mairead lay down, and Balor stretched out to face her. For a moment, she traced her hand along the edge of his cheek.

He closed his eyes, as if drinking in her touch. Then he pulled her body against his, the heat of his skin warming her. He kissed her, and the hard length of him pressed against her stomach. She reached down between them, feeling the smooth tip of his erection. When his tongue slid into her mouth, she moved her thumb over the ridge.

He caught her hand and raised it, along with the other one, pinning them above her head. 'Not yet.' He bent down to take her nipple in his mouth. 'I could taste you all day, Mairead. The sweetness of you.'

She couldn't move, but she opened her legs slightly, letting him rest against her intimately. The hunger and need rose up within her, and she tried to hold herself back as he suckled her, teasing her breasts with his fingers and mouth.

She savoured his touch, moving her legs until her knees were bent, and it would take nothing at all for him to be inside her. He was being so careful with her, exploring her body with his mouth when she wanted so much more.

'Balor, please,' she begged.

But he only slowed his pace, releasing one of her hands while he brought his fingers to her aching womanhood.

'Softly,' she urged. She showed him how she wanted to be touched, and he was quick to explore.

When he dipped his finger into her wetness, he cursed softly. 'I don't want to hurt you.'

You won't, she thought, but didn't say it. Instead, she said, 'Touch me the way you did before.'

But instead, he moved lower, kissing her navel. She began to tremble when his mouth drifted between her legs.

'I've been wanting to do this again,' he murmured, lifting her to his mouth.

A sudden surge of raw pleasure erupted within her as he explored her with his tongue. He kissed her intimately, and she arched against him, suddenly realizing that everything was different with this man. He treated her as if she meant everything to him. His mouth drove her higher, the rising storm pulling her under until she was drowning in him.

She had never felt like this in all her life, and Mairead gave herself up, surrendering as he pushed her over the edge again. Her hands dug into his hair, and she guided him up, reaching down to caress his hard length. More than anything, she wanted his body inside her.

He groaned as she explored him in the same way, stroking every part of him with her palm. Then he guided himself to her entrance and slid inside, joining them together. He hesitated a moment, but she kissed him, welcoming his thrust and squeezing him within her depths.

He shuddered, his own breath mirroring her own with

heavy panting. She took him in deep, lifting her knees and then wrapping her legs around his waist.

He was slow and careful at first, and though it frustrated her, slowly the penetrations began to reawaken her. She was dying a slow death, and just when she trembled, he sheathed himself fully, and she cried out as the ecstasy washed over her. She was shaking as he quickened his thrusts, covering her body with his own as he invaded again and again.

I want a life with him.

Tears spilled from her eyes at the fear of losing this man. Balor had fought alongside her, protecting her own life with his. She couldn't live with herself if anything happened to him.

His thrusting continued, and when his mouth covered her nipple again, she took his hips and ground herself against him. He lost control then and continued driving himself in hard until he gave a sharp exhale and pulled out as he released himself against her hip.

It startled her, though she realized the risk of pregnancy. Balor collapsed on top of her, and she caressed his back, pressing a kiss against his shoulder.

But a part of her was terrified that this night would be their last.

Chapter Nine

Balor barely slept that night. Not only because of their lovemaking, but also with a realization he didn't want to face. He had been truthful with Mairead, that he had never been intimate with a woman—he'd only learned how to give pleasure.

But he knew enough, from the stories of other soldiers, that there was usually blood and pain the first time. Yet for her, there had seemed to be no pain, no blood.

And he didn't know how to feel about it. Was he wrong? Was it simply his own ignorance causing suspicions? Or was there another reason, one he didn't want to admit?

She nestled against him in sleep, her body warm and soft. The urge came over him, to take her again and lose himself in her arms. But it felt as if an unspoken secret hung between them.

Did it matter if she'd been with another man first? The thought filled him with raw jealousy, and he tensed. Had it been her choice? Or had someone hurt her against her will? The thoughts swarmed over him, darkening his mood.

But then she turned to face him, resting her cheek against his heart. 'Are you awake?'

'I am.' His voice came out cooler than he'd intended, and he leaned in to kiss her softly. She kissed him back, winding her arms around his neck and pulling him down on top of her. His body instantly responded to the touch, and she opened to him.

A fierce jealousy made him want to drive every memory of any other man from her past and replace the man with himself. He wanted her to remember no one but him.

Balor took his rigid erection and slid it against the seam of her, tempting Mairead, just as he aroused himself. Then he bent to take her nipple in his mouth again, trying to pleasure her.

He wanted to be the one who could meet her needs, the one who consumed her thoughts. The edge of his jealousy was a shard that slashed through his control and left him hanging by a thread. She gasped as his tongue slid over her, tasting the sweetness of her nipple.

But then she guided him inside her, and he slid within her wetness. He pinned her wrists to the soft fur beneath her, thrusting slowly. He continued to tease one erect nipple, then the other, noticing how she moaned and tried to move her hips to take him.

'What is it, Balor?' she asked quietly. 'Something's wrong.'

She'd read him so easily, sensing his change in mood. But he forced his anger back and lied, 'It's nothing.' He gentled his pace, watching her expression as he took her slowly. He remembered how much she had liked it when he'd teased the hooded flesh above her entrance, so he brought his thumb there and circled slowly.

'Balor,' she whispered, closing her eyes. 'Gods above, don't stop.'

He obeyed, but when she met his thrusts with her own hips, welcoming him home, the insidious voice inside him whispered words he didn't want to hear.

You're not good enough for a king's daughter. You'll never be the man she needs you to be.

She opened her eyes again, shuddering as he kept pressing her closer and closer to fulfilment. Her gaze was filled with tenderness as he made love to her.

And then she pushed against him, rolling him to his back. She gave herself over, riding him and increasing the pace. He sat up, and the motion brought them even closer, her body moving atop his. She was squeezing him inside, and he couldn't stop himself from seizing her waist and quickening the penetrations until he was lost in her again.

'I love you,' she cried out.

The words washed over him, filling him with both joy and fear. He couldn't stop himself from claiming her body in the same way he wanted her heart.

He couldn't answer her, for words weren't enough. He knew he was a bastard for sharing this night with her, especially when she would likely marry someone else.

But those words completely broke him apart. With a few more strokes, she finished him off, and he didn't have time to pull out before he erupted inside her body, shuddering as the fast release barreled through him. Too fast, he realized. And as he rolled over, still inside her, he used his thumb to continue stroking her, feeling the way she arched to meet him, until a few moments later, she gave a cry and shuddered at her own completion.

There could be a child, he realized.

For so long, he'd avoided the risk. He'd not wanted to sire a bastard. And yet, she'd said she loved him.

If she did grow round from his baby, Mairead would never treat a child in the way he'd been treated. He could easily imagine her cradling an infant, kissing their child with love.

It shook him to the core.

But she was crying now, and he gathered her in his arms. 'What is it, *a mhurnín*? Did I hurt you?'

'No. But I knew I shouldn't have done this,' she wept. 'I don't want to let you go. Not anymore.'

Balor wiped at her tears and cradled her against his chest. He caressed her back, down her spine, soothing her without words until she calmed.

She stared at him with raw emotion. 'I'm so afraid of what will happen next.'

She was right. If her father learned that he'd taken her, Balor wouldn't face imprisonment—he'd be killed for daring to touch the king's daughter. But he didn't want those thoughts to torment her during their last moments together. Instead, he kissed the top of her head and held her in his embrace.

'Am I wrong to love you?' she whispered.

'Aye,' he answered. 'I was never the man you deserved. But for this night, at least, you're mine.' He continued touching her, moving his hands down to her bottom, cupping her even while he was still buried inside her body.

'You are the man I want.' She clung to him, pressing another kiss to his chest. 'I promise you that.'

He held her, breathing in the scent of her hair. The jealousy returned, despite his attempts to hold it back. He wanted to believe her, but the same suspicions kept rising.

'I'm not the only man you ever loved, am I?'

Her posture grew motionless. 'What do you mean?'

He stroked her spine and dared to ask, 'Who was he? The first man you loved.'

She pulled back to look at him, and the stricken expression on her face confirmed his fears. 'Why are you asking me this?'

Because he couldn't stop the dark jealousy gathering inside. He withdrew from her body and sat beside her.

'There was no blood or pain,' he said quietly. 'You were hoping I wouldn't notice, weren't you?' Balor locked his gaze with her, wondering if she would give him the truth.

Mairead reached for her *léine* and pulled it over her head, keeping her knees up. For a long moment, her face turned crimson before she turned away from him. The silence was enough to rekindle his jealousy. He'd wanted to be wrong.

But then she answered, 'H-his name was Diarmud.' Her emotions rose higher the moment she spoke the name.

He struggled to keep his voice even. 'Did your father know him?'

Her face paled, and she closed her eyes, releasing a shaky breath. 'He was one of my father's soldiers,' she answered at last. 'I had planned to marry him in secret.'

The heartbreak in her voice made him aware that she'd said *was*, not *is*.

'What happened?'

'My father forbade me to be with him.' She lowered her head. 'Diarmud was killed in a raid, trying to prove himself worthy of marrying me.' The grief and raw emotions on her face were real, revealing the feelings she still held within her.

He didn't know what to say now. He understood her fear that the same thing would happen again. Her father would never approve of a bastard like him. Balor sat up, wondering where he fit in. Did Mairead truly love him, as she'd said? He wanted to believe that her feelings were real. And yet, the thought seemed impossible.

The greater problem was that, even if he did keep her with him, he had no means of supporting her. Aye, she might find it romantic at first—until they lived in poverty.

The only way he could provide for her was to hire out his sword. And he simply couldn't imagine becoming a mercenary and forcing her into a life of hardship. Though she might claim it didn't matter, one day she would resent him for it. Hunger wasn't at all romantic—but it was a reality he'd endured.

He didn't know what to do. His brain warned that it was better to give her up to another nobleman than see her suffer. Wasn't that was love was? Doing what was right, even if the thought tore him apart inside?

But his heart wanted him to find another way of being with her.

Mairead's expression was somber as she faced him. 'I cannot change the past,' she said softly. 'But will you let it take away our future?'

Mairead could see the turmoil of emotions over his face. She'd bared her soul to him, hoping he could understand the reasons why she'd given herself to Diarmud. She had truly believed the man had been her first love.

But now she understood that those feelings were nothing compared to the way she felt about Balor. And fear roiled within her that he didn't feel the same way. From the way he was looking at her now, it seemed as if he wanted to end things between them.

'What do you want from me, Mairead?' he asked. 'Do you want to leave Éireann with me and go to England? Even if it means never seeing your family again?'

Her breath came out in a slow release, and she wasn't entirely sure what to say. But despite her feelings for him, the thought of leaving her homeland and all her family was unbearable.

'I don't know,' she whispered. But the more she thought

of it, the more she realized that it was no different from her other suitors. Lord Lowell wanted her to leave Éireann and live with him in England. The only difference was that her family approved of the earl.

And she didn't love him.

Balor had always listened to her opinions, treating her as an equal. Would Lord Lowell do the same? Somehow, she didn't think so.

Her emotions balled into an ache of misery inside. Balor's words weren't meant to fill her with hope—only to leave her heart bruised. He wasn't truly asking her to stay with him. He was showing her the hopelessness of their situation.

He was giving up on them before anything could start.

With her heart in her throat, she forced herself to answer. 'I would…hope that we could find a way to be together so I wouldn't have to choose between you and my family.'

His expression grew shuttered. 'I think we both know you were never meant to choose someone like me, *a mhuirnín*.'

Was he turning his back on her because she hadn't been innocent when she had given herself to him? Raw pain welled up in her eyes when Balor reached for his clothing and dressed in the darkness, giving her a glimpse of strong thighs and a ridged stomach.

But when she looked at him in the dim firelight—and caught a glimpse of regret on his face, she saw something else entirely.

Despite all Balor's efforts to cast himself as a villain, she saw the man he was. The broken boy whose father had beaten him. The strong warrior who had fought to survive. And the man who had utterly stolen her heart.

'I disagree.' She stood and went to his side. 'I think you are a man worth fighting for.'

'You're wrong, Mairead.' He handed her the fallen overdress in a silent command to dress herself. 'I know you've heard what they call me.'

She hesitated but nodded. 'The Demon of Éireann.'

He gave a nod. 'And do you know why I deserve that name?' There was a slight threat within his words, and she recognized that he was trying to frighten her and push her away.

She only met his gaze openly. 'Others don't know who you really are. You've never let them see.'

'Oh, I deserve to be called a demon, *a mhuirnín.* It's who I am. Who I've always been.'

She finished dressing, but even the extra layer of wool did nothing to allay the coldness threatening to cloak her.

'Then tell me. Why do they call you that? What did you do?' She turned back to face him, prepared for the worst.

He crossed his arms, still not facing her. 'I'm not a man of honour, Mairead. I know how to kill. I've killed many men—both Normans and Irishmen. And I'm very, very good at it.'

'When?' she dared to ask.

He remained quiet for a time. The silence between them was as heavy as an accusation, and it left her confused, almost as if her heart were being pulled apart in different directions.

'I was returning from my fostering, about a year ago,' he said. 'There was a raid, north of Dunmalus.'

Her heart faltered before she realized it wasn't the same raid that had claimed Diarmud's life. But he could read the fear in her eyes.

'I killed seven men that day,' he said softly. 'And I have no regrets.'

The words were meant to make her think less of him.

But she'd come to know him better than that. Balor would never stand aside and watch an innocent bystander be cut down, no matter the reason.

Mairead narrowed her gaze upon him and faced him down. 'Who were you protecting?'

The look of surprise on his face only confirmed her guess. His lips tightened as he stared back at her.

'Was it a woman?' she ventured.

His fists tightened at his sides, but he gave a nod. 'And her son.'

'You fought to defend them.' It wasn't a question.

Balor glanced away, and she dared to ask, 'Did you save them?'

He shook his head. 'Only the boy. I was too late to save her.' His voice was low and resonant, but the story came spilling out. 'She was caught in a fight between two clans, trying to escape after they killed her husband.'

His expression turned distant. 'They had already won the battle, but it wasn't enough for them.' He flexed his fingers and said, 'They wanted to kill his wife and child as well.'

With a dark expression, he added, 'I killed every man who dared to raise a weapon against them. One survived and ran away while I took the boy back to his clan.' His mouth twisted. 'They blamed me for the deaths and gave me that name.'

'The bards said you killed twenty men.'

He let out an exasperated sigh. 'They wanted a good story.' His gaze fixed upon her, his blue eyes heated. 'But the truth is, I *am* guilty of those deaths. And I would do it again.'

Before she could say a word, he added, 'There's a reason why your family wants me to stay away from you.'

She lowered her head, the numbness creeping over her.

This had nothing to do with his violent past and everything to do with his unwillingness to fight for her. Her words held heaviness as she answered, 'Why are you telling me this, Balor?'

'Because you need to know that you can't love someone like me. You love the idea of me, but not who I really am.' His voice held frustration and a hint of anger. 'My own family loathes the sight of me, Mairead. My mother sent me away to England for seven years, and they didn't want me to return. I know the sort of man I am. The sort of man I'll always be.'

Her heart bled as she struggled to reconcile the broken pieces of this man. He was telling her this to justify reasons why they shouldn't stay together. And she didn't like it—not at all.

'Enough,' she commanded. 'I don't want to hear any more.' She moved to face him and rested her hands on his heart. 'If you don't want to be with me, then just say it. If you don't love me in return, if you're giving up on us, then—'

He dragged her into his arms and kissed her hard, his mouth claiming hers to stop the words. She kissed him back in a silent challenge, daring him to voice how he truly felt.

'I've always wanted the things I can't have,' he said against her mouth. Then he slid his tongue inside, reminding her of the intimacy they'd shared.

Balor Ó Phelan was a man of action, not words. She'd witnessed that for herself, time and again. And as he continued to kiss her, pulling her body against his, she understood that he hadn't voiced his feelings to her because they made him vulnerable. For someone who believed no one had ever loved him, he seemed starved for it.

'Are you angry with me?' she demanded.

'No.' He drew his hands through her hair, cupping her face. 'I'm angry with myself because I can't give you the life you need. Not even a home.' He brushed her lips with his thumb. 'And I'm jealous of the man you once loved. I wanted to be your first,' he murmured. 'And maybe your last.'

The admission softened her own frustration, and she touched Balor's cheek. There weren't any answers for how to resolve this.

'I can't go back and change the past,' she said softly. Then she regarded him with her own silent anger. 'Neither can you.' Her own tears broke free, sliding down her cheeks. 'We've both made mistakes that we can't undo.'

He gently wiped her tears away, and the expression in his gaze was both fierce and tender.

'Did you mean what you said?' she murmured. 'About wanting me to leave with you? Or was that nothing at all?'

He rested his head against her forehead. 'Were it possible, I would take you away from here, Mairead. But I have no right to take you away from the life you deserve.'

'If I weren't the daughter of a king, would it be different?' she asked. 'Would you want to take me with you?'

He covered her hand with his and squeezed it. 'King's daughter or not, I would steal you away.' He lifted her palm to his mouth and kissed it.

She loved Balor and wished there was a way they could stay together. And perhaps that was the reason why she pulled him down for a kiss, pressing his body close to hers. She needed to savour whatever moments they had left.

He kissed her hard, cradling her face as he drew her to lie upon him. His hands moved down her spine, holding her body close to his. 'Before I go, remember the way it is between us, with my hands on your skin. The way I make you feel.'

He kissed her again, his tongue sliding against hers, and she answered with her own. He broke free and murmured, 'I'm going to find your brother and bring him back home again. It's the only thing I can give you.'

She wanted this man with every breath in her, and it took all her courage to pull away. 'Then come back to me, Balor Ó Phelan. Swear it.'

'On my life.'

And with that, he left the hut, filling her with the fear that she would never see him again.

In the darkness, Balor walked towards the ruined fortress, fully armed with a sword and blades hidden beneath his clothing. Although he'd come this far to gather information, he didn't plan on fighting unless someone attacked.

Part of him wished he hadn't left Mairead behind. But he'd given her blades of her own, and she was safe in the village. He continued walking through the darkness, listening to the sounds. As he drew closer, he wondered why he hadn't heard anyone talking. If Liam was guarded in this place, he would expect there to be many Normans, for the *tánaiste* was a strong fighter.

The silence was unnerving, stretching out in an invisible threat. Had his mother been telling the truth about where Liam had been taken? Or had they moved him already?

Balor rested his hand upon his sword, and every instinct within him sharpened. He crept closer, remaining in the shadows as the moon rose high above the land. There wasn't much light but enough to see how many men guarded the ruin. His hand tightened upon his sword when he dared risk a look inside.

But he found the fortress empty.

He let out a breath, his shoulders releasing the tension. In the darkness, he couldn't truly see much of anything, but he kept his back to the wall as he moved silently inside. There were the remains of a fire, but when he reached towards the hearth, it had been cold for some time. So someone *had* been there.

He continued along the edge of the wall, and as he drew close to the far corner, he found a large piece of wood with an iron ring, covering the ground. It must have been used for storing food, he guessed. But when he raised up the door, he heard a faint groan coming from inside.

They'd kept a prisoner within the earthen chamber. He didn't know how deep it was, but he bent down and called out, 'Is someone there?'

A coughing sound was his only answer. Balor tried again, 'Who are you?' But the prisoner didn't answer.

Light. He needed a torch, so he hurried back to the abandoned hearth. He gathered some of the unlit tinder and struck flint with his dagger, sparking a fire. It took some time to build it up, but eventually he made a makeshift torch from a half-burned stick of wood and a torn piece of his tunic as kindling. He brought the torch over to the pit and leaned into the darkness.

There, he saw Liam MacEgan, bound and gagged. A coldness caught him as he wondered how long the *tánaiste* had been kept prisoner here—and where were his captors?

'Can you stand?' Balor asked. 'I'm here to get you out.'

But Liam's expression was weak and glazed. It was likely the man hadn't had enough water, which was why he lacked the strength to free himself.

Balor studied the distance and then looked around the fortress. The pit appeared deep, which would make it difficult to lift Liam up without a ladder or a way of climbing back out. But there were a number of fallen stones and also the wood from the trap door.

'I'm going to free you,' he swore. But as he began gathering materials, he was starting to understand what Fergus had done. He'd paid men to bring Liam here as a prisoner, to prevent him from returning to Laochre. It seemed as if his Norman captors had abandoned the *tanáiste*, leaving him with hardly any food or water.

Or did they intend to return soon? It was possible, but Balor wasn't about to let Liam die.

He strained under the weight of several large stones, dropping them into the storage chamber. Then he ripped away the trap door, breaking it free of its hinges.

'Listen to me,' he told Liam. 'I'm going to lift you up so you can climb out.' He lowered himself into the pit and removed the man's gag, offering him a flask of water. 'Drink this slowly.'

Liam took the water and was careful with it, though from the way he drank, it was clear that he'd not had water in at least a day or two. Balor reached into a fold of his cloak and passed the man a crust of bread.

'Where is—' Liam's words were raw, barely more than a whisper.

'Your family?' Balor guessed as he arranged the stones against the wall. The man nodded.

'Your wife is safe with the queen. Your sister, Mairead, traveled with me here, and she's in the village. I imagine your father and his men are following us.'

He tried to help Liam stand, but the man's legs buckled under him. Balor supported his weight and then stepped on the first stone. He struggled to lift Liam, but he braced his leg against the second stone and used all his strength to lift the *tánaiste* up high to the edge of the pit.

'Climb out,' he commanded. 'On your hands and knees.'

Liam struggled, but his strength gave out. 'Not safe. You have to…get help.'

'Not until I get you out first.' Balor shoved the man over the edge. Only when Liam was out of the pit did he haul himself up.

A moment later, he discovered where Liam's captors were when a circle of torches illuminated the ruined fortress.

And Balor saw the faces of Norman soldiers staring back at him.

Mairead had followed Balor back to the fortress after he'd left. She'd been careful to keep a slight distance and had seen the Norman soldiers closing in. Her brother stood with his hands bound, appearing dizzy and weak, while Balor supported him with an arm under his shoulders.

'You're not taking the prince,' one of the men said. He motioned to some of the soldiers and added, 'He has to remain our prisoner.'

Mairead's heart beat faster as she stared at the men in the darkness. Balor had been so close. He'd nearly helped her brother escape.

But now, with the soldiers surrounding them, she was starting to sense another truth. They were going to punish Balor for this—and she would be forced to watch.

No. She had no intention of remaining in the shadows. Not if she could help.

Mairead pulled back her hood and strode into the fortress. She stood in front of Balor and her brother, eyeing the Normans. 'You will not lay a hand on either of them.'

Their leader's expression tightened. 'My lady, you would be wise to step away. We are following King John's orders, and His Highness does not want you harmed. You are not part of this.'

Her breath tightened, as she suspected the king still had plans for her arranged marriage. But she ignored them and squared her shoulders.

'My brother is your prisoner. I would say I'm very much a part of this.' She narrowed her gaze on them amid the flare of torches. 'My father and his men are on their way here now.' Though she couldn't be certain, she hoped it wasn't a lie. 'What do you think will happen to you, if he finds out you've harmed any of us?'

Balor leaned in close. In a low whisper, he said, 'Steal a horse from the man on the edge of the others and ride north to Banslieve, Mairead. Bring back your uncle Connor and his men as reinforcements while I fight to free Liam.'

Without turning her head, she saw which rider he meant. The man wasn't holding the reins, and he appeared distracted. There were only three horses, but if Balor could get himself and her brother to the other two, they had a chance.

A low ache caught in her stomach as she realized he meant to fight back against all of them. She turned to him and whispered back, 'If I leave, they could kill you. There are too many.'

'They'll likely take us prisoner,' he corrected. 'When I make a move, you run. Take the horse and go.'

She gave a faint nod, fear pooling within her. Though he spoke as if he believed he could succeed, part of her worried that this might be the last time she saw him alive. She traced her hand against his cheek and murmured, 'Don't die, Balor.'

He touched his forehead to hers and then moved her behind him as he unsheathed his sword.

He charged towards the left, and most of the men attacked him, leaving her a clean escape. Mairead raced to the horse and seized the man by his tunic, using her body weight to pull him off balance. When he tried to grab her, she slashed at him with her blade. He gripped his wounded arm, and she mounted the horse, urging it out of the fortress.

She rode hard, leaning against the mare as she turned it northward. It was the hardest thing she'd ever done, leaving Balor and Liam behind. But he was right. Their only hope was if she brought back reinforcements from Banslieve. Her cousins, Dylan and Finn MacEgan, would fight, along with her uncle Connor.

Mairead blamed herself for everything. They never should have stopped here. They should have asked for help from her cousins first and brought their own forces. And now it would be her fault if Balor died. The ache in her chest made her realize just how much he meant to her.

He was bold, rebellious, and fierce—a man who stole her breath with the slightest touch. Someone who wouldn't hesitate to stand up to her overprotective father.

Someone who would sacrifice himself for her freedom.

The tears streamed down her face as she rode through the meadows. Mairead vowed to herself that, if he survived this, she was going to fight for Balor.

Because maybe if she did, there was a chance they could have the future that wasn't promised.

Balor was fairly certain he was going to die. He was outnumbered by at least twelve men, and Liam MacEgan was far too weak to fight. But at least Mairead had escaped. He could console himself with that.

His sword clashed with theirs, the steel ringing against steel. He moved from one to the next, spinning and fighting back as he relied on his instincts and years of Norman training.

Memories of the past collided with present, and as he fought back, the years seemed to fall away. He remembered the fighter he'd been when he'd first arrived in England at Beaumont. Like Marcas, he'd been helpless at first. Unbalanced and weak—but rage had fueled his fighting.

He'd been furious at being sent away from Éireann. As far as he was concerned, he never wanted to see his family again.

But he'd kept his mother's ring. He didn't know why he'd ignored her demand that he deliver it to the Norman lord. It was meant to be payment for his fostering…and yet, it was the only thing he had left of Orla.

He'd always considered it a punishment to be sent away, and he'd been so angry with her. But maybe…his mother *had* been trying to help him. He'd finally had enough food to eat and a warm place to sleep. He'd joined another group of boys, letting everyone believe he was with them. And later, the captain of the guards had allowed Balor to work in the stables and care for the horses, in return for training.

Lord Beaumont hadn't seemed to mind. He'd allowed Balor to stay with his other foster sons. And he'd been grateful to the nobleman for the gift of instruction and learning to read and write.

When they'd begun training him, Balor had been knocked to the ground more than once, and the other boys had laughed at him. But he'd used their scorn to motivate him, to push past the resentment of his low birth to become stronger. Month after month, he'd trained for hours each day, determined to become a warrior of strength.

And somehow, he'd caught the eye of the earl. Lord Beaumont had been dismissive of the boys at first, occasionally watching them train. But one morning, after Balor had defeated all the others, he'd glanced up at the battlements, and the earl had given him a slight nod of approval with a faint smile.

No one had ever acknowledged him like that before—as if the man was proud of him. Balor had been ashamed that a single gesture had meant so much. But from that day forward, he'd poured himself into training, learning everything he could. The others stopped laughing at him and had grudgingly given him their respect. They'd treated him as a leader, despite his desire to remain in the shadows.

Sometimes he wished he'd taken the time to befriend the other boys. But the idea of reaching out to anyone put him at the risk of being mocked. And so he'd kept to himself, embracing a life of being alone.

Even then, a few of the soldiers had offered him words of encouragement during training. He'd become stronger, the warrior he'd always wanted to be.

And he'd kept the ring until the very last day. Before he'd departed England, he'd left his mother's silver ring upon the earl's carved wooden table within his chambers. He didn't really know why, but somehow it felt like he was releasing the fear he'd felt as a boy, embracing the man he'd become. Letting go of the past.

And now, as his sword grew heavy and he faced his final moments of life, regrets slid over him. He wished he'd had the chance to say farewell to Kenneth. But more than anything else, he wished he'd told Mairead what she'd meant to him. Never in his life had anyone touched him willingly, offering affection or pleasure. She didn't even know how much he'd savoured each moment with her.

She'd said she loved him. And he hadn't said it back when he'd had the chance, a regret he would carry with him until his last breath. It had seemed unthinkable that she could ever give her heart to him.

He wasn't worthy of a king's daughter. But *she* was worth dying for.

With renewed strength, Balor fought back, using his blade, his fists, and a stolen shield. He shifted the fighting away from Liam, ignoring the slash that cut through his cloak and skimmed his side. Blood flowed, but Balor paid it no heed at all. He would defend the *tánaiste*, for Mairead's sake.

Yet, as the soldiers closed in on him, hope began to dim. Balor concentrated on the memory of Mairead's smile and her kiss. He remembered her hands upon his skin and how it had felt to touch her.

Though his arms ached, he kept fighting. He'd slain several men, wounding others to keep them away from Liam. But as his strength began to wane, he heard the sounds of approaching horses. Was it the MacEgans, arriving at last?

No, it was far too soon for that.

When he saw the gleam of Norman armour and six more soldiers mounted on horseback, his spirits deflated. He defended himself from the soldier in front of him, but pain exploded in the back of his head, dropping him to his knees. Balor tasted blood in his mouth, and dizziness made the world sway while he braced himself for the killing blow.

And when the sword descended towards him, he saw nothing more.

Chapter Ten

Mairead's spirits sank as she reached Banslieve. She'd ridden as fast as she could, but when she reached the fortress, her father's men were already waiting inside. They must have ridden all day and night.

Patrick stood beside his brother Connor, and the moment she entered the gates, she dismounted and ran to them.

'Mairead—' he started to say.

'You have to bring your men to fight,' she interrupted. 'We—we found Liam.' Her words were rushed, for she was out of breath.

Her father paled at her words. 'Thank God he's alive.'

She nodded. 'But we have to hurry. He's being held captive at the ruined fortress. Fergus Ó Phelan sold him to the Normans.'

'Stay with your aunt Aileen,' her uncle Connor commanded. 'We'll go after him now.' The men seemed to dismiss her, but she wasn't about to leave Balor at risk.

'Balor found Liam and freed him, but they were attacked. Please. You have to protect him.'

Patrick turned to her. 'By rights, Ó Phelan should die for capturing *you*, Mairead. Along with his traitorous family.'

'I went willingly,' she argued. 'We found Liam because

of him. His mother betrayed Fergus to tell us both where Liam was. Balor deserves to live for saving my brother.'

Yet, from the rigid cast to his face, she knew her father wasn't going to listen. She would have to wait until after they were gone to do anything to help Balor. Frustration and grief made tears spill over her cheeks. 'Please...go now before they kill Liam.'

Her father's expression held a blend of pity and determination. He joined the others, followed by his brother Connor and his sons, Dylan and Finn.

Mairead stepped back with her aunt Aileen while they rallied the men and mounted their horses. She gripped her hands together, feeling utterly helpless. But her cousin Finn paused a moment, his wild dark hair falling against his face. 'Don't be afraid, Mairead. We'll save them both.'

Then he rode off, leaving her with her own fear that Balor would die, just as Diarmud had. She swiped at her tears, trying to hold herself together.

After they had gone, Aileen's hand came down on her shoulder. Her grey hair was bound back into a single braid, and the years had been kind to her, the gentle lines of her smile creasing her face. 'You care for him, don't you? This man named Balor.'

Mairead nodded numbly, but it went deeper than that. She didn't know how or when it had happened, but Balor had laid a quiet assault on her heart. The thought of losing him terrified her. And she promised herself that, if he somehow survived it, she would choose him as her husband.

Her aunt pulled her into an embrace, and the sudden love broke down her defences. Mairead began sobbing, and Aileen held her tightly.

'I don't want him to die,' she wept. 'It's my fault he came with me to help Liam. We never should have gone alone.'

'Come and sit with me,' Aileen soothed. 'I'll make tea, and you'll tell me all about it.' She led her into a small roundhouse with a thatched roof. The interior was warm from hot stones, and there was a low table with small stools around it. A pot of water hung near the hearth, and Aileen chose an assortment of dried herbs from a pouch at her waist.

'Chamomile and mint, I think.' She sprinkled the herbs into two wooden mugs, and after the water was hot, she poured it in, swirling the herbs around until a pleasant fragrance emanated from the steam.

'Is Rhiannon here? Or Emla?' Mairead asked. Her older cousin had been a friend over the years, and their daughter Emla had been like a sister to her.

'They are visiting family in the south. If you stay for a few days, they should return. Emla will want to see you, I know.' Aileen gave her a cup of tea and then poured one for herself.

Mairead sipped at the herbal tea, wishing it could calm the unrest in her heart. Her aunt gave a faint smile and remarked, 'Your father told me that a Norman earl wishes to wed you. And yet, you seem far more concerned about Balor Ó Phelan.'

'Lord Lowell was the man chosen by King John,' Mairead admitted. 'But I don't want to marry him.' To anyone else, it would seem like an advantageous betrothal. Yet, she had no interest in a man who was quiet, wealthy, and everything her family believed she wanted.

'Is there a reason why you won't consider the earl?' her aunt asked.

There was. But not the one Aileen would guess.

Deep inside, Mairead was becoming aware of another truth. Beneath her sheltered life as a king's daughter lay a woman who craved rebellion.

She liked being wicked. She liked breaking the rules and defying everyone else's expectations. A man like Balor—who represented everything her family didn't want—was exactly what she *did* want.

She straightened and regarded her aunt. 'My marriage should not be built upon the will of kings. My father promised I could choose my own husband.'

'And you've chosen Balor?' her aunt predicted.

She steeled herself. 'Balor has done nothing wrong. And he doesn't deserve to die for trying to rescue my brother.' Though it wasn't really an answer, she plunged forward and added, 'Fergus is responsible for this, and *he* should be the one to face the consequences.'

Aileen finished her tea, her eyes discerning. 'I imagine he will. But in the meantime, there may be wounded men returning to us tonight. Will you help me gather bandages and healing herbs while we wait?'

'Of course.' But a chill slid beneath her skin with the fear that someone she cared about would be hurt. Balor… Liam…or her father.

She could never tell her father of the feelings she held in her heart. If she told him the truth, Patrick would only make Balor leave, or worse. She could only pray that he would survive this night with the help of her father's men.

As she helped her aunt gather healing herbs and supplies, a plan began to shape within her mind of how to get what she wanted.

And that meant travelling back to Balor to save his life.

* * *

Balor awakened in darkness. His mouth was dry and cracked, and his head had a dull ache. When he reached up, he felt a bandage.

He didn't know where he was or who had brought him here. But when he tried to sit up, someone caught him by the shoulders and laid him back. 'Not yet.' The man spoke in the Norman tongue, but the voice seemed slightly familiar. It was too dark to see him.

'What happened?' Balor's voice came out in a rasp, and the Norman lifted a cup of water to his lips. Balor drank it, grateful to quench his thirst. Whoever this was, he didn't seem to want him dead, or he'd already be gone.

'You were surrounded and about to die. We took you here when King John's men arrived.'

So there had been more than one rescuer.

'How long have I been here?'

'A full day and a half,' he answered.

'Who are you?' Balor asked. 'It's too dark to see your face.'

'Gerald of Mowbray,' the man answered. 'We met at Laochre, along with my commander, Sir Edward of Baldwin.' The man lit a brazier, and soon enough, the dim light of the peat fire illuminated the tent.

A tightness caught within him. 'Why did you follow me here? Were your men the ones who took Liam?'

'No. We came here for you,' Gerald said. He left without explanation, and a moment later, Sir Edward entered.

Balor didn't truly believe him. But there was a reason why these men had saved his life—and a dark uneasiness clenched within him at the thought.

Sir Edward sat beside him, his demeanour cool. 'Do you know why we came to Éireann, Balor Ó Phelan?'

Balor struggled to sit up, still trying to hide his dizziness. He suspected they were connected to King John or Liam's disappearance, though he couldn't say that. 'I suppose you're going to tell me.'

'If you ask nicely,' Gerald responded drily.

'You came for Mairead's hand in marriage,' Balor said, even knowing it was false. He wanted to see how they would respond.

'That's not—' Sir Edward started to say. But he fell silent, holding back his words. Which made Balor even more suspicious.

'What do you know about the Liam MacEgan?' he interrupted. 'Is he—'

'He lives,' the man answered. 'The other soldiers took him to King John at Blarnan.'

'Why?' He'd thought Fergus had simply sold Liam into captivity. Now it seemed like part of something much larger.

'The men Fergus paid were the king's men. I imagine they saw an opportunity to make him a valuable hostage.'

And likely the English king would take advantage, Balor guessed. Probably by manipulating Patrick into doing his will, even though the King of Laochre had already travelled to see King John and had sworn his loyalty. Since the king's men had taken Liam MacEgan, it suggested that John didn't trust the MacEgans at all.

But there was a hidden opportunity, Balor realized. If he somehow broke Liam free of the king's custody and brought him back to Laochre in secret, he could ensure that Liam was crowned as the next Irish king and gain Patrick's favour. Since Fergus had been responsible for the capture, he would pay the price for his treason. Kenneth could become the next chieftain of the Ó Phelan clan.

Or you could.

The inner thought startled him. Mairead had asked him before why he didn't want it. He'd told her that the people would never want someone like him. But the truth was he'd never imagined taking command of his clan. He'd always believed that his people hated him. It still might be true.

And yet, becoming chieftain might give him a chance at wedding Mairead. It wasn't nearly as influential as being an earl, but it was something.

'You said that you were fostered at Beaumont,' Sir Edward began. 'Is that where you trained to fight in our style?'

Balor didn't truly understand why the man would ask such a question. 'It was,' he answered. 'I stayed there for seven years.'

'But you weren't there as a young child, were you?' Gerald remarked. 'Your mother sent you there when you were older.'

How did he know such a thing? And why would he care?

Balor's jaw tightened. 'I was eleven.' Far too old for fostering, since most children were sent away just after they learned to walk.

He didn't know how his mother had arranged his fosterage, since there were no family connections.

Unless there *was* a tie to his true father's family. A sudden wariness caught him at the thought.

'He sent you to find me, didn't he?' Balor guessed. 'My true father.' He leaned back on the bed, grimacing at the pain. It unnerved him to even think of it. In the dim light, he saw the men exchange cautious glances. 'I don't care if he did or not. I've no wish to see the Norman soldier who turned his back on my mother and me.'

Orla had claimed that she'd loved the man who had fathered him, that it hadn't been an attack at all. Regardless of whether the Norman had loved his mother in return, Orla had been forced to wed Fergus after they'd been abandoned. She'd lost all courage, becoming a shadow. She'd claimed her indifference was to keep Balor safe.

But he couldn't forgive her and simply let go of years of hurt and suffering. Not now.

The older man's stare grew intense. 'Have you ever asked yourself why your mother sent you so far away for your fostering?'

He already knew what the knight was implying but refused to consider it. Instead, he kept his expression neutral. 'Because she wanted me far away from Fergus.'

'She could have sent you across the sea, and it would have been far enough,' Sir Edward said quietly. 'Instead, she sent you farther away, to be fostered with your father.'

Balor gave a shrug. 'If that was her intent, it came to nothing. No one ever spoke of fathering me.'

'Your father didn't know who you were until you left your mother's ring behind on his desk.'

Silence hung between them, and his pulse quickened at the knight's words. The revelation sank around his shoulders with the weight of disbelief. No. Such a thing was completely impossible.

How had Orla ever fallen in love with a Norman earl? How would she even have met him? From what he understood, his mother had never been to England, had never left Éireann. But the ring must have been a gift from Lord Beaumont—one she had kept for twenty years.

He leaned back, staring up at the ceiling. 'Are you trying to tell me my father was the Earl of Beaumont?'

'He is, yes.'

A hollow ache caught his gut, a blend of regret and bitterness. Would anything have changed if he'd given the earl the ring sooner? Would he have known what it was to have a father? More questions rose up, but Balor dared to voice the most important one. 'Did he know she bore him a son?'

The knight shook his head. 'No. But a servant saw you put the ring on his desk. After the earl found it, he demanded to know who had put it there. When he learned it was you, Lord Beaumont sent us to find you.' Sir Edward paused a moment then added, 'And bring you home.'

Home.

Dunmalus had never really been a home. It was where he'd lived, where he'd endured the chieftain's years of hatred.

It was strange to imagine that there was another place where he might belong. Uncertainty sharpened within him, and an invisible heaviness seemed to bind across his chest. Balor remembered how proud he'd felt when he'd seen Lord Beaumont watching him fight. When the man had offered a nod of approval, something within him had shifted. He'd wanted to please the earl, to demonstrate his newfound strength and skill.

And now, to learn that Lord Beaumont was his father? Balor didn't know how to feel about it.

'How did they meet?' he asked.

'The earl travelled to Éireann on the king's orders, the year before you were born. He met your mother near her family's lands. He stayed there for a time, and she later saved his life during a raid,' Sir Edward continued. 'She sent him away by boat, and because of her bravery, he survived.'

The knight's confession seemed like a lie. His mother had always been hesitant—not at all the sort of woman who would step into battle and save a man's life. But she'd paid the price, hadn't she? That might have been why she had retreated into herself.

A thousand questions caught in Balor's mind, circling and spinning, but he couldn't bring himself to speak. Instead, he stared up at the thatched roof above him, realizing that none of it mattered. The truth was Orla had left her family's lands, married Fergus, and had never told Beaumont about his bastard son.

She'd told Fergus that she'd been violated, letting everyone believe a lie. And Balor didn't know if he could forgive her for that.

At last, he turned back to the Normans. 'What does the earl want from me?'

'Lord Beaumont wants to know you,' Sir Edward answered. 'To offer you the chance to return to England.'

Balor knew he ought to be grateful for the offer, but all he could think of was the powerful earl who had turned his back on the woman who had once loved him. 'Why would I want to know a man who abandoned us?'

The knight exchanged a look with Gerald. 'He didn't abandon you. When he returned for Orla and learned she had gone to Dunmalus, Fergus told him she was dead.'

That part seemed probable. The chieftain would have lied to a Norman soldier, especially if he believed the man was responsible for attacking her.

'The earl came back to England and grieved the loss of her,' Sir Edward continued. 'Lord Beaumont only learned Orla was alive just after you left her ring behind at the estate. The moment he realized who you were—he sent us to find both of you and bring you back.'

The knight added, 'After you've recovered, you should return with us to England. The earl would welcome you as his son.'

Maybe. But if that were true, why hadn't Lord Beaumont travelled here himself?

And yet…he couldn't reject the offer. As the bastard son of an earl, it increased his chances of winning Mairead's hand in marriage. Only a little, but if the earl allowed him to stay at Beaumont, it was possible that Balor could at least give her a home.

A sense of determination caught him, and he told the knight, 'Before I would consider travelling to England, there is something I need to do first.'

'And what is that?' Sir Edward asked.

'I need to free the *tánaiste* and bring him back to Laochre. Then, if she is willing, I intend to take King Patrick's daughter as my bride.'

Gerald exchanged a look with the knight. 'Ambitious, aren't you?'

'If I free Liam MacEgan, her father might consent to the marriage,' he answered.

'It's not a good idea,' Gerald countered. 'Liam will be heavily guarded at Blarnan. King John will want to use him as leverage against King Patrick.'

Outside, there came the sound of approaching horses, and Balor suspected his time was running out. 'We have to leave.' He struggled but managed to stand up. Dizziness flooded through him, and he stumbled forward a step before Gerald caught him.

'You're not strong enough to walk yet.'

Not yet, but he would regain that strength after he healed. Beneath his breath, he muttered, 'Take me to Blarnan and imprison me with Liam. Then I can break him out with your help.'

After a pause, Balor added, 'And in return, I'll go back to Beaumont with you.'

* * *

Balor sat in the darkness, alongside Liam. Sir Edward and Gerald had followed his request and had brought him as a prisoner to Blarnan at nightfall. He'd already given his share of food and water to the *tánaiste*, for he still appeared weak and hungry.

'Where is my sister?' Liam asked. His voice was hoarse, revealing his exhaustion.

'I sent her to Banslieve, to her uncle Connor,' Balor replied. 'She's safe.'

'Thank God.' For a long moment, Liam waited. Then he added, 'You should know that we're very protective of her.'

'As Mairead deserves,' he answered. A woman like her, one who viewed the world with a generous heart, was worth guarding with his life.

'Were you hoping she would choose you at the *aenach*?' Liam ventured.

Balor didn't miss the veiled threat from her older brother. 'I knew she wouldn't. Not when the king has already chosen her betrothed husband.' But that didn't mean he intended to stand aside and let that happen. He turned towards Liam and added, 'Mairead deserves the freedom to choose any man she desires.'

The *tánaiste* seemed to silently agree with him. Then he asked, 'Why did they capture you?'

Balor understood the unspoken question. 'You mean why did they bother bringing me here when they could have killed me?'

A faint smile tugged at Liam's mouth. 'Just so.'

'Perhaps the guards found me handsome,' Balor said drily.

The *tánaiste* gave a rough laugh. 'Do you know, I could almost like you, Ó Phelan.'

'It's probably not a good idea.' But Balor drew up his knees and added in a low voice, 'Are you feeling well enough to break out of this prison tonight?'

'Possibly. Are my father's men here to help us?'

'Not yet,' he answered. 'But soon. King Patrick followed when I escorted Mairead here.'

Liam let out a slow breath. 'That was a mistake. My father will kill you slowly for taking Mairead.'

'It was *her* idea to search for you,' he pointed out. 'And you wouldn't be alive if I hadn't agreed to it.'

The *tánaiste* gave a nod. 'You're right. I apologize for that.'

'Save your apology. What I want is Mairead's hand in marriage.' He saw no reason not to be honest with her brother. 'I'll help you escape, and in return, I want your support.'

'Mairead can make her own decisions,' Liam said quietly. 'I don't speak for her. But you have a greater problem with her betrothal to Lord Lowell.'

'And what if she doesn't want to wed him?' Balor demanded softly. When Liam gave no answer, he added, 'You don't think Mairead should have a choice in her marriage, the way you did? You would force her to sacrifice her future?' Balor fully understood the risks to her family, but she deserved a choice. And if she truly loved him, then he would move the world to keep her with him.

'Lowell is here right now,' Liam said softly. 'He came on King John's orders. And they are planning the wedding as we speak.'

'How do you know this?'

'I heard the soldiers talking about it. And the earl came to speak with me. King John has demanded a marriage alliance between Lord Lowell and our family.'

'And you're going to stand back and let that happen?' Balor asked softly. His mind began shifting through the possibilities. The more he thought of it, the more he realized he needed Gerald's and Sir Edward's help.

He didn't know how powerful Lord Beaumont's influence with King John was, but perhaps the earl could intervene, if the English king would allow Balor to marry Mairead instead. Or possibly, his father could grant them both sanctuary in England for a time.

His father. The words held a weight to it, even though Balor knew better than to trust a man he didn't know. He'd lived with Lord Beaumont for years, but the man had remained apart, keeping to himself. It could have been loneliness. Or indifference.

He shouldn't rely on one man. The earl might not have influence with King John, or he might refuse to speak with the monarch.

Balor knew it was better to solve his own problems. And maybe that meant abandoning everything and taking Mairead away to build their own lives.

A voice inside warned him that she might refuse to leave with him. It truly did mean asking her to choose between her family and him. And if she chose the MacEgans, their fragile relationship would be over.

Though he was inwardly prepared for it, he couldn't suppress the hollow ache. He wanted her, more than anything he'd ever wanted in his life.

But in the end, it had to be her decision. If she chose to marry the earl, he would respect her choice.

Balor moved in closer to Liam. 'Listen to me. There are two Norman guards who can free both of us. They are the ones who kept me alive.' He described Sir Edward and

Gerald, adding, 'After we break out of this prison, we will leave with them. They will take us back to Laochre.'

'No,' Liam said at last. 'You need to escape first. If you trust these guards, then let them help you.'

He was about to protest, but the *tánaiste* continued, 'My father is going to bring Mairead here. If you truly want to wed her, then you'll need to be free first. And, if anything goes wrong, you can help from the outside.'

Liam was right. If King John was planning to witness a wedding between Mairead and the earl, then Balor had to leave tonight.

And find a way to stop it from happening.

Chapter Eleven

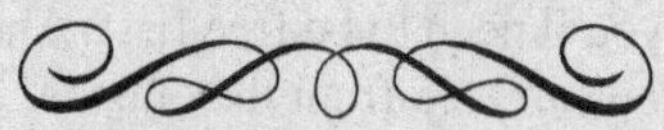

Mairead rode alongside her cousin Finn while a small escort of MacEgan soldiers accompanied her to Blarnan. The summer morning air was crisp, and the wind brushed against her face, trying to pull her hair free from its arrangement. Her aunt Aileen had given her a deep blue silk gown to wear—and it felt like wearing another kind of armour.

Her emotions were barely held together, twisted with worry and fear for Balor. She'd tried to go back to the ruins after he hadn't returned, only to be stopped by her father.

He and his men hadn't reached them in time, and Balor and Liam were now prisoners.

We'll find them, her father had sworn. *Stay with your aunt Aileen until I send word.*

And at last, he had.

He'd asked them to travel to the fortress of Blarnan where Liam and Balor were both being held hostage by King John.

Although Mairead kept her head held high as they rode, behaving like the king's daughter she was, it felt as if her life no longer belonged to her. If she made the wrong decision or behaved in the wrong way, the man she loved might suffer the consequences.

Her heartbeat stuttered at the thought of what lay ahead. She could feel the invisible chains tightening around what was left of her freedom. This was a battle she didn't know how to fight—or even if she could.

The journey to Blarnan had lasted all morning, but they never stopped once. Her cousin Finn escorted her through the gates, and as Mairead rode past, she noted their surroundings. Both Irish and Norman soldiers guarded the space while stonemasons worked to build the large square tower within the fortress. A soldier stepped forward to take her horse as she dismounted, and she was shocked to see her cousin Alanna standing nearby, wearing a green silk gown.

Mairead didn't truly understand why Alanna had traveled such a far distance, but when she saw her father standing beside the Earl of Lowell at the top of the stairs, her heart sank.

Had Lord Lowell come for the reason she suspected? Was this about fulfiling the betrothal King John wanted?

The earl met her gaze, and a faint smile reached his mouth, one that appeared to be relief. He wore a blue silk tunic with darker trews, clothing that befitted a king's audience.

Mairead couldn't smile in return. The thought of a forced marriage tightened every part of her body in silent rebellion. For this man wasn't Balor. He wasn't the man who had worshipped her with his hands and mouth, only a few nights ago. He wasn't the man who had fought against all odds to save her and then, to save her brother.

And by God, she would not stand aside and be a pawn in a royal game of political power. She walked closer, and when she reached Alanna, the woman embraced her warmly.

'What are you doing here?' Mairead breathed.

'I came because you need me here,' her cousin answered. 'My father sent his men, and I accompanied them.'

Mairead didn't understand. Why would Alanna believe she needed her?

'Are you all right?' her cousin murmured.

'I don't know,' Mairead answered honestly. She had travelled here to plead for Balor's life—and now it was starting to feel like a trap closing in around her.

Alanna took her hand and led her up the stairs. 'The king is waiting inside. You will be presented to him before you have a formal…audience with him in the morning.'

She didn't quite understand why her cousin had phrased it that way, but when she reached her father, Patrick reached out to cup her cheek. Relief flooded through his features. 'I am glad you've come, *a iníon.*'

'Where are they?' she whispered.

'Chained below ground,' her father answered. 'By the order of King John.' His voice held a cool tightness, and she understood that he could not speak freely here.

But she would help in whatever way she could, as long as Balor and her brother escaped.

The earl took her hand and greeted her, kissing her wrist. Though it was a courtesy, she fought the urge to pull away. There were too many of the king's entourage surrounding them, so she veiled her emotions.

'Lord Lowell,' she greeted him softly.

'I am glad to see you are unharmed, Lady Mairead.' His features remained stoic, but she didn't miss his own strained demeanour. He was likely angry with her for leaving Rionallís with Balor. But despite the king's wishes for a betrothal, the earl was not her husband yet—and she would not wed him if she could find a way around it.

She needed to see Balor with her own eyes to know that

he was safe—and yet, she didn't know if her father had plans for their escape. And if that meant pretending to be obedient while they freed the men, so be it.

'Thank you,' she answered Lord Lowell. He offered his arm, and she took it while accepting her father as another escort.

As they walked inside the Great Chamber, servants were busy hanging up greenery and summer flowers. Bright yellow gorse and heather adorned the space, and when she glanced at her father, he said only, 'For the wedding.'

Her skin turned icy, even as blood rushed to her face. '*Whose* wedding?'

Her father didn't answer, and Lord Lowell's hand tightened upon hers. King John was seated on a dais at the far end of the Great Chamber, and his gaze fixed upon her as she walked with her father and the earl.

In desperation, she turned to Patrick. 'This isn't happening *now*, is it?'

He gave a slight shake of his head. 'In the morning.' He took her hand in a tight grip of warning. In a quiet voice, he said, 'Don't do anything reckless.'

I have to leave, she thought desperately. But how?

Her cheeks flamed scarlet, but she stopped walking, remaining at the back of the Great Chamber. To her father, she demanded, 'I don't understand. I thought we came to free Liam. Why would you bring the earl here?'

Lord Lowell appeared taken aback by her words. But after a slight pause, he added, 'I was summoned by King John, Lady Mairead. And despite what you may believe, I'm not your enemy. I never was.'

'I wanted a choice in my marriage,' she whispered, stepping away from both of them. It felt as if a future she never wanted was closing in on her.

Patrick caught her by the arm. 'Don't, Mairead. This is not about you or your wishes. It's about far more than that.'

She wrenched herself free, staring at him with defiance. But before she could speak, he continued, 'You defied orders that were meant to keep you safe,' he snapped. 'And now, according to King John, Liam will remain his hostage until you wed Lord Lowell.' He dropped his voice even softer. 'I don't think you have a choice anymore.'

The world seemed to tilt beneath her feet. 'Why does King John care? Why does it matter who I wed? I will never be queen.'

Patrick's face remained stony. 'It's his way of controlling our family.' He straightened and added, 'If you obey his orders and marry Lord Lowell, then the king has promised to let Liam go free.'

It was just as she'd feared—there had never truly been a choice. She stared back at her father in disbelief that he would allow himself to be manipulated. King John would never keep his word.

'And if I refuse?'

Her father's face turned to stone. 'Then his other prisoner, Balor Ó Phelan, will die.'

Shock and horror flooded through her. Mairead's entire body froze, and a ringing sounded in her ears. Did they intend to manipulate her by threatening his life? Or was this King John's decision? She'd never imagined her father would be this ruthless.

Before she could speak, Patrick gave her over to the earl. Lord Lowell took her hand, and she let him lead her forward to stand before the king. She was barely aware of what was happening, and her vision seemed to blur.

There was danger here, Mairead realized, even as she curtseyed out of respect for the English monarch.

King John's eyes gleamed, and he regarded her. 'We can see why you are your father's jewel, Lady Mairead.'

'Thank you, Your Grace,' she murmured, lowering her gaze.

'I look forward to an alliance between Lord Lowell and your family,' the king continued. 'In the morning, we will celebrate your nuptials.' He gave a slight wave of dismissal, and Lord Lowell bowed in response.

It would never be a celebration, Mairead thought. Only a prison.

The earl led her away from the others and lowered his voice. 'I know you do not want to marry me, Lady Mairead,' he began. 'And although I had…hoped you might reconsider, I am aware that you've no interest in me at all.'

His voice was quiet, and when she glanced at the earl, part of her turned sympathetic. He wasn't an unattractive man, though he was older.

'This marriage isn't fair to either of us,' she admitted. 'But I don't understand why you would want to wed me—especially now.'

'Am I so distasteful to you?' he asked. 'Have I done anything to offend you?'

She shook her head and lowered her voice. 'It's only that… I'm in love with someone else.'

'The Irishman,' he predicted.

'My father said that if I do not wed you, they will execute him.' Her voice held the weight of her anguish, and she didn't bother to hide it.

The earl squeezed her hand. 'I suppose that's not the best beginning to a marriage, is it?' He offered his arm. 'Shall we walk where there aren't so many others around to overhear our conversation?'

There really wasn't much of a choice, so she took his

arm and walked alongside him. When she glanced back at her father and the king, they both seemed pleased with her decision.

'So, what is it you wish to do?' the earl asked.

'I want you to let me go,' she murmured. 'If you refuse to wed me—'

'—they will punish you for it and execute your lover anyway.' His gaze sharpened. 'I presume he *is* your lover?'

Her cheeks burned, but she gave a faint nod. The earl's face was a mask, but he said nothing. It was only the tension in his posture that gave it away.

'So you see why I cannot wed you,' Mairead said. 'I am sorry, but it wouldn't be right or fair to you.'

'But you would do it to save his life?' the earl asked quietly.

She closed her eyes, feeling a wash of grief. 'If it meant Balor could live, then yes.' Everything within her went numb at the thought. 'But I beg of you, please don't ask that of me.'

His gaze fixed upon her. 'The king will settle for nothing less than a MacEgan alliance.' Then he led her back to her father. He murmured a quiet farewell before he returned among the king's retainers. Numbness cloaked Mairead as she joined Patrick.

She didn't know what the earl planned to do. Although he'd seemed to understand her reluctance, her confession gave him a strong reason to call off any sort of betrothal.

Her father escorted her outside the keep, gripping her wrist hard, as if to stop her from running away. Then he stopped, his gaze fixed upon the opposite stone wall.

'I am sorry, Mairead,' he told her. 'I'm trying to find a way out of this, but I cannot see another path forward.'

'Do you think the king would truly kill Balor if I refuse to wed Lord Lowell?'

'I don't know,' Patrick answered. In a quiet voice, he added, 'I have several of my men watching the prisoners, regardless of the king's promises. But if you refuse the wedding—even if we get Liam out—then King John will see it as an act of betrayal. I won't risk your lives. No throne is worth that cost.'

The wedding was meant to satisfy the king's wishes. If she obeyed, then her brother's life would be safe.

Patrick's voice sounded tired, and he relaxed his grip, slipping his hand from her wrist to her palm. 'It might not be so bad, Mairead. I was forced to wed Isabel, when it was the last thing either of us wanted. But the lives of my kinsmen depended on the marriage. I obeyed, and she turned out to be the woman I love more than anything in the world.'

He was trying to reassure her, but his words only held the weight of resignation.

'But you weren't in love with someone else,' she said softly.

Invisible walls seemed to enclose her, along with grief over the life she'd wanted. Mairead didn't bother to hide her tears. It broke her apart, knowing that Balor's life rested in her hands. And the only way to save him was to marry a man she didn't love.

They were relying on her to make the sacrifice, and it infuriated her. John wasn't her king. And this was *her* life, not theirs.

Her father's face had gone stoic, as if he didn't like this any more than she did. 'Why does Ó Phelan mean so much to you, Mairead?'

She had to choose her words carefully. 'Because he saw

the woman I am, not a king's daughter.' Her voice grew strained. 'He didn't care about me for his own ambitions. Unlike so many others.'

'I cannot allow you to wed Balor Ó Phelan,' her father said. 'He's not right for you, Mairead. And I think you know it.'

It wasn't true, but she also knew better than to push her father. He was nearing his breaking point, so she simply said, 'I won't do anything until I know he's still alive.' That much was a reasonable request. 'And if he is, then at least allow me to say goodbye to him before I obey your command.'

Patrick grew somber. 'Wait here.' Slowly, he walked towards one of the towers and spoke quietly to a soldier. Then he returned to her side and led her a short distance away while they waited.

'I'm not taking you inside that prison. But I have asked the soldiers to let you see Balor here, for a moment.' His gaze remained steady, and he rested his hand on her shoulder. 'To say farewell.'

Mairead stared back at him, her heart sinking. There were far too many guards for an escape. And still…she wondered if Patrick had done this on purpose, to give Balor a glimpse at his surroundings.

There was no doubt her father believed the stories of Balor's reputation as a killer. But Balor *was* a man of honour, even if no one believed it but her. It shattered her to think of abandoning the man she loved for the sake of duty.

The seed of rebellion took root and began to deepen. There had to be another way.

After a little while, a group of soldiers emerged with Balor between them, his hands bound behind his back. His dark hair hung against his cheeks, and traces of dried blood marred his jawline. She longed to run to him, but as the tears welled up in her eyes, she forced herself to wait.

Her father released her hand. 'I will wait here and let you speak with him. And then you will return and do your duty on the morrow. In return, I will try to arrange his release.'

She turned to look at him and softly murmured, 'Thank you.'

Her heart was breaking as she crossed the space to Balor. His eyes drank in the sight of her, and she steeled herself for what might become another loss.

To the soldiers, she commanded. 'Step back and let me speak with him alone.'

'We cannot, my lady,' one argued. But she was not about to let her last moments with Balor be witnessed by strangers.

'That was an order,' she demanded. 'Not a request.'

They glanced at her father, who nodded and signalled for them to obey. Even so, they stood close by.

'Are you all right?' Balor asked quietly.

The ache inside her seemed to crack open, even as she tried to hold back tears. 'No,' she admitted, forcing herself to meet his gaze. 'My father is allowing me to say farewell to you before King John commands me to wed Lord Lowell in the morning.'

She stepped in close and wrapped her arms around his neck, resting her head beneath his chin. He couldn't return the embrace with his bound hands, but she murmured, 'I love you. I need you to know that, no matter what happens.'

Balor dropped his voice low. 'You don't have to marry him, Mairead.'

'I don't know what to do,' she confessed. 'If I disobey the king's orders, your life is in danger.'

'Don't wed him,' he murmured. 'I have others who will help me escape.'

She risked a glance at the soldiers in disbelief. No, Balor wasn't safe at all. Not when they were using him as leverage to force her obedience.

'Find a way to refuse the marriage,' he said softly. Against her ear, he whispered, 'I intend to save your brother and bring him back to Laochre. After he is free, I want you to wed me instead.'

His words wove a blend of hope and terror within her. She wanted to believe him, wanted to believe that she could somehow gain the marriage she'd dreamed of. But if she made a single mistake, Balor's life would be forfeit. And possibly her brother's, too.

The risk was far too grave. She'd grieved the loss of Diarmud, blaming herself. And rightfully so. He never would have gone to fight, if he hadn't wanted to prove himself.

Balor was doing the same thing. He felt the need to help save her brother, possibly to show her father that he was a man of worth. But this wasn't his fight. He didn't have to risk his life—not for her family. If anything happened to him, she wouldn't grieve.

She would break apart into a thousand pieces that could never be mended.

And so she answered his offer of marriage with the truth. 'I don't know if I can.'

The words were an arrow, slicing through him. She saw it in the barest flinch before he shielded his demeanour back into a mask of indifference, guarding his own feelings. He believed she was turning her back on him, just as everyone else had done.

The tears fell freely, but she forced herself to voice the

truth. 'I would rather wed another man than watch you die. I couldn't bear it. Not again.'

Every muscle in his body stiffened, and he took a step back from her, his gaze stony.

Maybe she shouldn't have alluded to Diarmud, but he needed to know that her feelings for him were far stronger. 'I will do whatever I must, to save your life.' If marrying Lord Lowell meant that Balor survived, she would do it without hesitation.

'Don't you have any faith in me?' His expression darkened as he took another step back, forcing her to look at him. 'I am not Diarmud.'

'Balor.' Her voice was anguished, but when she tried to touch his cheek, he turned it away.

'It doesn't matter what I say or how hard I fight for us, does it?' Bitterness lined his tone, and his eyes glittered with anger. 'I'll still only ever be a bastard. Someone you could never wed.'

That wasn't true. How could he even think that? 'I never cared if you were a prince or a serf,' she insisted. 'I only want you to live. But I don't know how to fight back against the King of England.' She swiped at her tears and faced him. 'I would rather marry a man I don't love, to save the man I do.'

She didn't know what she'd expected from him. Pride made him straighten, his shoulders back as he faced her, revealing all the frustration and anger she had caused. Even as bruised and bleeding as he'd been, he carried himself like a nobleman.

'I don't need your martyrdom,' he said coldly. 'Either fight for us or walk away, Mairead.'

He didn't understand. And she closed her eyes for a moment, gathering what was left of her courage. 'I lost someone I loved and could do nothing to stop it. This time, I *will* save you—no matter what it costs me.'

But in his eyes, she saw the bleak resignation. And maybe he was right. Maybe sacrificing herself was the wrong decision. It would take courage greater than she'd ever had to defy two kings.

If she dared take the risk, Balor had to be gone where no one could harm him.

When she reached to embrace him one last time, she discreetly slid a small blade beneath his tunic at his waist. It was the only weapon she could give him. Beneath her breath, she murmured, 'You need to leave tonight. Take my brother with you, if you can. And then disappear to a place where no one will ever find you.'

His eyes gleamed with raw emotion as she pulled back. 'Don't marry him, Mairead. Swear it.'

He was asking her to refuse the commands of the most powerful men in England and Éireann—to find the courage to reach for what *she* wanted instead of what they demanded of her. She wanted to, more than anything. But fear held her back. She needed more time to think, time to consider.

She reached out to touch his cheek once more. 'I love you.'

Mairead couldn't stop the tears from falling as she walked back to her father. It might be the last time she saw Balor, and she didn't know what to do. The guards took him away, and it felt as if *she* were the one in chains.

Patrick reached out to touch her hair, but she pulled away. 'Don't.'

She strode towards the keep, not wanting to watch the soldiers as they led Balor back to the prison. But a short distance away, she saw Alanna standing alone. Her cousin seemed to sense how badly Mairead needed to leave. Within moments, her cousin crossed the inner bailey.

She took Mairead's hand in silent support, pretending as if she didn't see the tears. 'You must be weary.' Alanna glanced at Patrick and asked, 'May I escort my cousin to my chamber where she can rest and refresh herself before the wedding in the morning?'

Mairead suspected it was simply an excuse to let her leave, and she was grateful for it.

Her father gave a nod of assent, and Alanna led her inside the fortress and up a narrow staircase.

'Are you all right?' Alanna asked in a low voice.

Mairead followed her up the stairs and into a tiny bedchamber. 'No. I am not.' She told her cousin about Balor's plan to help Liam escape and her fears that he would die.

She wanted to curl into a ball on the bed and sob out her heartache. Just like before, she felt helpless to do anything. And worse, Balor believed she was turning her back on him, that she was giving up.

Alanna put her arm around her, sitting beside her. 'Is there anything I can do for you?'

Mairead started to shake her head. She had to find a way to solve this problem herself. But no matter how she thought of ways to help Balor and Liam escape, she couldn't stop the sense of looming failure.

She understood Balor's intentions—if he escaped with her brother, then the king held no leverage over her, nothing that would force the marriage. But it was only a temporary solution. King John wanted a marriage alliance and would not stop until he achieved that goal.

Abruptly, she stared at her cousin through her tears and

straightened. Alanna had travelled for days, seemingly for no reason. But *was* there a way her cousin could help?

She tried not to get her hopes up, but she asked, 'Why did you really come to Blarnan, Alanna?'

Her cousin's expression softened. 'Maybe because I wanted to help you. When you were at Rionallís, I saw you with Balor. He was the man you saw through your May crown, wasn't he?'

Mairead didn't really understand why Alanna had brought it up. Did she believe that Fate or the gods had decreed that Balor was the man she was meant to be with?

'I believe he was,' she answered. He had been there that morn, watching over her. 'But that doesn't mean anything.'

And yet…she wondered if there was another reason for the question? She turned to Alanna, sensing something else. Her gaze sharpened. 'I saw you talking with the earl while I was at Rionallís.'

And there it was—the faint blush on her cousin's cheeks. 'What of your own future, Alanna?' Mairead ventured. 'Is there something you would wish for? Or *someone*?'

Her cousin raised her eyes, and Mairead saw the truth within them. And suddenly, the path ahead seemed clearer. She knew what she wanted for her own future—a different life. And maybe her cousin wanted the same thing—a change.

She'd let fear cloud her thinking in the past. She couldn't live her life based on that. Balor had accused her of having no faith in him. Maybe she needed to consider every path, not just the one that meant surrender.

Her mind started piecing together the choices ahead. And although she'd felt utterly trapped, forced into a marriage she didn't want, another idea took shape within her mind.

God help her, she seized upon it. It was reckless and dangerous. But maybe it would work.

'What are you thinking?' Alanna asked, her expression wary.

'I'm thinking about other ways to save my brother and Balor. And I no longer care what the English king wants. This is *my* life. *My* future.'

She was starting to understand how passive she'd become. She'd let Diarmud go off into battle, even knowing how inexperienced he was. And she'd cloaked herself in blame for his death. She couldn't stand aside and wait for someone else to make decisions for her.

'There is…another way,' Mairead said slowly. 'But we must speak with the earl first. He might be able to help us.'

Her cousin ventured a slight smile. 'What did you have in mind?'

The soldiers escorted Balor below ground, leaving Gerald and Sir Edward to stand guard. After they were alone, Sir Edward leaned in and spoke quietly. 'You'll stay here until nightfall when we make our move.'

Balor inclined his head, veiling his own frustration. He recoiled against the idea of leaving Mairead behind while he saved her brother—especially when they were trying to force her to marry the earl. He wanted to take Mairead away and damn the consequences—even taking her against her will. He couldn't imagine standing aside and doing nothing.

But *she* had to be the one to decide her fate, not him.

If he tried to steal her away from her wedding, it meant certain death. There were too many guards. Too many kings. He could do nothing without an army to back him up.

She didn't choose you, his mind warned. *You always knew she wouldn't.*

He'd nearly told her about his true father, Lord Beaumont, but something had stopped him. He didn't want this to be about status or nobility. Mairead had claimed it didn't matter whether he was a prince or a serf, but he needed to know if she'd meant it.

A darkness settled in his gut as he forced himself to face the inevitable. There was still the chance that he wasn't enough—that she didn't want to marry him and leave her family. And he might have to accept that.

Their last embrace haunted him still. She'd said she loved him as she'd wept. The words had resonated inside, filling up the hollow spaces of the lonely years. If she'd truly meant it, how could he walk away from her?

His mind settled upon the undeniable truth. Mairead still had the choice of whether to wed for duty or love. And if he took away that choice, then there was nothing left for them.

He would escape this place with her brother and undermine the kings' control over her. And when they could not force her to marry, Balor would know the truth of whether she truly wanted to be with him.

'Don't do anything reckless,' Gerald warned. 'I can see that you're considering it.'

The soldier wasn't wrong. But no matter how Balor considered a way to save Mairead, it came down to trust.

A fierce emptiness gripped him, for he had to walk away and hope that she loved him enough to stand firm and refuse the match. It was the greatest risk he'd ever imagined taking. Because he would likely lose her.

'There are two horses tethered in the woods outside the gate,' Sir Edward continued.

'Ride south towards the coast and hire a boat.' The knight gave him a handful of silver and paused. 'Unless you'd rather return with us now to Beaumont? You don't owe the MacEgans your loyalty.'

He'd considered it. But another part of him wanted to hold on to the barest hint of hope, that Mairead might choose to defy her family, unlikely though it might be. 'No. I'll bring the *tánaiste* back to Laochre first.'

The way Balor saw it, there was no other way to gain King Patrick's favour. If he helped Liam return, then there was the barest hope that he could win Mairead's hand in marriage. A thin thread, yes, but it was still a chance.

'I am grateful for your help,' Balor admitted to the Norman soldiers. 'Were it not for both of you, I would be dead already.' Somehow, he would ensure that these men were rewarded.

It seemed strange, leaving Éireann to become the bastard son of a man he hardly knew. He didn't think Beaumont had any other sons, so likely he could make a place for himself in the earl's household. It wasn't the life he'd anticipated, but it was all he had to offer Mairead if she refused Lord Lowell.

'We'll come for you at nightfall,' Edward said. 'I'll help you get outside the gates with Liam.'

Balor straightened, flexing his wrists against the ropes. 'Leave it to me.'

'Do you think this will work?' Liam asked quietly.

Balor pulled the chainmail shirt over his head. 'I do.'

Sir Edward and Gerald had removed the manacles and chains earlier. Then they'd brought armour so Balor and Liam could disguise themselves among the guards. During the next rotation, the pair of them would stand guard at the castle entrance. As long as they behaved like the other soldiers and kept their features hidden in the darkness, no one would notice.

The armour was heavy, and Balor grimaced at the weight of it against his wounds. It was the cowl and helm that hurt the most, though he bore the pain.

Liam struggled with his own armour and then glanced at him. 'We're a pair, aren't we? I feel a thousand years old.'

So did Balor, but his weariness was more about his regret for what he'd said to Mairead. He'd let his pride get in the way, and he'd lashed out without meaning to. But the thought of losing her was worse than he could ever have imagined.

Even now, he remembered the softness of her hair, the scent of her skin. He remembered what it was to love her, to hear her soft sighs as he'd touched her. It was killing him to imagine her wedding someone else.

'Can you ride?' he asked Liam.

The *tánaiste* gave a nod. 'I'll do whatever I must to get home again.' He leaned back against the wall. 'I need to see my wife and the children.' After a pause, he said, 'I owe you my life, Ó Phelan. I would have been dead if you hadn't found me that night.'

'It's lucky I did,' Balor admitted.

After a slight pause, the *tánaiste* asked, 'Why *did* you travel all this way to help me?'

'Because your sister asked me to,' he answered honestly. The truth was he would have done anything Mairead wanted. There didn't need to be any other reason.

'You care for her, don't you?'

He nodded. 'I do, aye. But it doesn't matter. Your father would never allow us to marry.' His words exposed the bitterness he felt, and he didn't care. For it didn't matter. One way or the other, Mairead would make her choice. And so would he, by bringing her brother home to claim his throne.

Liam seemed to consider the answer. Then he asked, 'What reward do you want for saving my life?'

There was only one thing he wanted, but Balor said, 'What I want is something you cannot give.'

He wanted Mairead as his wife. He wanted to give her children, to hear their laughter in their home. And he wanted to love her.

'I am sorry,' Liam said solemnly. 'If it means anything at all, I will ensure that my father knows all that you've done for me and my family.'

Balor thought about it again and said, 'There is something else. If it's within your power to grant this, I want Fergus removed as chieftain. Especially after what he did to you.'

'Oh, he will be removed, rest assured.' Liam's voice held a quiet threat. 'Were you hoping to take his place?'

Balor shook his head. 'My half brother should replace him. If Kenneth becomes chieftain, it's enough for me.'

'What about you?' Liam asked. 'Where will you go?'

'I am going back to England.'

There had been a time when he never would have considered returning to Beaumont, even though he'd learned how to fight there. But he no longer belonged in Éireann. The thought of staying here, where every familiar place evoked memories of Mairead, wasn't possible anymore. Better to begin anew somewhere else.

Liam cast a sidelong look at him. 'Why England?'

Balor hesitated, wondering whether to tell him the truth. In the end, he admitted, 'Because I am the bastard son of a Norman lord. He sent two of his men to bring me back—

they are the soldiers helping us tonight. I've been offered a home there.'

'What of your family here?'

Balor shrugged. 'No one will miss the Demon of Éireann.'

The *tánaiste* regarded him with a long look. 'I am grateful for your help, Ó Phelan. And I will do what I can. Whether that means helping your brother or helping you.' After a pause, he asked, 'Who is your father?'

'William Fleming de Beaumont.'

Liam's expression turned interested. 'You're *Beaumont's* bastard son? Our family is on good terms with him.'

Before he could say anything further, Sir Edward and Gerald arrived. Both wore chainmail armour with conical helms and swords at their waist. The older knight said quietly, 'It's time. Walk to the main gate and take your positions. Hurry.'

'Won't they ask questions about who we are?' Liam asked.

'I told them King John's men would guard the gate, so they don't need to recognize you. You'll stay for a time, and when Gerald and I approach, you'll go through the gates while we take your places. No one will question it.'

Balor set aside his chains, but he couldn't stop the wariness or the sense of danger that kept his gaze fixed upon the spiral stairs in the distance. Liam, too, shadowed the wall as they joined the Norman soldiers.

Abruptly, torches flared at the end of the hall, and they froze in place as soldiers emerged in the darkness. Balor couldn't tell how many men were descending the stairs—possibly four. He recognized one of them as a guard who had kept watch over them yestereve and today. The man immediately unsheathed his weapon and regarded them. 'Trying to escape, are you?'

Sir Edward and Gerald unsheathed their weapons, stepping forward. Balor inwardly cursed that he had only the small blade Mairead had given him. It would have to be enough until he could disarm one of them.

Balor lunged forward and slashed his blade, drawing blood. The fighting blurred around him, but he released his frustration and rage. Every emotion brimming within him descended into this fight. He wasn't going to let these be his last moments. Not while he was still breathing.

He charged forward, dodging a blow while Gerald blocked a strike meant for him.

Balor seized his assailant's shield, barely in time to defend another slice towards his head. But he used the wooden shield as its own weapon, swinging it hard until the soldier crashed to the ground. Sir Edward was struggling, and Balor ignored the protests of his body, reaching for a sword.

This was more than a fight to live—it was a fight against those who despised him, against those who would keep him from the future he wanted with Mairead at his side.

He unleashed himself, guarding Liam and Sir Edward while Gerald fought alongside him. And when the soldiers lay wounded or dead on the ground, Balor kept his weapon drawn, blood spilling over the blade.

'Put the survivors in chains,' Liam advised.

'We'll take care of it,' Sir Edward vowed. 'You need to go now before anyone else arrives.'

Footsteps approached, and Balor led Liam up the ladder, keeping his hand upon his stolen sword. Darkness cloaked the keep with only a few torches set in iron sconces. Liam stumbled slightly, and ahead of them, Balor spied King Patrick. The man's eyes widened as he recognized his son. But a heartbeat later, Patrick took a step towards them, drawing the dagger at his waist.

The world seemed to shift slightly, and Balor sensed the subtle threat. Time stilled, and he seized Liam, pulling him out of the way just as the king threw his blade.

The weapon struck its mark—in the heart of the soldier who had slipped behind them, his own weapon raised to cut them down. The man fell backwards towards the shadowed tower where he had stood poised to strike.

Gods above, the king had just saved their lives.

Balor raised a knee in silent deference, and Patrick met their gaze for a moment, giving his own nod as they approached the gates.

But as he took his place to guard the castle, Balor glanced towards the battlements. And there, he saw Mairead speaking softly to Lord Lowell. Behind her stood her cousin, Alanna.

Jealousy settled in Balor's gut as he watched over the woman who had captured his own heart and claimed it for her own. From her intent conversation and bearing, he watched as she took the earl's hand.

She didn't at all look like a woman who intended to walk away from a marriage of duty. He pushed aside the angry hurt and told himself it was only what he deserved. It didn't matter what choice she'd made.

That choice wasn't him. And he simply had to live with it.

Chapter Twelve

The next morning, a cold dullness seemed to encircle Mairead, distancing her from those around her. The wedding was prepared, and the guests were gathered outside the small chapel. She waited beside her cousin Alanna, who was clad in her own finery.

'Are you certain about this?' Although Mairead tried to keep her courage up, her nerves tangled up inside her.

Her cousin's hands were as cold as her own. 'I am. And though this path is a troubled one for you, it is the right one. I believe that.'

Mairead embraced her cousin. 'We've always been there for each other from the moment I was a small child. And… although this is a risk, maybe you'll find love, too, one day.'

'It's unlikely.' Alanna's voice held a hint of sadness. 'I know what they say about me. Everyone believes I am mad.'

'Not everyone,' Mairead reassured her. 'You were always one of my favourite cousins.'

Alanna gave a slight nod, though her expression grew strained. She took a deep breath and ventured, 'Are you ready for what lies ahead?'

'No,' she answered honestly. 'I'm more afraid of what will happen this day than anything else I've ever done.'

'You needn't be,' Alanna said. 'All the wedding arrangements are in place. But in the end, you still have a choice. If you don't want to do this—'

'No matter what I decide, it's the wrong choice.' And the slightest defiance could mean Balor's death. She couldn't bear for that to happen, regardless of his wishes.

His words haunted her even now, with his demand that she refuse the match and marry him instead. She wanted to, with everything in her. The idea of sharing her life with Balor filled her with such bittersweet joy, even if it meant leaving her family. But she didn't know if it could ever happen.

She gripped her cousin's hand for silent support, and Alanna ventured a smile. 'It will be all right, I promise you. Lord Lowell is a good man.'

Mairead took a deep breath and gave a nod. She was careful as they descended the spiral stairs and walked towards the open doors outside where the ceremony would be held before the later feasting in the Hall.

Rain was pouring outside, and Alanna lifted up her hood to hide her hair and face. 'This is a good omen.'

'It is.' Mairead raised her own hood and stepped away from her cousin. King John of England sat a goodly distance away with her father on a covered dais while Lord Lowell stood close to the chapel doors.

Then she walked towards the earl alone, her face and hair concealed by the hood, to take her place as the bride.

After sailing all night, the coastline of Laochre emerged in the morning sunlight. Liam had slept for part of the journey, leaving Balor troubled with thoughts of Mairead. The cold wind cut into him, but he didn't feel it at all.

As he stared out into the bleak grey morning, he forced himself to face the truth. She'd likely married the earl since none of the soldiers had pursued them thus far. There was an emptiness at the thought, a gnawing ache of loneliness that he pushed aside.

She'd told him she loved him. And he hadn't given back the words, hadn't told her the raw feelings in his own heart.

He'd let his pride get in the way, accusing her of martyrdom when she'd only been trying to save him. The bitter emptiness flooded through him with regret.

He wished he could tell her the words now.

Maybe he hadn't said them because he didn't believe that this beautiful, kind woman could ever love someone like him. He didn't really know what love was—but he knew he would walk through fire for Mairead.

He would never forget the way she'd made him feel, the moments of joy in her arms, no matter how fleeting. Her smile would haunt him until he drew his last breath.

All he could do was harden his heart to the emptiness. He would save her brother before he returned to England to live an unknown future without her. And perhaps one day, he would learn to let her go.

As dawn broke across the horizon, dying torches lined the island fortress of Ennisleigh, lighting a path towards the channel near the mainland. The water was calm with only the slightest waves lapping against the shore. Behind them, the sky was creased with rose and amber as the sun began to rise.

The boat reached the edge of the pier, and Balor tied it off, securing the vessel. He followed the *tánaiste*, keeping his hand upon his sword. The morning sunlight lifted above the horizon, illuminating the fields as he walked up the hillside behind Liam. When they reached the top of the outcropping, the limestone walls of Laochre Castle gleamed in the distance.

They walked through the fields in silence, but as they drew closer, Liam changed his direction away from the gates and led them towards a small, thatched roundhouse on the outer edge. When they walked inside the small hut, it appeared deserted.

'Why are we stopping here?' Balor asked.

'Something's wrong.' Liam glanced over at the castle. 'It's too quiet. I want to find out what's happening inside Laochre.'

Balor paused to listen and realized the *tánaiste* was right. There should have been more voices, the sounds of activity or even the low hum of conversation. Instead, it did seem unnaturally quiet.

Liam raised up an opening in the floor and revealed a ladder that went down into an underground storage chamber. 'This leads underground towards the castle. Follow me.'

Balor climbed down below, and Liam moved storage baskets out of the way, shoving against a wall until a passageway opened.

Then he stopped to regard Balor. 'I'll need your help once we're inside. If anyone—Fergus especially—has harmed my wife or if my children are in any danger, I will end him.'

'My sword is yours,' Balor agreed.

But before they continued through the passageway, Liam studied him. 'I think many people misjudged you, Ó Phelan. I'll admit that I was wrong. You would have been a strong defender for my sister.'

'I would have died for her,' Balor said quietly.

Liam reached out and gripped his arm. 'I'd rather have you among my fighting men. If you would rather stay here, instead of in England with Beaumont, I would offer you a place here, at Laochre.'

He understood that it was honour being asked, but it was too soon to make that decision. He needed to know what sort of future lay ahead for him. And he didn't know if he could stand to see Mairead married to someone else. It might be better to remain in England.

But for now, he said, 'I will think on it.'

Then he followed the *tánaiste* into the castle, neither knowing what lay ahead.

Mairead sat within the boat, her back rigid as they approached Laochre. Inside, she felt numb to everything that had happened. It was as if she were living another woman's life, and she could feel the shadow of uneasiness. Her father sat beside her while their men rowed behind them. In the king's bearing, she perceived his own unrest.

She and Alanna had upended King John's plans—but it was her cousin who had taken the greatest risk and had married Lord Lowell in her place.

Mairead had been startled that the earl had agreed to their proposition the night before the wedding. But Lord Lowell and Alanna were closer in age, and it seemed that there *was* the foundation of a friendship between them. She hadn't realized that they had talked together on several occasions. She suspected that Alanna *did* care for Lord Lowell. And maybe both would find joy in their union.

Alanna had wanted to wed the earl, unlike herself.

After the two had married the next morn, her cousin's happiness had been undeniable. The earl, too, seemed satisfied with the match.

King John had been furious at their wedding switch, but he could not deny that a MacEgan alliance had taken place, just as he'd wanted. The only trace of acceptance amid the king's rage was the fact that he had let them go. She'd learned from her father that Liam and Balor had left the castle the night before, so both were free.

But even so, Mairead knew she had weakened her father's position. And she didn't know what that meant for them now.

When she glanced at Patrick, she saw the weariness in his eyes as they approached the coast. His face held the lines of so many years, and from the way he stared towards Laochre, she could tell that he was missing Isabel.

Mairead had always admired her parents' union. No, she hadn't obeyed King John's command. But how could she, when her own parents knew what love was? She wanted that kind of marriage for herself. And no matter that the earl had been kind, it hadn't been fair to him, either.

'You didn't sleep last night, did you?' her father said at last, breaking the silence.

She shook her head. 'No.' How could she when she didn't know whether Balor had arrived safely? Until she saw him with her own eyes, the worry would remain.

Although Patrick hadn't blamed her for refusing Lord Lowell, she didn't truly know what would happen now. It didn't matter if she had to give up the life of a king's daughter. She was willing to live in poverty if it meant being with the man she loved. But did Balor love her in return? He'd never said the words.

Perhaps it was time to simply be honest with her father. 'Balor asked me to marry him, the night before he left.'

She didn't miss her father's tension, but Patrick ventured, 'And did you agree?'

Her feelings were held together by the barest thread. 'If he's still alive, I do want that. If he'll still have me.'

Her father chose his words carefully. 'I've only ever wanted what's best for you, Mairead. I want you to be happy.'

'So do I,' she managed. But at least he hadn't said anything about Balor or disapproving of him. It gave her a trace of hope.

When they reached the pier, her father helped her out of the boat while one of their men tied up the vessel. They walked along the path leading up the hillside, and it wasn't long before they were greeted by a few men with horses.

'King Patrick, you must hurry,' one of the men said as he dismounted. 'The *brehons* and chiefs held a gathering, and they have brought out the stone chair to choose a new king.'

'What of Liam?' Patrick asked. 'Is he here?'

The soldier's face turned grim. 'We have not seen him. But Fergus Ó Phelan is attempting to claim the throne for himself.'

'I won't allow that. Not while I am still the king.' Patrick mounted his horse before he turned to them. 'No one will take my throne before I willingly give it up.' He squared his shoulders and leaned in to urge his horse faster.

Mairead followed behind, but worry rooted within her. Where were Liam and Balor? They had left earlier, so they should already be here. But if no one had seen her brother, what did that mean? The knot of worry tightened inside, threatening to choke her.

As they approached Laochre, the sun rose higher in the sky, but the air held a bitter coldness. The moment her father reached the gates, the soldiers raised a knee as a gesture of respect. They stepped aside to let him ride through, and Mairead followed. She held back from her father and saw that the stone chair had indeed been brought to the center of the inner bailey.

A crowd of MacEgans had gathered in the inner bailey, but she did not see her family among them, which only intensified her fear.

Fergus Ó Phelan stood at the top of the stairs, and when the chieftain spied them, his mouth curved in a smile. Orla stood behind her husband. She wore a grim expression on her face, revealing the hatred she felt towards Fergus.

'Patrick,' the chieftain greeted him. 'We didn't expect to see you so soon.'

'That much is clear, Fergus,' her father answered. 'I believe it's time you returned to Dunmalus.'

Dread gripped Mairead's stomach as Patrick approached the chieftain alone. Everything within her tensed, and she scanned the soldiers, searching for Balor. What if…he and Liam hadn't escaped? What if something had happened to them?

The environment within Laochre was charged with fear, and she didn't know who was truly in command. Why weren't her father's men attacking Fergus?

Mairead discreetly dismounted her horse and slipped back towards the stone inner wall while everyone else was distracted. Her heart thundered in her chest, and right now she didn't trust anyone. She kept her back to the wall, moving slowly to the first guard tower. The MacEgan soldiers rested their hands on their swords, as if to protect her, when she passed by them.

But as she drew close to the second tower entrance, her back pressed against the wall and a strong arm pulled her inside. Before she could make a sound, she saw Balor's face in the darkness. He wore chainmail armour and was alive and whole.

Mairead threw herself into his arms and gripped him hard, a sob escaping her. 'You're here.' Her heart flooded with relief and love as he returned the embrace. She hadn't known how much she'd needed to see him until now.

There was tension in his bearing, even as he stroked her hair back. 'I'm here.' He slowly released her from the embrace and asked quietly, 'Where is your…husband?'

So that was the reason for his hesitancy. She reached out to touch his cheek as she faced him. 'I didn't marry the earl. Alanna did.' Her voice broke, but there was not time to tell him all the words caught inside her.

In the darkness, he covered her hand with his own. Against her mouth, he murmured, 'Thank God.' Then he kissed her, and his mouth was a healing balm, soothing the pain of the past two days. She yielded to him, holding his body close to hers.

'I'm glad you didn't wed him,' Balor said. 'Because I want you to marry me when this is over.'

'Yes,' she whispered. 'No matter what happens.'

His mouth descended on hers again, claiming another reckless kiss as she held him in the darkness. Balor's tongue slid against hers, and the familiar aching need stole her breath and weakened her knees. She wanted this man, craved his touch on her bare skin.

With reluctance, he broke off the kiss, his arms still around her waist. 'Stay here, where it's safe,' he warned. 'This isn't finished yet.'

'My brother—' she started to ask.

'Liam took Adriana and your mother to Rionallís, along with his children. He's gathering forces with his uncle and will bring back more soldiers.'

A tremulous smile broke over her with relief. But then he stepped back and raised his hood. 'Stay alive, Mairead.'

Her emotions brimmed over with thankfulness, even as she feared what would happen now. Though she understood he needed to confront Fergus to set aside the shadows of his past, she didn't know what dangers lay ahead.

She stepped to the edge of the tower entrance to listen. The chieftain was still speaking to her father, but her attention was fully focused on Balor.

'I have been chosen as the new King of Laochre,' Fergus continued. 'The *brehons* have spoken.'

There was an icy rage upon her father's face. 'I have not surrendered my crown,' Patrick argued. 'And you are not the king, Fergus.' To his men, he ordered, 'Escort him outside the castle gates.'

The captain of the MacEgan soldiers unsheathed his sword and strode forward to obey the order, determination lining his face. But before he reached the stairs, an arrow struck him in the back.

The captain crumpled to the ground, and several women screamed, huddling against the rest of the crowd.

Mairead bit back her own cry and sank back against the wall, her pulse pounding with terror. Enemies surrounded them everywhere, and now she understood why the soldiers were hesitant to intervene. If Ó Phelan archers had taken command of the parapets, more would die if they dared defend the MacEgans.

'Do you see what happens to those who defy me?' Fergus said. He began walking down the stairs, towards the stone chair.

She pressed her knuckles to her mouth, her gaze searching for Balor. But instead of moving within the crowd towards Fergus, he disappeared into one of the towers. She knew, then, what he was doing—removing the threat of the archers.

Fergus was speaking again, but she paid him no heed, instead watching the cloaked figure as Balor moved across the parapets. Just as another archer took aim to release another arrow, Balor shoved him over the edge. The man's body hit the ground, bleeding out.

Cries of shock broke out in the crowd before they realized the dead man was the archer who had shot the captain. A second archer crumpled upon the parapets in silence, his bow falling. The third dropped his weapons and fled.

Balor's swift vengeance had had made its mark, unsettling the Ó Phelans. He'd earned his reputation as the Demon of Éireann.

But she didn't fear him. This was the man who had travelled with her for days, across land and sea, to keep her safe. The same man she'd held in her arms while he'd stared at her as if she was the reason his heart kept beating.

And the man she had welcomed into her body, joining with him until her pleasure took her under, drowning her in the feeling of his skin against hers.

She loved Balor more than she'd ever thought possible. Mairead unsheathed her own blade and emerged from the shadows. She would fight to be with him, no matter the cost. And she began walking towards her father.

The crowd grew restless, now that the seeds of chaos had been sown. Fergus was trying to call out orders, but no one was listening.

Instead, Balor crossed through the crowd as he forged a path towards Fergus. 'You will never be King of Laochre or any king of mine.' His voice was strong and clear, breaking through the noise of the crowd. He unsheathed a sword with his right hand, keeping his shield in his left.

Balor was buying time, trying to distract Fergus while Liam had gone to Rionallís to gather forces. But it left him alone to defend Patrick's crown with the remainder of the MacEgan men. And with the Ó Phelans closing in, he didn't know how much time they had left before reinforcements arrived.

The unrest of the MacEgan crowd was what they needed now, to weaken Fergus and distract the Ó Phelans.

'You will never wear a crown,' he told Fergus. 'Not when the rightful king is standing before you. You should leave now while you're still breathing.'

When he risked a look back at King Patrick, he found Mairead standing beside her father.

Sunlight illuminated her face, and she wore a dark cloak and a rose-colored gown. Her dark hair was braided back, the wind sliding the loose strands against her cheeks.

An ache caught inside him at the sight of her, along with a fierce burst of hope. He could see the worry in her expression, but he wasn't afraid—he had a reason to fight. She had defied her family for their sake. And that realization was a flame igniting his sense of purpose.

King Patrick stared back at him, as if taking his measure. Then the MacEgan soldiers gathered around their king in silent defence. Balor knew what that meant—they would not intervene in this fight. But he intended to face the chieftain and end Fergus's reign once and for all.

He kept his sword steady, circling the chieftain. Waiting for the first strike.

Fergus slashed his own blade downward, and their swords rang out in the stillness. Balor blocked the strikes with his shield, just as he slashed with his own blade.

'Why would you believe you can win this fight, Balor?' Fergus taunted. 'My men will defend me and cut you down.'

Two Ó Phelans charged up the stairs, but Balor's blade flowed like water, cutting through flesh and bone as he moved. Bodies slumped to the ground, but it was a familiar dance with death. And one he intended to win.

Fergus had always been a strong fighter, ruthless in his methods. He didn't seem to care about the fallen men but swung his sword again. As steel clashed against steel, Balor remembered the frightened boy he'd once been, years ago. That boy was gone now, honed by Norman training from the man who was his true father—the man who had once shown pride in Balor's skills.

'You'll never win,' Fergus taunted. With a glance at the people surrounding them, he added, 'No one will fight for you. You're nothing but a bastard no one wanted.'

The words were meant to be another slice at his pride. But the word *bastard* no longer stung, as it once had. Lord Beaumont had sent men to find him and bring him back. And now Balor had a possible future to offer Mairead. Even if she was the only person who ever wanted him, it would be enough.

More of the Ó Phelans closed in, their forces locked together with spears while the MacEgans remained to guard Patrick and Mairead. And when he saw the resolution on their faces, he suddenly understood that Fergus intended for him to continue fighting his own kinsmen, killing them while everyone watched.

'This isn't your fight,' he warned the Ó Phelan men. 'Stay back.' Several understood and obeyed.

'Balor!'

Mairead's voice was a sharp warning. And before he could react, he felt the iron kiss of a spear against the back of his neck.

Chapter Thirteen

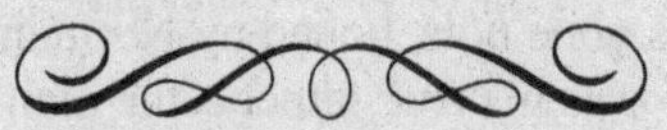

Mairead froze at the fighter who had used the distraction to move into place with his spear. Fergus Ó Phelan held his sword on the other side of Balor's neck, and the sight of it shattered her. Even if Balor fought back, he was outnumbered.

Her father's men would never reach him in time. Bile rose up in her throat, and she'd never been so furious—or helpless—in all her life. In that moment, she grew aware of every person within Laochre, every enemy and every ally.

'You've been a problem since the moment you were born,' Fergus said to Balor. 'Now I'm going to end your life—and she can watch.'

Not again. She had already lost one man she'd cared for, even if it hadn't truly been love. Her heart completely belonged to Balor Ó Phelan, and if she lost him, it would shatter her. Of every man here, he'd had the courage to stand up for her father. And he didn't deserve to die for it.

She refused to stand back and do nothing. Mairead unsheathed her own blade, even as three men stepped closer to keep her away from the fight. 'Let me go!'

Balor was staring at her as if he held no regrets. There was resignation in his posture, and yet, his face held peace.

'Mairead, if your face is the last one I see in this world, it's enough for me.'

'It's not enough for me,' she shot back.

She tried to lunge towards him, but someone else caught her from behind. 'Don't move, Mairead.' She struggled, only to realize it was her brother, Liam, who was now holding her back. The people murmured among themselves, while her father's relief was palpable.

Soldiers poured into the inner bailey, led by her uncle Bevan, fully armed and prepared to kill anyone who threatened their family.

And among them was Kenneth Ó Phelan. Fergus appeared stunned by the sight, and he hesitated with his blade.

Mairead fought to break free, but her brother's grip only tightened. His gaze locked on the men, and he pressed her behind him. Although she realized he was keeping the Ó Phelans distracted, giving the MacEgan men time to move into place, her heart was breaking.

'Liam, I beg you, help Balor.' This wasn't supposed to be their ending. She was supposed to marry Balor, waking beside him each morn, and building a life at his side. Perhaps having children of their own.

The tears slid down her cheeks as she stared back at him. Balor believed he was about to die. And she simply couldn't accept it.

Kenneth stepped forward and called out to his father, 'Let my brother go.'

Fergus dug his blade into the side of Balor's neck and blood welled against his skin. 'No.'

Mairead's scream of anguish caught in the back of her throat as she pressed her fist to her own mouth, horrified at the thought of watching him die.

Then suddenly, Fergus froze, the sword falling from his

hands. His face paled, and he dropped to his knees, blood spilling over him. The other soldier spun with his spear, only to see Orla standing behind the body of her husband, gripping a blade. She paled, her husband's blood covering her shaking hands.

Balor took advantage of the distraction and disarmed the soldier, forcing him back. The man raised his hands in surrender as he retreated.

Balor turned to his mother, and Orla gripped her waist, as if she couldn't believe what she'd done. For a moment, she looked as if she wanted to embrace her son but didn't dare move.

'Are you…all right?' Orla asked, her voice barely above a whisper. Balor gave a nod.

At that, Mairead broke free of Liam's hold and ran across the space, not even caring about the other soldiers as she threw herself into Balor's arms. He gripped her tightly, breathing in the scent of her hair as she embraced him.

'I love you,' he murmured against her cheek. 'I should have said it sooner.'

She wept in his arms, and he kissed her, even as they were surrounded by the MacEgans. 'I love you, too. Don't ever let me go.'

'I won't,' he promised, resting his forehead against hers. 'I'll steal you away if I have to, and I won't give you back. No one will come between us again.'

She couldn't seem to get close enough to him, needing to feel his body against hers. 'I'm never leaving you again. Wherever you go, I go.' She didn't care if she had to live in poverty for the rest of her life. If Balor was with her, she would be the richest woman in the world.

He embraced her tightly, and she was dimly aware of

the Ó Phelan men pulling back, surrendering to the MacEgan fighters.

Her father stepped forward and straightened. The moment King Patrick faced the Ó Phelans, they dropped to their knees. 'After your rebellion, you don't deserve to live.' His voice was filled with fury. 'But you will each receive a fair trial, and the *brehons* will judge your guilt or innocence.'

Patrick turned his attention to Balor. Mairead clung to the man she loved, prepared to fight for him. But before the king could speak, Liam interrupted, saying, 'I owe my life to Balor Ó Phelan. And he deserves to be rewarded for his bravery today.' With a faint smile, he suggested, 'Perhaps the hand of my sister in marriage?'

Mairead couldn't stop her radiant smile. Her father's gaze softened upon them, and he nodded his permission. 'After the Demon of Éireann fought for us, he has proven his loyalty.'

Joy broke through her at his words, and she smiled through her tears. 'Thank you,' she breathed. She held Balor fiercely, feeling as if the broken pieces of her heart had mended together at last.

'I will provide a place for them here, at Laochre,' Patrick offered.

'They likely won't need it,' Liam interrupted. Mairead didn't understand what her brother meant, but he continued, 'Balor *is* the bastard son of the Earl of Beaumont, after all.'

She pulled back to stare at Balor. His expression turned slightly uncomfortable, but he murmured, 'It's true. I only just learned of it.' He brushed a hand over her hair and added, 'But if you would rather live in Éireann instead of England…'

'I don't care where we live,' she answered, tracing her fingers along his jaw. 'As long as we're together.'

He kissed her again, and there were cheers and applause all around them. When the noise died down, Orla stepped forward. She was gripping her hands together, but she spoke up loud enough for everyone to hear. 'Balor is not a bastard.'

She cast an apologetic look towards her son, and Mairead tightened her embrace around Balor.

'What are you trying to say?' Patrick asked. The question seemed to hang within the space, the weight of their future lying in the balance.

'I mean that Balor is the legitimate son of Lord William Fleming de Beaumont. My husband.'

Within her arms, Mairead could feel the change in Balor's posture. There was tension there, laced with shock.

'Tell me everything.' Balor's voice held iron as he stared at his mother.

Orla walked forward, her steps heavy. She faced him, and in her eyes, Balor read the heartbreak. 'I…met William when he travelled here twenty years ago.' A flush suffused her face, and she admitted, 'I loved him from the moment I met him. We married in secret at Fearna, and he gave me a silver ring.'

Balor's hand moved into Mairead's hair, and he stroked it gently, even as he listened to his mother's story. It felt as if he were standing outside himself, as if none of it were real. If he was the earl's legitimate son—then it meant that her marriage to Fergus had been invalid.

And she'd known that. She'd always known. Why had Orla stayed with him for so long?

His anger started to rise, but then Mairead rested her cheek against his heart, lacing his hands with hers. She calmed him, and he realized that none of it mattered anymore. Anger wouldn't change the past, but if he was the heir to an earldom, then he could now give Mairead the life he'd always wanted her to have.

Orla straightened, clenching her hands together. 'For weeks, we were so happy together until the Ó Phelans attacked William and his men.'

Pain laced her words, but she continued, 'I stayed away from the fighting, and the only way I could save William's life was with a lie.' Her tone grew heavy, filled with sadness. 'I told Fergus I had been violated by one of the Normans and begged him to keep me safe.'

Her voice grew thick with more tears. 'He believed me, and he was so distracted that they escaped by boat.'

Orla openly wept and added, 'I was terrified that, even if I did find a way to reach Beaumont, no one would believe me. Why would an earl wed a poor Irish maiden?' She straightened slightly and added, 'I—I told myself that William was lost to me now. All I had left of him was his child. And so, I pretended to marry Fergus. I needed his protection since my own family lived so far away. I tried to make the best of the life I had, even though it wasn't with the man I wanted.'

In her words, Balor could hear the wrenching heartache. Although he'd hated her for treating him differently from Kenneth, he was starting to understand that she, too, had suffered.

Mairead reached up to touch his cheek, and he covered her hand, bringing it to his lips. And he understood her silent reassurance. Unlike his mother, they *had* fought for a life together. Even if he'd had nothing at all, he would never stop fighting for the woman he loved. He was hers, just as she was his.

He traced his hand over Mairead's face. It seemed impossible that he had won the heart of a king's daughter, that she had defied her family to be with him. But he would spend each day of the rest of his life making her happy.

Tears streamed down Orla's face as she turned towards Balor. 'I am so sorry for the way Fergus treated you. And for my cowardice.'

Some of Balor's frustration eased, knowing that Orla's decision to remain silent was borne out of fear. So many years had been lost.

'Why didn't you send me to England sooner?' he asked.

'Because Fergus wouldn't allow it. I was so afraid of him. But…after that time when he beat you so badly, I knew if I didn't send you away, he would kill you one day,' she answered. 'I had to give you up, to save you.'

'You sent me with your wedding ring, didn't you? That was what you wanted me to give the earl.'

She nodded. 'I wanted William to know who you were.'

'I never showed it to him,' Balor admitted. 'Not until I left the ring behind, just before I returned to Éireann.' He'd been so angry with Orla for abandoning him, and yet, the ring was the only thing he'd had left of her. Surrendering it had felt like letting go of the life he'd known. After a slight pause, he asked, 'Do you want to see Beaumont again?'

His mother closed her eyes, as if gathering her emotions. 'I've made so many mistakes over the years because of fear. I am guilty of the sin of adultery and abandoning my marriage. Even if I came to England, William wouldn't want me now.'

'If you want to go, we will take you there,' Balor offered. 'And you can decide what to do after that.'

Orla seemed so broken, but she gave a weary nod. 'So be it.'

* * *

Mairead stared outside the window in her chamber while the moonlight shone over the keep. Her father and brother had begun making plans for Liam's coronation, which would be held within a few weeks, followed by her wedding to Balor.

She could hardly believe it. It was even stranger to realize that Balor was the son and heir of an earl. But she would have married him, even if he'd been nothing but a serf.

A faint knock caught her attention, and she pulled a warm *brat* to cover her linen shift. When she opened the door, Balor was standing there. 'I needed to see you, Mairead.'

She smiled at him and opened the door wider. 'Come here.' After he was inside, she lowered the bar to give them privacy.

Silvery moonlight spilled across his handsome features. He drew her into his arms, and she held him close as she murmured, 'I don't know if I can wait to be married to you.'

'Oh, we won't be waiting, *a mhuirnín*,' he said. 'I came here with the intent of spending all hours of the night with my mouth upon your skin.'

His wicked words sent a rush of sensation through her. But she touched his face and asked the question that had been bothering her for so long. 'Have you forgiven me, Balor? For what happened in the past…' Her words broke off as she chose them carefully.

He captured her mouth, pulling her body close until his hardness rested against her softness. 'The past doesn't matter anymore. I'm going to spend every day of the rest of our lives loving you.' He cupped her nape and spoke against her mouth. 'Starting tonight, if you're willing.'

His hand moved against her breast, gently stroking it

through the delicate linen. Her body reacted instantly, rising against his touch as she went liquid between her legs.

In answer, Mairead let the *brat* slide from her shoulders. Then she loosened the ties of her shift and let it fall away until she stood naked before him. She needed him to lie with her this night, to drive away the shadows and remind her of the happiness yet to come.

Balor stripped away his leather armour and tunic, followed by his weapons and trews. And when he, too, was naked before her, she couldn't resist the urge to touch him. Hunger roared through her, along with the thankfulness that he was here with her now.

'Do you remember the day I first rescued you?' he asked as he drew her towards her bed. 'The day I tried to take you away?'

'Yes.' Her words were breathless as he slid his hands over her breasts, caressing the nipples with his thumbs.

'I didn't want to give you back,' he admitted. 'I saw you once when we were children, and you waved at me. I never forgot that, and I think I always wanted you to be mine.'

'I am yours now,' she said softly. 'And always will be.'

He drew his hands to her waist, then pulled her tightly against him. She loved the feeling of his hard body against her own.

'I never imagined you would love someone like me.' He caressed her spine, stealing another kiss.

She cupped his face and looked into his eyes. 'How could I not? When you saw me as a woman and not a king's daughter?'

A smile caught his mouth as he continued guiding her back towards the bed. He pressed her to sit and asked, 'Do you know what a man must do when he's with a king's daughter?'

A sudden rise of nerves caught her, but she shook her head. 'He has to kneel.'

And with that, he laid her back, pulling her legs to rest on his shoulders as he knelt at the foot of her bed.

His breath warmed her intimate flesh, and the anticipation made her body yearn for his touch. He kissed her inner thigh, and she bit her lip, trying to gather the shreds of her own control.

But when he used his tongue to worship her, tasting her flesh, she let out a shattering moan and arched against him. Her fingers dug into her coverlet as he feasted, and never in her life had she felt so powerless…and yet, he was doing this for her. With his mouth, he kissed her softly, sucking against the bundle of nerves while his wicked tongue invaded.

She went over the edge within moments, heat and wild sensation pulsing through her until she was hardly able to breathe. She cried out in gratitude as the release tore through her.

Then he kissed a path up her stomach as his erection came into contact between her thighs. She tried to reach for him, but he pinned her wrists above her head.

'This is what I've been dreaming of since the first night I touched you.' He leaned his weight against her, and she yearned to join their bodies together. His mouth covered one breast while he teased the other nipple, and she felt the slow burn of another release rising within her.

'I've wanted to taste every part of you,' he said, moving his mouth to the other breast.

'So have I,' she answered, gripping his hair. He suckled her nipples, his fingers sliding into her wetness. 'I want to take you into my mouth.' She imagined running her tongue over his thick length, savouring him.

'Later,' he promised, before he began a gentle thrusting rhythm with his fingers. He teased her with shallow strokes before his fingers slid in deep. But even as he pleasured her, she whispered the words he needed to hear.

'You are the man I've been waiting for, all my life, Balor. And I want nothing more than to be at your side. I love you with everything I am. And everything I have yet to become.'

He groaned as she found his velvet length at last, caressing him with her palm and guiding him to her entrance. His face turned pained with ecstasy as she used her thumb to coat the essence of him against the blunt head.

'I love you, Mairead.' His words turned into a blend of Gaelic and Norman endearments. And when she squeezed him, he rewarded her by finding her slick opening and driving in deep. He found a rhythm, thrusting until she lost where he ended and she began.

God above, she loved the feeling of his body inside hers. But more than that, his gaze burned into hers, his blue eyes captivating her.

'You're mine,' he said. And he slowed down, lifting her hips with one hand while he gently pressed against her stomach with the other. The sensation intensified, her body rising and falling with the rhythm of his thrusts. As he made love to her, she could only squeeze him from within, meeting his body with her own.

When the second wave of release broke over her, her body erupted against his. He seemed insatiable, his mouth everywhere, while his hands brought her such pleasure.

'Your turn,' she commanded. 'Take me.'

And heaven help her, he obeyed. He lifted one of her legs, pressing it back to gain deeper access. Mairead watched him enter her body, and she could only hold him as he thrust hard, marking her as his own as he invaded and withdrew.

'I'm going to marry you,' she told him. 'And you won't ever be free of me.'

'I don't want to be,' he admitted. He thrust within her, claiming her body as his own as she gave him everything she had. At last, his own release took him under, and he flooded her deep inside. Against her damp skin, she could feel his heartbeat pounding.

The aftershocks of their lovemaking still made her clench around him, and he rested above her with a sleepy smile, tracing slow circles over her spine.

'Do you know, Alanna was right? She told me I would meet my future husband if I gazed through my May crown at dawn. And I did.'

'I wasn't the sort of husband you expected, was I?' he said against her throat.

'No,' she agreed. 'You were far more than I ever dreamed of.'

The morning of his wedding, Balor awoke at dawn, feeling restless. Although he'd spent each day at Mairead's side, it felt as if, at any moment, this gift would be taken from him. He could hardly believe that he'd won her heart and that she would become his wife this day.

During the past few weeks, Patrick had begun passing on his duties until Liam was crowned the new King of Laochre, only a day ago. The former king had also begun teaching Balor how to govern a large household.

The idea of looking after so many people intimidated him. It seemed impossible that he'd gone from a bastard son, unwanted by anyone, to becoming the heir of Beaumont.

Balor dressed in his wedding finery, the silk tunic trimmed with silver thread, and he wore darker trews. His cloak was woven of the finest wool, fastened with a golden brooch Mairead had given him.

A quiet knock sounded at the door, and he went to open it. His mother stood there, and she offered a nervous smile. 'You look very handsome, Balor.'

'You look beautiful as well,' he answered. It was true. She wore a gown the color of the sea, and the blue brought out the colour of her eyes. Orla had woven yellow gorse into her hair, and she ventured a smile at him as she murmured her thanks.

Their relationship had been strained, and he was trying to forgive her. She came to visit often, though she was helping Kenneth assume his duties as the new chieftain of Dunmalus.

'There is…someone I've been wanting to introduce to you.' She stepped aside, and then an older man stepped through the doorway.

Balor found himself staring at the man who had watched over him during all the years he'd trained—Lord Beaumont.

'This is your father,' she said softly. 'William Fleming de Beaumont.'

The earl offered a hesitant smile. His hair held hints of silver amid the dark color, and Balor found himself studying the man's features. They shared the same nose and mouth and were the same height.

Balor hadn't truly noticed their resemblance in the past, since the earl had only watched his foster sons from a distance. But now there was no denying that Lord Beaumont was his true father.

'I am…humbled to be here for your wedding,' William said. 'I wish I could have been there for all the years I missed.' He extended his hand, and Balor gripped it. Even when he relaxed his hand, his father didn't let go.

'You were there as my foster father,' Balor said. 'Those years mattered a great deal.' He glanced at his mother, who was smiling through her tears. He only wished Orla had sent him there far sooner.

'You were always the strongest fighter of all the boys,' William said. 'And my favourite to watch. I wonder if a part of me guessed that you were my son.' At last, he released Balor's arm and he asked, 'Will you bring your royal bride home to Beaumont?'

'I will. But she will want to visit her family at Éireann often.'

'Of course.' William reached for his wife's hand. 'Just as I know Orla will want to visit Kenneth.' There was affection and forgiveness in his eyes, as if he'd set aside the lost years and was focused on rebuilding their future together.

Balor walked with his parents down the stairs, as they continued outside to where the horses waited. He mounted the stallion that had been a gift from King Patrick. Orla and William followed as he rode towards the coast. The crowd of guests lined a pathway to the sea, and each person carried a sprig of yellow gorse, Mairead's favourite flower.

When he reached the shore, Balor dismounted and waited beside the priest. Isabel was already seated, and King Liam and Queen Adriana waited beside her, along with their children.

Balor smiled at the sight of Marcas. The boy beamed at him, and he proudly wore the leather bracers Balor had given him, to protect his arms while practicing archery. Liam had agreed to let them foster Marcas at Beaumont, and they would travel back to England together.

The sun rose above them, the light glittering upon the sea in waves of gold. Balor waited for Mairead, and at last, she arrived on her own white horse, escorted by King John of England on one side and her father on the other.

The sight of his bride made Balor's heart ache, and she wore her elder wood May crown woven with heather, gorse, and yellow roses.

Her smile mirrored his own, and King John led her to him, a bemused expression on his face. It had taken weeks of negotiation to heal the bruised relations, but the new alliances among the MacEgans, Lord Lowell, and Lord Beaumont had softened the king's resentment.

Balor took Mairead's hands in his as the priest gave the opening blessing. It was unusual to speak vows here, beside the sea, but he'd wanted to give her a gift upon her wedding day. It was also a reminder of the journeys they'd shared and the journeys yet to come.

They spoke their vows, and then the priest offered up the Mass for all the guests. Balor held his wife's hands in his during the celebration as he stared into her green eyes. As a boy, he'd never imagined that he would one day marry a king's daughter. Or that she would love him as fiercely as he loved her.

When the Mass was over, he kissed her in front of everyone. Then he lifted her on his horse and swung up behind her. As they rode past hundreds of cheering guests, he leaned in. 'I know this is our wedding, but I'm tempted to steal you away right now.'

She leaned back against him, happiness lighting up her face. 'Do you promise?'

As they rode back to Laochre, he leaned to kiss her cheek, overwhelmed by all the precious gifts he'd been given.

And of all those yet to come.

* * * * *

If you enjoyed this story, make sure to catch up on the previous instalments of The Legendary Warriors miniseries

The Iron Warrior Returns
The Untamed Warrior's Bride
Her Warrior's Redemption

And why not check out Michelle Willingham's other historical romances

The Taming of the Countess
The Highlander and the Wallflower
The Highlander and the Governess